Eight Cousins

The Louisa May Alcott Library

Jo's Boys

Eight Cousins

An Old-Fashioned Girl

Eight Cousins

or, The Aunt Hill

Louisa May Alcott

GRAMERCY BOOKS
New York • Avenel

Foreword copyright © 1995 by Random House Value Publishing, Inc.

This edition is published by Random House Value Publishing, Inc.,
40 Engelhard Avenue, Avenel, New Jersey 07001.

Printed and bound in the United States of America

Library of Congress Cataloging-in-Publication Data

Alcott, Louisa May, 1832–1888.
    Eight cousins / Louisa May Alcott.
       p.   cm.
    Sequel: Rose in bloom.
    Summary: Orphaned Rose Campbell finds it difficult to fit in when she goes to live
with her six aunts and seven mischievous boy cousins.
    ISBN 0–517–14810–2
    [1. Orphans—Fiction. 2. Cousins—Fiction. 3. Family life—Fiction.] I. Title.
PZ7.A335E   1995
[Fic]—dc20
    95–17766
    CIP
    AC

8 7 6 5 4 3 2 1

FOREWORD

THE ORIGINAL DEDICATION to *Eight Cousins* reads, "To the many boys and girls whose letters it has been impossible to answer, this book is dedicated as a peace offering by their friend."

Author Louisa May Alcott wrote those words in response to the enormous popularity her *Little Women* and *Little Men* had already received. Today, for many, the popularity of these classics has overshadowed the fact that Alcott was a prolific writer who also wrote dozens of articles, short stories, and novels—including the delightful, exuberant, and romantic *Eight Cousins*.

Written several years after the world had been introduced to Meg and Beth, Jo and Amy, and all the rest of the March family, *Eight Cousins* tells the tale of young heiress Rose Campbell, an orphan who is grieving over the death of the two people in the world she loved most: her mother and father. Imagine her dismay when she is whisked away from her proper boarding school and sent to live with her six aunts, with such names as Aunt Plenty and Aunt Peace! Worse, they even have seven sons among them, tow-haired, blue-eyed, energetic boy cousins who all live in various houses and cottages on a mountain nicknamed "Aunt Hill" in the countryside outside Boston.

Solitary Uncle Alec, brown-bearded and outspoken, promised Rose's father that he would take care of her, and take care of her he does—by tossing her hot, fresh morning coffee out the window! He sets down the rules from the moment she comes to live with him: No coffee. No corsets. No proper teas and no dating. Instead Rose Campbell is to eat oatmeal every morning. She's to get plenty of fresh air and exercise. And she is to give up her silks and petticoats for comfortable—and frumpy—loose brown garments.

For those of us in modern times, fresh air, oatmeal, exercise, and comfortable clothes are a way of life. But think about the customs and culture one hundred years ago. Wealthy girls were supposed to be young adults, wearing the same corsets and bustles as their mothers, talking of debuts, balls, and the boys from fine families whom they would ultimately marry.

Certainly no "proper" girl would live on "Aunt Hill" amid—count them—seven boy cousins! In fact, the first time the boys come to visit, Rose is so terrified to meet the noisy crew that she pretends to be sick.

But soon their love of life, their enthusiasm, and their high spirits get the best of Rose. She is drawn to them all—from Archie, at sixteen, the oldest of the group, and Jamie, the Baby, to Mac, called "Worm" because he reads most of the time. In fact, when Worm gets sick it is Rose who reads to him in his darkened bedroom, just as it is Worm—and the rest of the clan—who visits her when she lies sick with pneumonia.

Then there's Uncle Alec, so different, and yet so much like her parents in the way he really cares. Louisa May Alcott used the character of Uncle Alec to give her society a message about education. Although we take equality in school for granted, in her day a "proper" girl's education did not consist of learning to row a boat or go fishing on a lake. And certainly no girl grew as confident, independent, and strong as Rose did!

On the other hand, although Louisa May Alcott was a firm believer in liberty and freedom for all, she used some of the insensitive and stereotyping language of her time. Thus, within these pages, you will find references to Rose's Asian friend as a "slanty-eyed Chinaman." But you'll also see the seven cousins introduce themselves by dancing a Highland jig, complete with kilts, socks, and bagpipes.

However, despite the cultural differences, in this long-ago world of innocence, Louisa May Alcott's true and timeless magic comes through: in her fascination with enjoyment and her understanding of everyday family life. Like the Marches, Rose Campbell and her clan have that magic. You can feel the breeze from the lake coming through the trees of "Aunt Hill." You can taste the crusty bread Rose so proudly bakes and takes out of the oven. You can smell the wildflowers and frescia in the peaceful countryside. And you can hear Rose's soft voice, raising and lowering in cadence as she reads beloved classics to Worm by candlelight in his darkened room.

And within this story, among these sights and sounds and adventures, lies the perfect balance between the innocence of a bygone era and the growing independence of women. Alcott, a longtime admirer of Thoreau and his Walden Pond, was, like Thoreau, able to turn one small New England hill into a country all its own and, in turn, make its everyday life poetry.

As each of us, in every new generation, discovers Louisa May Alcott, we are glad for this magic poetry. And in *Eight Cousins,* she does not disappoint us. We find a young, timid, and oh-so-polite-and-refined young girl who becomes strong and independent through love, care, and, yes, plenty of oatmeal and fresh air, too!

Enjoy the magic.

KARLA DOUGHERTY

Montclair, New Jersey
1995

Eight Cousins

TO

*The many boys and girls
whose letters it has been impossible to answer,
this book is dedicated
as a peace offering by their friend*

LOUISA MAY ALCOTT

CHAPTER 1

TWO GIRLS

ROSE SAT ALL ALONE in the big best parlor with her little handkerchief laid ready to catch the first tear, for she was thinking of her troubles, and a shower was expected. She had retired to this room as a good place in which to be miserable; for it was dark and still, full of ancient furniture, somber curtains, and hung all round with portraits of solemn old gentlemen in wigs, severe-nosed ladies in top-heavy caps, and staring children in little bobtailed coats or short-waisted frocks. It *was* an excellent place for woe; and the fitful spring rain that pattered on the windowpane seemed to sob, "Cry away: I'm with you."

Rose really did have some cause to be sad; for she had no mother and had lately lost her father also, which left her no home but this with her great-aunts. She had been with them only a week, and though the dear old ladies had tried their best to make her happy, they had not succeeded very well, for she was unlike any child they had ever seen, and they felt very much as if they had the care of a low-spirited butterfly.

They had given her the freedom of the house, and for a day or two she had amused herself roaming all over it, for it was a capital old

1

mansion and was full of all manner of odd nooks, charming rooms, and mysterious passages. Windows broke out in unexpected places, little balconies overhung the garden most romantically, and there was a long upper hall full of curiosities from all parts of the world; for the Campbells had been sea captains for generations.

Aunt Plenty had even allowed Rose to rummage in her great china closet—a spicy retreat, rich in all the "goodies" that children love; but Rose seemed to care little for these toothsome temptations; and when that hope failed, Aunt Plenty gave up in despair.

Gentle Aunt Peace had tried all sorts of pretty needlework, and planned a doll's wardrobe that would have won the heart of even an older child. But Rose took little interest in pink satin hats and tiny hose, though she sewed dutifully till her aunt caught her wiping tears away with the train of a wedding dress, and that discovery put an end to the sewing society.

Then both old ladies put their heads together and picked out the model child of the neighborhood to come and play with their niece. But Annabel Bliss was the worst failure of all, for Rose could not bear the sight of her and said she was so like a wax doll, she longed to give her a pinch and see if she would squeak. So prim little Annabel was sent home, and the exhausted aunties left Rose to her own devices for a day or two.

Bad weather and a cold kept her indoors, and she spent most of her time in the library where her father's books were stored. Here she read a great deal, cried a little, and dreamed many of the innocent bright dreams in which imaginative children find such comfort and delight. This suited her better than anything else, but it was not good for her, and she grew pale, heavy-eyed, and listless, though Aunt Plenty gave her iron enough to make a cooking stove, and Aunt Peace petted her like a poodle.

Seeing this, the poor aunties racked their brains for a new amusement and determined to venture a bold stroke, though not very hopeful of its success. They said nothing to Rose about their plan for this Saturday afternoon, but let her alone till the time came for the grand surprise, little dreaming that the odd child would find pleasure for herself in a most unexpected quarter.

Before she had time to squeeze out a single tear, a sound broke the stillness, making her prick up her ears. It was only the soft twitter of a bird, but it seemed to be a peculiarly gifted bird, for while she listened the soft twitter changed to a lively whistle, then a trill, a coo, a chirp, and ended in a musical mixture of all the notes, as if the bird burst out laughing. Rose laughed also and, forgetting her woes, jumped up, saying eagerly, "It is a mockingbird. Where is it?"

Running down the long hall, she peeped out at both doors, but saw nothing feathered except a draggle-tailed chicken under a burdock leaf. She listened again, and the sound seemed to be in the house. Away she went, much excited by the chase, and following the changeful song it led her to the china-closet door.

"In there? How funny!" she said. But when she entered, not a bird appeared except the everlastingly kissing swallows on the Canton china that lined the shelves. All of a sudden Rose's face brightened, and softly opening the slide, she peered into the kitchen. But the music had stopped, and all she saw was a girl in a blue apron scrubbing the hearth. Rose stared about her for a minute, and then asked abruptly, "Did you hear that mockingbird?"

"I should call it a Phebe bird," answered the girl, looking up with a twinkle in her black eyes.

"Where did it go?"

"It is here still."

"Where?"

"In my throat. Do you want to hear it?"

"Oh, yes! I'll come in." And Rose crept through the slide to the wide shelf on the other side, being too hurried and puzzled to go round by the door.

The girl wiped her hands, crossed her feet on the little island of carpet where she was stranded in a sea of soapsuds, and then, sure enough, out of her slender throat came the swallow's twitter, the robin's whistle, the blue jay's call, the thrush's song, the wood dove's coo, and many another familiar note, all ending as before with the musical ecstasy of a bobolink singing and swinging among the meadow grass on a bright June day.

Rose was so astonished that she nearly fell off her perch, and when the little concert was over clapped her hands delightedly.

"Oh, it was lovely! Who taught you?"

"The birds," answered the girl with a smile as she fell to work again.

"It is very wonderful! I can sing, but nothing half so fine as that. What is your name, please?"

"Phebe Moore."

"I've heard of phebe birds, but I don't believe the real ones could do that," laughed Rose, adding, as she watched with interest the scattering of dabs of soft soap over the bricks, "May I stay and see you work? It is very lonely in the parlor."

"Yes, indeed, if you want to," answered Phebe, wringing out her cloth in a capable sort of way that impressed Rose very much.

"It must be fun to swash the water round and dig out the soap. I'd love to do it, only Aunt wouldn't like it, I suppose," said Rose, quite taken with the new employment.

"You'd soon get tired, so you'd better keep tidy and look on."

"I suppose you help your mother a good deal?"

"I haven't got any folks."

"Why, where do you live, then?"

"I'm going to live here, I hope. Debby wants someone to help round, and I've come to try for a week."

"I hope you *will* stay, for it is very dull," said Rose, who had taken a sudden fancy to this girl who sang like a bird and worked like a woman.

"Hope I shall; for I'm fifteen now, and old enough to earn my own living. You have come to stay a spell, haven't you?" asked Phebe, looking up at her guest and wondering how life *could* be dull to a girl who wore a silk frock, a daintily frilled apron, a pretty locket, and had her hair tied up with a velvet snood.

"Yes, I shall stay till my uncle comes. He is my guardian now, and I don't know what he will do with me. Have you a guardian?"

"My sakes, no! I was left on the poorhouse steps a little mite of a baby, and Miss Rogers took a liking to me, so I've been there ever since. But she is dead now, and I take care of myself."

"How interesting! It is like Arabella Montgomery in the *Gypsy's Child*. Did you ever read that sweet story?" asked Rose, who was fond of tales of foundlings and had read many.

"I don't have any books to read, and all the spare time I get I run off into the woods; that rests me better than stories," answered Phebe as she finished one job and began on another.

Rose watched her as she got out a great pan of beans to look over, and wondered how it would seem to have life all work and no play. Presently Phebe seemed to think it was her turn to ask questions, and said wistfully, "You've had lots of schooling, I suppose?"

"Oh, dear me, yes! I've been at boarding school nearly a year, and I'm almost dead with lessons. The more I got, the more Miss Power gave me, and I was so miserable I 'most cried my eyes out. Papa never gave me hard things to do, and he always taught me so pleasantly, I loved to study. Oh, we were *so* happy and so fond of one another! But now he is gone, and I am left all alone."

The tear that would not come when Rose sat waiting for it came now of its own accord—two of them in fact—and rolled down her cheeks, telling the tale of love and sorrow better than any words could do it.

For a minute there was no sound in the kitchen but the little daughter's sobbing and the sympathetic patter of the rain. Phebe stopped rattling her beans from one pan to the other, and her eyes were full of pity as they rested on the curly head bent down on Rose's knee, for she saw that the heart under the pretty locket ached with its loss, and the dainty apron was used to dry sadder tears than any she had ever shed.

Somehow, she felt more contented with her brown calico gown and blue-checked pinafore; envy changed to compassion, and if she had dared she would have gone and hugged her afflicted guest.

Fearing that might not be considered proper, she said, in her cheery voice, "I'm sure you ain't all alone with such a lot of folks belonging to you, and all so rich and clever. You'll be petted to pieces, Debby says, because you are the only girl in the family."

Phebe's last words made Rose smile in spite of her tears, and she looked out from behind her apron with an April face, saying in a tone of comic distress, "That's one of my troubles! I've got six aunts, and they all want me, and I don't know any of them very well. Papa named this place the Aunt Hill, and now I see why."

Phebe laughed with her as she said encouragingly, "Everyone calls it so, and it's a real good name, for all the Mrs. Campbells live handy by and keep coming up to see the old ladies."

"I could stand the aunts, but there are dozens of cousins, dreadful boys all of them, and I detest boys! Some of them came to see me last Wednesday, but I was lying down, and when Auntie came to call me I went under the quilt and pretended to be asleep. I shall *have* to see them some time, but I do dread it so." And Rose gave a shudder, for having lived alone with her invalid father, she knew nothing of boys and considered them a species of wild animal.

"Oh! I guess you'll like 'em. I've seen 'em flying round when they come over from the Point, sometimes in their boats and sometimes on horseback. If you like boats and horses, you'll enjoy yourself first-rate."

"But I don't! I'm afraid of horses, and boats make me ill, and I *hate* boys!" And poor Rose wrung her hands at the awful prospect before her. One of these horrors alone she could have borne, but all together were too much for her, and she began to think of a speedy return to the detested school.

Phebe laughed at her woe till the beans danced in the pan, but tried to comfort her by suggesting a means of relief.

"Perhaps your uncle will take you away where there ain't any boys. Debby says he is a real kind man, and always brings heaps of nice things when he comes."

"Yes, but you see that is another trouble, for I don't know Uncle Alec at all. He hardly ever came to see us, though he sent me pretty things very often. Now I belong to him, and shall have to mind him, till I am eighteen. I may not like him a bit, and I fret about it all the time."

"Well, I wouldn't borrow trouble, but have a real good time. I'm sure I should think I was in clover if I had folks and money and nothing to do but enjoy myself," began Phebe, but got no further, for a sudden rush and rumble outside made them both jump.

"It's thunder," said Phebe.

"It's a circus!" cried Rose, who from her elevated perch had caught glimpses of a gay cart of some sort and several ponies with flying manes and tails.

The sound died away and the girls were about to continue their confidences when old Debby appeared, looking rather cross and sleepy after her nap.

"You are wanted in the parlor, Miss Rose."

"Has anybody come?"

"Little girls shouldn't ask questions, but do as they are bid," was all Debby would answer.

"I do hope it isn't Aunt Myra; she always scares me out of my wits asking how my cough is and groaning over me as if I was going to die," said Rose, preparing to retire the way she came, for the slide, being cut for the admission of bouncing Christmas turkeys and puddings, was plenty large enough for a slender girl.

"Guess you'll wish it *was* Aunt Myra when you see who has come. Don't never let me catch you coming into my kitchen that way again, or I'll shut you up in the big biler," growled Debby, who thought it her duty to snub children on all occasions.

CHAPTER 2

THE CLAN

ROSE SCRAMBLED into the china closet as rapidly as possible, and there refreshed herself by making faces at Debby while she settled her plumage and screwed up her courage. Then she crept softly down the hall and peeped into the parlor. No one appeared, and all was so still she felt sure the company was upstairs. So she skipped boldly through the half-open folding doors, to behold on the other side a sight that nearly took her breath away.

Seven boys stood in a row—all ages, all sizes, all yellow-haired and blue-eyed, all in full Scotch costume, and all smiling, nodding, and saying as with one voice, "How are you, cousin?"

Rose gave a little gasp and looked wildly about her as if ready to fly, for fear magnified the seven and the room seemed full of boys. Before she could run, however, the tallest lad stepped out of the line, saying pleasantly, "Don't be frightened. This is the clan come to welcome you; and I'm the chief, Archie, at your service."

He held out his hand as he spoke, and Rose timidly put her own into a brown paw, which closed over the white morsel and held it as the chief continued his introductions.

"We came in full rig, for we always turn out in style on grand occasions. Hope you like it. Now I'll tell you who these chaps are, and then we shall be all right. This big one is Prince Charlie, Aunt Clara's boy. She has but one, so he is an extra good one. This old fellow is Mac, the bookworm, called Worm for short. This sweet creature is Steve the Dandy. Look at his gloves and topknot, if you please. They are Aunt Jane's lads, and a precious pair you'd better believe. These are the Brats, my brothers, Geordie and Will, and Jamie the Baby. Now, my men, step out and show your manners."

At this command, to Rose's great dismay, six more hands were offered, and it was evident that she was expected to shake them *all*. It was a trying moment to the bashful child; but remembering that they were her kinsmen come to welcome her, she tried her best to return the greeting cordially.

This impressive ceremony being over, the clan broke ranks, and both rooms instantly appeared to be pervaded with boys. Rose hastily retired to the shelter of a big chair and sat there watching the invaders and wondering when her aunt would come and rescue her.

As if bound to do their duty manfully, yet rather oppressed by it, each lad paused beside her chair in his wanderings, made a brief remark, received a still briefer answer, and then sheered off with a relieved expression.

Archie came first, and, leaning over the chair back, observed in a paternal tone, "I'm glad you've come, cousin, and I hope you'll find the Aunt Hill pretty jolly."

"I think I shall."

Mac shook his hair out of his eyes, stumbled over a stool, and asked abruptly, "Did you bring any books with you?"

"Four boxes full. They are in the library."

Mac vanished from the room, and Steve, striking an attitude which displayed his costume effectively, said with an affable smile, "We were sorry not to see you last Wednesday. I hope your cold is better."

"Yes, thank you." And a smile began to dimple about Rose's mouth as she remembered her retreat under the bedcover.

Feeling that he had been received with distinguished marks of attention, Steve strolled away with his topknot higher than ever, and Prince Charlie pranced across the room, saying in a free and easy tone, "Mamma sent her love and hopes you will be well enough to come over for a day next week. It must be desperately dull here for a little thing like you."

"I'm thirteen and a half, though I *do* look small," cried Rose, forgetting her shyness in indignation at this insult to her newly acquired teens.

"Beg pardon, ma'am; never should have guessed it." And Charlie went off with a laugh, glad to have struck a spark out of his meek cousin.

Geordie and Will came together, two sturdy eleven- and twelve-year-olders, and, fixing their round blue eyes on Rose, fired off a question apiece as if it were a shooting match and she the target.

"Did you bring your monkey?"

"No, he is dead."

"Are you going to have a boat?"

"I hope not."

Here the two, with a right-about-face movement, abruptly marched away, and little Jamie demanded with childish frankness, "Did you bring me anything nice?"

"Yes, lots of candy," answered Rose, whereupon Jamie ascended into her lap with a sounding kiss and the announcement that he liked her very much.

This proceeding rather startled Rose, for the other lads looked and laughed, and in her confusion she said hastily to the young usurper, "Did you see the circus go by?"

"When? Where?" cried all the boys in great excitement at once.

"Just before you came. At least I thought it was a circus, for I saw a red and black sort of cart and ever so many little ponies, and—"

She got no farther, for a general shout made her pause suddenly, as Archie explained the joke by saying in the middle of his laugh, "It was our new dogcart and the Shetland ponies. You'll never hear the last of your circus, cousin."

"But there were so many, and they went so fast, and the cart was so very red," began Rose, trying to explain her mistake.

"Come and see them all!" cried the Prince. And before she knew what was happening, she was borne away to the barn and tumultuously introduced to three shaggy ponies and the gay new dogcart.

She had never visited these regions before, and had her doubts as to the propriety of her being there now, but when she suggested that "Auntie might not like it," there was a general cry of, "She told us to amuse you, and we can do it ever so much better out here than poking round in the house."

"I'm afraid I shall get cold without my sacque," began Rose, who wanted to stay but felt rather out of her element.

"No, you won't! We'll fix you," cried the lads, as one clapped his cap on her head, another tied a rough jacket round her neck by the sleeves, a third nearly smothered her in a carriage blanket, and a fourth threw open the door of the old barouche that stood there, saying with a flourish, "Step in, ma'am, and make yourself comfortable while we show you some fun."

So Rose sat in state enjoying herself very much, for the lads proceeded to dance a Highland fling with a spirit and skill that made her clap her hands and laugh as she had not done for weeks.

"How is that, my lassie?" asked the Prince, coming up all flushed and breathless when the ballet was over.

"It was splendid! I never went to the theater but once, and the dancing was not half so pretty as this. What clever boys you must be!" said Rose, smiling upon her kinsmen like a little queen upon her subjects.

"Ah, we're a fine lot, and that is only the beginning of our larks. We haven't got the pipes here or we'd

> Sing for you, play for you
> A dulcy melody,"

answered Charlie, looking much elated at her praise.

"I did not know we were Scotch; Papa never said anything about it, or seemed to care about Scotland, except to have me sing the old ballads," said Rose, beginning to feel as if she had left America behind her somewhere.

"Neither did we till lately. We've been reading Scott's novels, and all of a sudden we remembered that our grandfather was a Scotchman. So we hunted up the old stories, got a bagpipe, put on our plaids, and went in, heart and soul, for the glory of the clan. We've been at it some time now, and it's great fun. Our people like it, and I think we are a pretty canny set."

Archie said this from the other coach step, where he had perched, while the rest climbed up before and behind to join in the chat as they rested.

"I'm Fitzjames and he's Roderick Dhu, and we'll give you the broadsword combat someday. It's a great thing, you'd better believe," added the Prince.

"Yes, and you should hear Steve play the pipes. He makes 'em skirl like a good one," cried Will from the box, eager to air the accomplishments of his race.

"Mac's the fellow to hunt up the old stories and tell us how to dress right, and pick out rousing bits for us to speak and sing," put in Geordie, saying a good word for the absent Worm.

"And what do you and Will do?" asked Rose of Jamie, who sat beside her as if bound to keep her in sight till the promised gift had been handed over.

"Oh, I'm the little foot-page, and do errands, and Will and Geordie are the troops when we march, and the stags when we hunt, and the traitors when we want to cut any heads off."

"They are very obliging, I'm sure," said Rose, whereat the "utility men" beamed with modest pride and resolved to enact Wallace and Montrose as soon as possible for their cousin's special benefit.

"Let's have a game of tag," cried the Prince, swinging himself up to a beam with a sounding slap on Stevie's shoulder.

Regardless of his gloves, Dandy tore after him, and the rest swarmed in every direction as if bent on breaking their necks and dislocating their joints as rapidly as possible.

It was a new and astonishing spectacle to Rose, fresh from a prim boarding school, and she watched the active lads with breathless interest, thinking their antics far superior to those of Mops, the dear departed monkey.

Will had just covered himself with glory by pitching off of a high loft head first and coming up all right, when Phebe appeared with a cloak, hood, and rubbers, also a message from Aunt Plenty that "Miss Rose was to come in directly."

"All right; we'll bring her!" answered Archie, issuing some mysterious order, which was so promptly obeyed that, before Rose could get out of the carriage, the boys had caught hold of the pole and rattled her out of the barn, round the oval and up to the front door with a cheer that brought two caps to an upper window and caused Debby to cry aloud from the back porch, "Them harum-scarum boys will certainly be the death of that delicate little creter!"

But the "delicate little creter" seemed all the better for her trip and ran up the steps looking rosy, gay, and disheveled, to be received with lamentation by Aunt Plenty, who begged her to go and lie down at once.

"Oh, please don't! We have come to tea with our cousin, and we'll be as good as gold if you'll let us stay, Auntie," clamored the boys, who not only approved of "our cousin," but had no mind to lose their tea, for Aunt Plenty's name but feebly expressed her bountiful nature.

"Well, dears, you can; only be quiet and let Rose go and take her iron and be made tidy, and then we will see what we can find for supper," said the old lady as she trotted away, followed by a volley of directions for the approaching feast.

"Marmalade for me, Auntie."

"Plenty of plum cake, please."

"Tell Debby to trot out the baked pears."

"I'm your man for lemon pie, ma'am."

"Do have fritters; Rose will like 'em."

"She'd rather have tarts, *I* know."

When Rose came down fifteen minutes later, with every curl

smoothed and her most beruffled apron on, she found the boys
loafing about the long hall, and paused on the halfway landing to
take an observation, for till now she had not really examined her
newfound cousins.

There was a strong family resemblance among them, though some
of the yellow heads were darker than others, some of the cheeks
brown instead of rosy, and the ages varied all the way from sixteen-
year-old Archie to Jamie, who was ten years younger. None of them
were especially comely but the Prince, yet all were hearty, happy-
looking lads, and Rose decided that boys were not as dreadful as she
had expected to find them.

They were all so characteristically employed that she could not
help smiling as she looked. Archie and Charlie, evidently great cro-
nies, were pacing up and down, shoulder to shoulder, whistling
"Bonnie Dundee"; Mac was reading in a corner, with his book close
to his nearsighted eyes; Dandy was arranging his hair before the oval
glass in the hatstand; Geordie and Will investigating the internal
economy of the moon-faced clock; and Jamie lay kicking up his heels
on the mat at the foot of the stairs, bent on demanding his sweeties
the instant Rose appeared.

She guessed his intention and forestalled his demand by dropping
a handful of sugarplums down upon him.

At his cry of rapture the other lads looked up and smiled involuntarily, for the little kinswoman standing there above was a winsome
sight with her shy, soft eyes, bright hair, and laughing face. The black
frock reminded them of her loss and filled the boyish hearts with a
kindly desire to be good to "our cousin," who had no longer any
home but this.

"There she is, as fine as you please," cried Steve, kissing his hand
to her.

"Come on, Missy; tea is ready," added the Prince encouragingly.

"*I* shall take her in." And Archie offered his arm with great dignity, an honor that made Rose turn as red as a cherry and long to
run upstairs again.

It was a merry supper, and the two elder boys added much to the fun by tormenting the rest with dark hints of some interesting event which was about to occur. Something uncommonly fine they declared it was, but enveloped in the deepest mystery for the present.

"Did I ever see it?" asked Jamie.

"Not to remember it; but Mac and Steve have, and liked it immensely," answered Archie, thereby causing the two mentioned to neglect Debby's delectable fritters for several minutes while they cudgeled their brains.

"Who will have it first?" asked Will with his mouth full of marmalade.

"Aunt Plenty, I guess."

"When will she have it?" demanded Geordie, bouncing in his seat with impatience.

"Sometime on Monday."

"Heart alive! What is the boy talking about?" cried the old lady from behind the tall urn, which left little to be seen but the topmost bow of her cap.

"Doesn't Auntie know?" asked a chorus of voices.

"No, and that's the best of the joke, for she is desperately fond of it."

"What color is it?" asked Rose, joining in the fun.

"Blue and brown."

"Is it good to eat?" asked Jamie.

"Some people think so, but I shouldn't like to try it," answered Charlie, laughing so he spilt his tea.

"Who does it belong to?" put in Steve.

Archie and the Prince stared at one another rather blankly for a minute, then Archie answered with a twinkle of the eye that made Charlie explode again, "To Grandfather Campbell."

This was a poser, and they gave up the puzzle, though Jamie confided to Rose that he did not think he could live till Monday without knowing what this remarkable thing was.

Soon after tea the clan departed, singing "All the blue bonnets are over the border" at the tops of their voices.

"Well, dear, how do you like your cousins?" asked Aunt Plenty as the last pony frisked round the corner and the din died away.

"Pretty well, ma'am, but I like Phebe better." An answer which caused Aunt Plenty to hold up her hands in despair and trot away to tell her sister Peace that she never *should* understand that child, and it was a mercy Alec was coming soon to take the responsibility off their hands.

Fatigued by the unusual exertions of the afternoon, Rose curled herself up in the sofa corner to rest and think about the great mystery, little guessing that she was to know it first of all.

Right in the middle of her meditations, she fell asleep and dreamed she was at home again in her own little bed. She seemed to wake and see her father bending over her; to hear him say, "My little Rose"; to answer, "Yes, Papa"; and then to feel him take her in his arms and kiss her tenderly. So sweet, so real, was the dream that she started up with a cry of joy to find herself in the arms of a brown, bearded man, who held her close and whispered in a voice so like her father's that she clung to him involuntarily: "This is my little girl, and I am Uncle Alec."

CHAPTER 3

UNCLES

WHEN ROSE WOKE next morning, she was not sure whether she had dreamed what occurred the night before, or it had actually happened. So she hopped up and dressed, although it was an hour earlier than she usually rose, for she could not sleep any more, being possessed with a strong desire to slip down and see if the big portmanteau and packing cases were really in the hall. She seemed to remember tumbling over them when she went to bed, for the aunts had sent her off very punctually because they wanted their pet nephew all to themselves.

The sun was shining, and Rose opened her window to let in the soft May air fresh from the sea. As she leaned over her little balcony, watching an early bird get the worm and wondering how she should like Uncle Alec, she saw a man leap the garden wall and come whistling up the path. At first she thought it was some trespasser, but a second look showed her that it was her uncle returning from an early dip into the sea. She had hardly dared to look at him the night before, because whenever she tried to do so she always found a pair of keen blue eyes looking at her. Now she could take a good stare at him as he lingered along, looking about him as if glad to see the old place again.

A brown, breezy man, in a blue jacket, with no hat on the curly head which he shook now and then like a water dog; broad-shouldered, alert in his motions, and with a general air of strength and stability about him which pleased Rose, though she could not explain the feeling of comfort it gave her. She had just said to herself, with a sense of relief, "I guess I *shall* like him, though he looks as if he made people mind," when he lifted his eyes to examine the budding horse-chestnut overhead and saw the eager face peering down at him. He waved his hand to her, nodded, and called out in a bluff, cheery voice, "You are on deck early, little niece."

"I got up to see if you had really come, Uncle."

"Did you? Well, come down here and make sure of it."

"I'm not allowed to go out before breakfast, sir."

"Oh, indeed!" with a shrug. "Then I'll come aboard and salute," he added; and to Rose's great amazement, Uncle Alec went up one of the pillars of the back piazza hand over hand, stepped across the roof, and swung himself into her balcony, saying, as he landed on the wide balustrade: "Have you any doubts about me now, ma'am?"

Rose was so taken aback, she could only answer with a smile as she went to meet him.

"How does my girl do this morning?" he asked, taking the little cold hand she gave him in both his big warm ones.

"Pretty well, thank you, sir."

"Ah, but it should be *very well*. Why isn't it?"

"I always wake up with a headache and feel tired."

"Don't you sleep well?"

"I lie awake a long time, and then I dream, and my sleep does not seem to rest me much."

"What do you do all day?"

"Oh, I read, and sew a little, and take naps, and sit with Auntie."

"No running about out-of-doors, or housework, or riding, hey?"

"Aunt Plenty says I'm not strong enough for much exercise. I drive out with her sometimes, but I don't care for it."

"I'm not surprised at that," said Uncle Alec, half to himself, adding, in his quick way: "Who have you had to play with?"

"No one but Annabel Bliss, and she was *such* a goose I couldn't bear her. The boys came yesterday, and seemed rather nice; but, of course, I couldn't play with them."

"Why not?"

"I'm too old to play with boys."

"Not a bit of it: that's just what you need, for you've been mollycoddled too much. They are good lads, and you'll be mixed up with them more or less for years to come, so you may as well be friends and playmates at once. I will look you up some girls also, if I can find a sensible one who is not spoiled by her nonsensical education."

"Phebe is sensible, I'm sure, and I like her, though I only saw her yesterday," cried Rose, waking up suddenly.

"And who is Phebe, if you please?"

Rose eagerly told all she knew, and Uncle Alec listened with an odd smile lurking about his mouth, though his eyes were quite sober as he watched the face before him.

"I'm glad to see that you are not aristocratic in your tastes, but I don't quite make out why you like this young lady from the poorhouse."

"You may laugh at me, but I do. I can't tell why, only she seems so happy and busy, and sings so beautifully, and is strong enough to scrub and sweep, and hasn't any troubles to plague her," said Rose, making a funny jumble of reasons in her efforts to explain.

"How do you know that?"

"Oh, I was telling her about mine, and asked if she had any, and she said, 'No, only I'd like to go to school, and I mean to someday.' "

"So she doesn't call desertion, poverty, and hard work, troubles? She's a brave little girl, and I shall be proud to know her." And Uncle Alec gave an approving nod that made Rose wish she had been the one to earn it.

"But what are these troubles of yours, child?" he asked after a minute of silence.

"Please don't ask me, Uncle."

"Can't you tell them to me as well as to Phebe?"

Something in his tone made Rose feel that it would be better to speak out and be done with it, so she answered, with sudden color and averted eyes, "The greatest one was losing dear Papa."

As she said that, Uncle Alec's arm came gently round her, and he drew her to him, saying, in the voice so like Papa's, "That *is* a trouble which I cannot cure, my child; but I shall try to make you feel it less. What else, dear?"

"I am so tired and poorly all the time, I can't do anything I want to, and it makes me cross," sighed Rose, rubbing the aching head like a fretful child.

"That we *can* cure and we *will*," said her uncle with a decided nod that made the curls bob on his head, so that Rose saw the gray ones underneath the brown.

"Aunt Myra says I have no constitution and never shall be strong," observed Rose in a pensive tone, as if it were rather a nice thing to be an invalid.

"Aunt Myra is a—ahem!—an excellent woman, but it is her hobby to believe that everyone is tottering on the brink of the grave; and, upon my life, I believe she is offended if people don't fall into it! We will show her how to make constitutions and turn pale-faced little ghosts into rosy, hearty girls. That's my business, you know," he added, more quietly, for his sudden outburst had rather startled Rose.

"I had forgotten you were a doctor. I'm glad of it, for I do want to be well, only I hope you won't give me much medicine, for I've taken quarts already and it does me no good."

As she spoke, Rose pointed to a little table just inside the window, on which appeared a regiment of bottles.

"Ah, ha! Now we'll see what mischief these blessed women have been at." And, making a long arm, Dr. Alec set the bottles on the wide railing before him, examined each carefully, smiled over some, frowned over others, and said, as he put down the last: "Now I'll show you the best way to take these messes." And as quick as a flash, he sent one after another smashing down into the posy beds below.

"But Aunt Plenty won't like it; and Aunt Myra will be angry, for she sent most of them!" cried Rose, half frightened and half pleased at such energetic measures.

"You are my patient now, and I'll take the responsibility. My way of giving physic is evidently the best, for you look better already," he said, laughing so infectiously that Rose followed suit, saying saucily, "If I don't like your medicines any better than those, I shall throw them into the garden, and then what will you do?"

"When I prescribe such rubbish, I'll give you leave to pitch it overboard as soon as you like. Now what is the next trouble?"

"I hoped you would forget to ask."

"But how can I help you if I don't know them? Come, let us have number three."

"It is very wrong, I suppose, but I do sometimes wish I had not *quite* so many aunts. They are all very good to me, and I want to please them; but they are so different, I feel sort of pulled to pieces among them," said Rose, trying to express the emotions of a stray chicken with six hens all clucking over it at once.

Uncle Alec threw back his head and laughed like a boy, for he could entirely understand how the good ladies had each put in her oar and tried to paddle her own way, to the great disturbance of the waters and the entire bewilderment of poor Rose.

"I intend to try a course of uncles now, and see how that suits your constitution. I'm going to have you all to myself, and no one is to give a word of advice unless I ask it. There is no other way to keep order aboard, and I am captain of this little craft, for a time at least. What comes next?"

But Rose stuck there, and grew so red, her uncle guessed what that trouble was.

"I don't think I *can* tell this one. It wouldn't be polite, and I feel pretty sure that it isn't going to be a trouble anymore."

As she blushed and stammered over these words, Dr. Alec turned his eyes away to the distant sea and said so seriously, so tenderly, that she felt every word and long remembered them, "My child, I don't expect you to love and trust me all at once, but I do want you to believe that I shall give my whole heart to this new duty; and if I make mistakes, as I probably shall, no one will grieve over them more bitterly than I. It is my fault that I am a stranger to you, when I want to be your best friend. That is one of my mistakes, and I never repented it more deeply than I do now. Your father and I had a trouble once, and I thought I never could forgive him; so I kept away for years. Thank God, we made it all up the last time I saw him, and he told me then, that if he was forced to leave her he should bequeath his little girl to me as a token of his love. I can't fill his place, but I shall try to be a father to her; and if she learns to love me half as well as she did the good one she has lost, I shall be a proud and happy man. Will she believe this and try?"

Something in Uncle Alec's face touched Rose to the heart, and when he held out his hand with that anxious, troubled look in his eyes, she was moved to put up her innocent lips and seal the contract with a confiding kiss. The strong arm held her close a minute, and she felt the broad chest heave once as if with a great sigh of relief; but not a word was spoken till a tap at the door made both start.

Rose popped her head through the window to say "Come in," while Dr. Alec hastily rubbed the sleeve of his jacket across his eyes and began to whistle again.

Phebe appeared with a cup of coffee.

"Debby told me to bring this and help you get up," she said, opening her black eyes wide, as if she wondered how on earth "the sailor man" got there.

"I'm all dressed, so I don't need any help. I hope that is good and strong," added Rose, eyeing the steaming cup with an eager look.

But she did not get it, for a brown hand took possession of it as her uncle said quickly, "Hold hard, my lass, and let me overhaul that dose before you take it. Do you drink all this strong coffee every morning, Rose?"

"Yes, sir, and I like it. Auntie says it 'tones' me up, and I always feel better after it."

"This accounts for the sleepless nights, the flutter your heart gets into at the least start, and this is why that cheek of yours is pale yellow instead of rosy red. No more coffee for you, my dear, and by and by you'll see that I am right. Any new milk downstairs, Phebe?"

"Yes, sir, plenty—right in from the barn."

"That's the drink for my patient. Go bring me a pitcherful, and another cup; I want a draft myself. This won't hurt the honeysuckles, for they have no nerves to speak of." And to Rose's great discomfort, the coffee went after the medicine.

Dr. Alec saw the injured look she put on, but took no notice, and presently banished it by saying pleasantly, "I've got a capital little cup among my traps, and I'll give it to you to drink your milk in, as it is made of wood that is supposed to improve whatever is put into it —something like a quassia cup. That reminds me; one of the boxes Phebe wanted to lug upstairs last night is for you. Knowing that I was coming home to find a ready-made daughter, I picked up all sorts of odd and pretty trifles along the way, hoping she would be able to find something she liked among them all. Early tomorrow we'll have a grand rummage. Here's our milk! I propose the health of Miss Rose Campbell—and drink it with all my heart."

It was impossible for Rose to pout with the prospect of a delightful boxful of gifts dancing before her eyes; so, in spite of herself, she smiled as she drank her own health, and found that fresh milk was not a hard dose to take.

"Now I must be off, before I am caught again with my wig in a toss," said Dr. Alec, preparing to descend the way he came.

"Do you always go in and out like a cat, Uncle?" asked Rose, much amused at his odd ways.

"I used to sneak out of my window when I was a boy, so I need not disturb the aunts, and now I rather like it, for it's the shortest road, and it keeps me limber when I have no rigging to climb. Good-bye till breakfast." And away he went down the waterspout, over the roof, and vanished among the budding honeysuckles below.

"Ain't he a funny guardeen?" exclaimed Phebe as she went off with the cups.

"He is a very kind one, I think," answered Rose, following, to prowl round the big boxes and try to guess which was hers.

When her uncle appeared at sound of the bell, he found her surveying with an anxious face a new dish that smoked upon the table.

"Got a fresh trouble, Rosy?" he asked, stroking her smooth head.

"Uncle, *are* you going to make me eat oatmeal?" asked Rose in a tragic tone.

"Don't you like it?"

"I de-test it!" answered Rose with all the emphasis which a turned-up nose, a shudder, and a groan could give to the three words.

"You are not a true Scotchwoman if you don't like the 'parritch.' It's a pity, for I made it myself, and thought we'd have such a good time with all that cream to float it in. Well, never mind." And he sat down with a disappointed air.

Rose had made up her mind to be obstinate about it, because she did heartily "detest" the dish; but as Uncle Alec did not attempt to make her obey, she suddenly changed her mind and thought she would.

"I'll try to eat it to please you, Uncle; but people are always saying how wholesome it is, and that makes me hate it," she said, half ashamed at her silly excuse.

"I do want you to like it, because I wish my girl to be as well and strong as Jessie's boys, who are brought up on this in the good old fashion. No hot bread and fried stuff for them, and they are the biggest and bonniest lads of the lot. Bless you, Auntie, and good morning!"

Dr. Alec turned to greet the old lady, and with a firm resolve to eat or die in the attempt, Rose sat down.

In five minutes she forgot what she was eating, so interested was she in the chat that went on. It amused her very much to hear Aunt Plenty call her forty-year-old nephew "my dear boy"; and Uncle Alec was so full of lively gossip about all creation in general, and the Aunt Hill in particular, that the detested porridge vanished without a murmur.

"You will go to church with us, I hope, Alec, if you are not too tired," said the old lady when breakfast was over.

"I came all the way from Calcutta for that express purpose, ma'am. Only I must send the sisters word of my arrival, for they don't expect me till tomorrow, you know, and there will be a row in church if those boys see me without warning."

"I'll send Ben up the hill, and you can step over to Myra's yourself; it will please her, and you will have plenty of time."

Dr. Alec was off at once, and they saw no more of him till the old barouche was at the door, and Aunt Plenty just rustling downstairs in her Sunday best, with Rose like a little black shadow behind her.

Away they drove in state, and all the way Uncle Alec's hat was more off his head than on, for everyone they met smiled and bowed and gave him as blithe a greeting as the day permitted.

It was evident that the warning had been a wise one, for in spite of time and place, the lads were in such a ferment that their elders sat in momentary dread of an unseemly outbreak somewhere. It was simply impossible to keep those fourteen eyes off Uncle Alec, and the dreadful things that were done during sermon time will hardly be believed.

Rose dared not look up after a while, for these bad boys vented their emotions upon her till she was ready to laugh and cry with mingled amusement and vexation. Charlie winked rapturously at her behind his mother's fan; Mac openly pointed to the tall figure beside her; Jamie stared fixedly over the back of his pew, till Rose thought his round eyes would drop out of his head; George fell over a stool and dropped three books in his excitement; Will drew sailors and Chinamen on his clean cuffs, and displayed them, to Rose's great tribulation; Steve nearly upset the whole party by burning his nose with salts as he pretended to be overcome by his joy; even dignified Archie disgraced himself by writing in his hymnbook, "Isn't he *blue* and *brown*?" and passing it politely to Rose.

Her only salvation was trying to fix her attention upon Uncle Mac —a portly, placid gentleman who seemed entirely unconscious of the iniquities of the clan and dozed peacefully in his pew corner. This was the only uncle Rose had met for years, for Uncle Jem and Uncle Steve, the husbands of Aunt Jessie and Aunt Clara, were at sea, and Aunt Myra was a widow. Uncle Mac was a merchant, very rich and busy, and as quiet as a mouse at home, for he was in such a minority among the womenfolk he dared not open his lips, and let his wife rule undisturbed.

Rose liked the big, kindly, silent man who came to her when Papa died, was always sending her splendid boxes of goodies at school, and often invited her into his great warehouse, full of teas and spices, wines and all sorts of foreign fruits, there to eat and carry away whatever she liked. She had secretly regretted that he was not to be her guardian; but since she had seen Uncle Alec she felt better about it, for she did not particularly admire Aunt Jane.

When church was over, Dr. Alec got into the porch as quickly as possible, and there the young bears had a hug all round, while the sisters shook hands and welcomed him with bright faces and glad hearts. Rose was nearly crushed flat behind a door in that dangerous passage from pew to porch; but Uncle Mac rescued her and put her into the carriage for safekeeping.

"Now, girls, I want you all to come and dine with Alec; Mac also, of course. But I cannot ask the boys, for we did not expect this dear fellow till tomorrow, you know, so I made no preparations. Send the lads home, and let them wait till Monday, for really I was shocked at their behavior in church," said Aunt Plenty as she followed Rose.

In any other place the defrauded boys would have set up a howl; as it was, they growled and protested till Dr. Alec settled the matter by saying, "Never mind, old chaps, I'll make it up to you tomorrow, if you sheer off quietly; if you don't, not a blessed thing shall you have out of my big boxes."

CHAPTER 4

AUNTS

ALL DINNERTIME ROSE FELT that she was going to be talked about, and afterward she was sure of it, for Aunt Plenty whispered to her as they went into the parlor, "Run up and sit awhile with Sister Peace, my dear. She likes to have you read while she rests, and we are going to be busy."

Rose obeyed, and the quiet rooms above were so like a church that she soon composed her ruffled feelings and was unconsciously a little minister of happiness to the sweet old lady, who for years had sat there patiently waiting to be set free from pain.

Rose knew the sad romance of her life, and it gave a certain tender charm to this great-aunt of hers, whom she already loved. When Peace was twenty, she was about to be married; all was done, the wedding dress lay ready, the flowers were waiting to be put on, the happy hour at hand, when word came that the lover was dead. They thought that gentle Peace would die too; but she bore it bravely, put away her bridal gear, took up her life afresh, and lived on—a beautiful, meek woman with hair as white as snow and cheeks that never bloomed again. She wore no black, but soft, pale colors, as if always ready for the marriage that had never come.

For thirty years she had lived on, fading slowly, but cheerful, busy, and full of interest in all that went on in the family; especially the joys and sorrows of the young girls growing up about her, and to them she was adviser, confidante, and friend in all their tender trials and delights. A truly beautiful old maiden, with her silvery hair, tranquil face, and an atmosphere of repose about her that soothed whoever came to her!

Aunt Plenty was utterly dissimilar, being a stout, brisk old lady with a sharp eye, a lively tongue, and a face like a winter apple. Always trotting, chatting, and bustling, she was a regular Martha, cumbered with the cares of this world and quite happy in them.

Rose was right; and while she softly read psalms to Aunt Peace, the other ladies were talking about her little self in the frankest manner.

"Well, Alec, how do you like your ward?" began Aunt Jane as they all settled down, and Uncle Mac deposited himself in a corner to finish his doze.

"I should like her better if I could have begun at the beginning, and so got a fair start. Poor George led such a solitary life that the child has suffered in many ways, and since he died she has been going on worse than ever, judging from the state I find her in."

"My dear boy, we did what we thought best while waiting for you to wind up your affairs and get home. I always told George he was wrong to bring her up as he did; but he never took my advice, and now here we are with this poor dear child upon our hands. I, for one, freely confess that I don't know what to do with her any more than if she was one of those strange, outlandish birds you used to bring home from foreign parts." And Aunt Plenty gave a perplexed shake of the head which caused great commotion among the stiff loops of purple ribbon that bristled all over her cap like crocus buds.

"If *my* advice had been taken, she would have remained at the excellent school where I placed her. But our aunt thought best to remove her because she complained, and she has been dawdling about ever since she came. A most ruinous state of things for a morbid, spoiled girl like Rose," said Mrs. Jane severely.

She had never forgiven the old ladies for yielding to Rose's pathetic petition that she might wait her guardian's arrival before beginning another term at the school, which was a regular Blimber hotbed, and turned out many a feminine Toots.

"*I* never thought it the proper school for a child in good circumstances—an heiress, in fact, as Rose is. It is all very well for girls who are to get their own living by teaching, and that sort of thing; but all *she* needs is a year or two at a fashionable finishing school, so that at eighteen she can come out with *éclat*," put in Aunt Clara, who had been a beauty and a belle and was still a handsome woman.

"Dear, dear! how shortsighted you all are to be discussing education and plans for the future, when this unhappy child is so plainly marked for the tomb," sighed Aunt Myra with a lugubrious sniff and a solemn wag of the funereal bonnet, which she refused to remove, being afflicted with a chronic catarrh.

"Now, it is my opinion that the dear thing only wants freedom, rest, and care. There is a look in her eyes that goes to my heart, for it shows that she feels the need of what none of us can give her—a mother," said Aunt Jessie with tears in her own bright eyes at the thought of her boys being left, as Rose was, to the care of others.

Uncle Alec, who had listened silently as each spoke, turned quickly toward the last sister and said, with a decided nod of approval, "You've got it, Jessie; and with you to help me, I hope to make the child feel that she is not quite fatherless and motherless."

"I'll do my best, Alec; and I think you *will* need me, for wise as you are, you cannot understand a tender, timid little creature like Rose as a woman can," said Mrs. Jessie, smiling back at him with a heart full of motherly goodwill.

"I cannot help feeling that *I,* who have had a daughter of my own, can best bring up a girl; and I am *very* much surprised that George did not entrust her to me," observed Aunt Myra with an air of melancholy importance, for she was the only one who had given a daughter to the family, and she felt that she had distinguished herself, though ill-natured people said that she had dosed her darling to death.

"I never blamed him in the least, when I remember the perilous experiments you tried with poor Carrie," began Mrs. Jane in her hard voice.

"Jane Campbell, I will *not* hear a word! My sainted Caroline is a sacred subject," cried Aunt Myra, rising as if to leave the room.

Dr. Alec detained her, feeling that he must define his position at once and maintain it manfully if he hoped to have any success in his new undertaking.

"Now, my dear souls, don't let us quarrel and make Rose a bone of contention—though upon my word, she *is* almost a bone, poor little lass! You have had her among you for a year and done what you liked. I cannot say that your success is great, but that is owing to too many fingers in the pie. Now, I intend to try my way for a year, and if at the end of it she is not in better trim than now, I'll give up the case and hand her over to someone else. That's fair, I think."

"She will not be here a year hence, poor darling, so no one need dread future responsibility," said Aunt Myra, folding her black gloves as if all ready for the funeral.

"By Jupiter, Myra, you are enough to damp the ardor of a saint!" cried Dr. Alec with a sudden spark in his eyes. "Your croaking will worry that child out of her wits, for she is an imaginative puss and will fret and fancy untold horrors. You have put it into her head that she has no constitution, and she rather likes the idea. If she had not had a pretty good one, she *would* have been 'marked for the tomb' by this time, at the rate you have been going on with her. I will not have any interference—please understand that; so just wash your hands of her and let me manage till I want help, then I'll ask for it."

"Hear, hear!" came from the corner where Uncle Mac was apparently wrapped in slumber.

"You were appointed guardian, so we can do nothing. But I predict that the girl will be spoiled, utterly spoiled," answered Mrs. Jane grimly.

"Thank you, sister. I have an idea that if a woman can bring up two boys as perfectly as you do yours, a man, if he devotes his whole mind to it, may at least attempt as much with one girl," replied Dr.

Alec with a humorous look that tickled the others immensely, for it was a well-known fact in the family that Jane's boys were more indulged than all the other lads put together.

"*I* am quite easy, for I really do think that Alec will improve the child's health; and by the time his year is out, it will be quite soon enough for her to go to Madame Roccabella's and be finished off," said Aunt Clara, settling her rings and thinking, with languid satisfaction, of the time when she could bring out a pretty and accomplished niece.

"I suppose you will stay here in the old place, unless you think of marrying, and it's high time you did," put in Mrs. Jane, much nettled at her brother's last hit.

"No, thank you. Come and have a cigar, Mac," said Dr. Alec abruptly.

"Don't marry; women enough in the family already," muttered Uncle Mac; and then the gentlemen hastily fled.

"Aunt Peace would like to see you all, she says," was the message Rose brought before the ladies could begin again.

"Hectic, hectic!—dear me, dear me!" murmured Aunt Myra as the shadow of her gloomy bonnet fell upon Rose, and the stiff tips of a black glove touched the cheek where the color deepened under so many eyes.

"I am glad these pretty curls are natural; they will be invaluable by and by," said Aunt Clara, taking an observation with her head on one side.

"Now that your uncle has come, I no longer expect you to review the studies of the past year. I trust your time will not be *entirely* wasted in frivolous sports, however," added Aunt Jane, sailing out of the room with the air of a martyr.

Aunt Jessie said not a word, but kissed her little niece with a look of tender sympathy that made Rose cling to her a minute and follow her with grateful eyes as the door closed behind her.

After everybody had gone home, Dr. Alec paced up and down the lower hall in the twilight for an hour, thinking so intently that sometimes he frowned, sometimes he smiled, and more than once he stood still in a brown study. All of a sudden he said, half aloud, as if he had made up his mind, "I might as well begin at once and give the child something new to think about, for Myra's dismals and Jane's lectures have made her as blue as a little indigo bag."

Diving into one of the trunks that stood in a corner, he brought up, after a brisk rummage, a silken cushion, prettily embroidered, and a quaint cup of dark carved wood.

"This will do for a start," he said as he plumped up the cushion and dusted the cup. "It won't do to begin too energetically, or Rose will be frightened. I must beguile her gently and pleasantly along till I've won her confidence, and then she will be ready for anything."

Just then Phebe came out of the dining room with a plate of brown bread, for Rose had been allowed no hot biscuit for tea.

"I'll relieve you of some of that," said Dr. Alec, and helping himself to a generous slice, he retired to the study, leaving Phebe to wonder at his appetite.

She would have wondered still more if she had seen him making that brown bread into neat little pills, which he packed into an attractive ivory box, out of which he emptied his own bits of lovage.

"There! If they insist on medicine, I'll order these, and no harm will be done. I will have my own way, but I'll keep the peace, if possible, and confess the joke when my experiment has succeeded," he said to himself, looking very much like a mischievous boy as he went off with his innocent prescriptions.

Rose was playing softly on the small organ that stood in the upper hall, so that Aunt Peace could enjoy it; and all the while he talked with the old ladies Uncle Alec was listening to the fitful music of the child and thinking of another Rose who used to play for him.

As the clock struck eight, he called out, "Time for my girl to be abed, else she won't be up early, and I'm full of jolly plans for tomorrow. Come and see what I have found for you to begin upon."

Rose ran in and listened with bright, attentive face while Dr. Alec said, impressively, "In my wanderings over the face of the earth, I have picked up some excellent remedies, and as they are rather agreeable ones, I think you and I will try them. This is an herb pillow, given to me by a wise old woman when I was ill in India. It is filled with saffron, poppies, and other soothing plants; so lay your little head on it tonight, sleep sweetly without a dream, and wake tomorrow without a pain."

"Shall I really? How nice it smells." And Rose willingly received the pretty pillow, and stood enjoying its faint, sweet odor as she listened to the doctor's next remedy.

"This is the cup I told you of. Its virtue depends, they say, on the drinker filling it himself; so you must learn to milk. I'll teach you."

"I'm afraid I never can," said Rose; but she surveyed the cup with favor, for a funny little imp danced on the handle, as if all ready to take a header into the white sea below.

"Don't you think she ought to have something more strengthening than milk, Alec? I really shall feel anxious if she does not have a tonic of some sort," said Aunt Plenty, eyeing the new remedies suspiciously, for she had more faith in her old-fashioned doses than all the magic cups and poppy pillows of the East.

"Well, ma'am, I'm willing to give her a pill, if you think best. It is a very simple one, and very large quantities may be taken without harm. You know hashish is the extract of hemp? Well, this is a preparation of corn and rye, much used in old times, and I hope it will be again."

"Dear me, how singular!" said Aunt Plenty, bringing her spectacles to bear upon the pills, with a face so full of respectful interest that it was almost too much for Dr. Alec's gravity.

"Take one in the morning, and a good night to you, my dear," he said, dismissing his patient with a hearty kiss.

Then, as she vanished, he put both hands into his hair, exclaiming, with a comical mixture of anxiety and amusement, "When I think what I have undertaken, I declare to you, Aunt, I feel like running away and not coming back till Rose is eighteen!"

CHAPTER 5

A BELT AND A BOX

When Rose came out of her chamber, cup in hand, next morning, the first person she saw was Uncle Alec standing on the threshold of the room opposite, which he appeared to be examining with care. When he heard her step, he turned about and began to sing, "Where are you going, my pretty maid?"

"I'm going a-milking, sir, she said," answered Rose, waving the cup; and then they finished the verse together in fine style.

Before either spoke, a head, in a nightcap so large and beruffled that it looked like a cabbage, popped out of a room farther down the hall, and an astonished voice exclaimed, "What in the world are you about so early?"

"Clearing our pipes for the day, ma'am. Look here, Auntie, can I have this room?" said Dr. Alec, making her a sailor's bow.

"Any room you like, except sister's."

"Thanks. And may I go rummaging round in the garrets and glory holes to furnish it as I like?"

"My dear boy, you may turn the house upside down if you will only stay in it."

37

"That's a handsome offer, I'm sure. I'll stay, ma'am; here's my little anchor, so you will get more than you want of me this time."

"That's impossible! Put on your jacket, Rose. Don't tire her out with antics, Alec. Yes, sister, I'm coming!" and the cabbage vanished suddenly.

The first milking lesson was a droll one; but after several scares and many vain attempts, Rose at last managed to fill her cup, while Ben held Clover's tail so that it could not flap, and Dr. Alec kept her from turning to stare at the new milkmaid, who objected to both these proceedings very much.

"You look chilly in spite of all this laughing. Take a smart run round the garden and get up a glow," said the doctor as they left the barn.

"I'm too old for running, Uncle; Miss Power said it was not lady-like for girls in their teens," answered Rose primly.

"I take the liberty of differing from Madame Prunes and Prisms, and as your physician, I *order* you to run. Off with you!" said Uncle Alec with a look and a gesture that made Rose scurry away as fast as she could go.

Anxious to please him, she raced round the beds till she came back to the porch where he stood, and dropping down upon the steps, she sat panting, with cheeks as rosy as the rigolette on her shoulders.

"Very well done, child; I see you have not lost the use of your limbs though you *are* in your teens. That belt is too tight; unfasten it, then you can take a long breath without panting so."

"It isn't tight, sir; I can breathe perfectly well," began Rose, trying to compose herself.

Her uncle's only answer was to lift her up and unhook the new belt of which she was so proud. The moment the clasp was open, the belt flew apart several inches, for it was impossible to restrain the involuntary sigh of relief that flatly contradicted her words.

"Why, I didn't know it was tight! It didn't feel so a bit. Of course it would open if I puff like this, but I never do, because I hardly ever run," explained Rose, rather discomfited by this discovery.

"I see you don't half fill your lungs, and so you can wear this absurd thing without feeling it. The idea of cramping a tender little waist in a stiff band of leather and steel just when it ought to be growing," said Dr. Alec, surveying the belt with great disfavor as he put the clasp forward several holes, to Rose's secret dismay, for she was proud of her slender figure and daily rejoiced that she wasn't as stout as Luly Miller, a former schoolmate, who vainly tried to repress her plumpness.

"It will fall off if it is so loose," she said anxiously as she stood watching him pull her precious belt about.

"Not if you keep taking long breaths to hold it on. That is what I want you to do, and when you have filled this out we will go on enlarging it till your waist is more like that of Hebe, goddess of health, and less like that of a fashion plate—the ugliest thing imaginable."

"How it does look!" and Rose gave a glance of scorn at the loose belt hanging round her trim little waist. "It will be lost, and then I shall feel badly, for it cost ever so much, and is real steel and Russia leather. Just smell how nice."

"If it is lost I'll give you a better one. A soft silken sash is much fitter for a pretty child like you than a plated harness like this; and I've got no end of Italian scarfs and Turkish sashes among my traps. Ah! that makes you feel better, doesn't it?" and he pinched the cheek that had suddenly dimpled with a smile.

"It is very silly of me, but I can't help liking to know that"—here she stopped and blushed and held down her head, ashamed to add, "you think I am pretty."

Dr. Alec's eyes twinkled, but he said very soberly, "Rose, are you vain?"

"I'm afraid I am," answered a very meek voice from behind the veil of hair that hid the red face.

"That is a sad fault." And he sighed as if grieved at the confession.

"I know it is, and I try not to be; but people praise me, and I can't help liking it, for I really don't think I am repulsive."

The last word and the funny tone in which it was uttered were too much for Dr. Alec, and he laughed in spite of himself, to Rose's great relief.

"I quite agree with you; and in order that you may be still less repulsive, I want you to grow as fine a girl as Phebe."

"Phebe!" and Rose looked so amazed that her uncle nearly went off again.

"Yes, Phebe; for she has what you need—health. If you dear little girls would only learn what real beauty is, and not pinch and starve and bleach yourselves out so, you'd save an immense deal of time and money and pain. A happy soul in a healthy body makes the best sort of beauty for man or woman. Do you understand that, my dear?"

"Yes, sir," answered Rose, much taken down by this comparison with the girl from the poorhouse. It nettled her sadly, and she showed that it did by saying quickly, "I suppose you would like to have me sweep and scrub, and wear an old brown dress, and go round with my sleeves rolled up, as Phebe does?"

"I should very much, if you could work as well as she does and show as strong a pair of arms as she can. I haven't seen a prettier picture for some time than she made of herself this morning, up to the elbows in suds, singing like a blackbird while she scrubbed on the back stoop."

"Well, I do think you are the queerest man that ever lived!" was all Rose could find to say after this display of bad taste.

"I haven't begun to show my oddities yet, so you must make up your mind to worse shocks than this," he said with such a whimsical look that she was glad the sound of a bell prevented her showing more plainly what a blow her little vanities had already received.

"You will find your box all open up in Auntie's parlor, and there you can amuse her and yourself by rummaging to your heart's content; I've got to be cruising round all the morning getting my room to rights," said Dr. Alec as they rose from breakfast.

"Can't I help you, Uncle?" asked Rose, quite burning to be useful.

"No, thank you. I'm going to borrow Phebe for a while, if Aunt Plenty can spare her."

"Anybody—anything, Alec. You will want me, I know, so I'll give orders about dinner and be all ready to lend a hand"; and the old lady bustled away full of interest and goodwill.

"Uncle will find that *I* can do some things that Phebe can't; so now!" thought Rose with a toss of the head as she flew to Aunt Peace and the long-desired box.

Every little girl can easily imagine what an extra good time she had diving into a sea of treasures and fishing up one pretty thing after another, till the air was full of the mingled odors of musk and sandalwood, the room gay with bright colors, and Rose in a rapture of delight. She began to forgive Dr. Alec for the oatmeal diet when she saw a lovely ivory workbox; became resigned to the state of her belt when she found a pile of rainbow-colored sashes; and when she came to some distractingly pretty bottles of attar of rose, she felt that they almost atoned for the great sin of thinking Phebe the finer girl of the two.

Dr. Alec meanwhile had apparently taken Aunt Plenty at her word, and *was* turning the house upside down. A general revolution was evidently going on in the green room, for the dark damask curtains were seen bundling away in Phebe's arms; the airtight stove retiring to the cellar on Ben's shoulder; and the great bedstead going up garret in a fragmentary state, escorted by three bearers. Aunt Plenty was constantly on the trot among her storerooms, camphor chests, and linen closets, looking as if the new order of things both amazed and amused her.

Half the peculiar performances of Dr. Alec cannot be revealed; but as Rose glanced up from her box now and then she caught glimpses of him striding by, bearing a bamboo chair, a pair of ancient andirons, a queer Japanese screen, a rug or two, and finally a large bathing pan upon his head.

"What a curious room it will be," she said as she sat resting and refreshing herself with Lumps of Delight, all the way from Cairo.

"I fancy *you* will like it, deary," answered Aunt Peace, looking up with a smile from some pretty trifle she was making with blue silk and white muslin.

Rose did not see the smile, for just at that moment her uncle paused at the door, and she sprang up to dance before him, saying, with a face full of childish happiness, "Look at me! Look at me! I'm so splendid I don't know myself. I haven't put these things on right, I dare say, but I do like them *so* much!"

"You look as gay as a parrot in your fez and *cabaja,* and it does my heart good to see the little black shadow turned into a rainbow," said Uncle Alec, surveying the bright figure before him with great approbation.

He did not say it, but he thought she made a much prettier picture than Phebe at the washtub, for she had stuck a purple fez on her blond head, tied several brilliant scarfs about her waist, and put on a truly gorgeous scarlet jacket with a golden sun embroidered on the back, a silver moon on the front, and stars of all sizes on the sleeves. A pair of Turkish slippers adorned her feet, and necklaces of amber, coral, and filigree hung about her neck, while one hand held a smelling bottle, and the other the spicy box of Oriental sweetmeats.

"I feel like a girl in the *Arabian Nights* and expect to find a magic carpet or a wonderful talisman somewhere. Only I don't see how I ever *can* thank you for all these lovely things," she said, stopping her dance as if suddenly oppressed with gratitude.

"I'll tell you how—by leaving off the black clothes that never should have been kept so long on such a child, and wearing the gay ones I've brought. It will do your spirits good, and cheer up this sober old house. Won't it, Auntie?"

"I think you are right, Alec, and it is fortunate that we have not begun on her spring clothes yet, for Myra thought she ought not to wear anything brighter than violet, and she is too pale for that."

"You just let me direct Miss Hemming how to make some of these things. You will be surprised to see how much I know about piping hems and gathering armholes and shirring biases," began Dr. Alec, patting a pile of muslin, cloth, and silk with a knowing air.

Aunt Peace and Rose laughed so that he could not display his knowledge any further till they stopped, when he said good-naturedly, "That will go a great way toward filling out the belt, so laugh away, Morgiana, and I'll go back to my work, or I never shall be done."

"I couldn't help it; 'shirred biases' were so very funny!" Rose said as she turned to her box after the splendid laugh. "But really, Auntie," she added soberly, "I feel as if I ought not to have so many nice things. I suppose it wouldn't do to give Phebe some of them? Uncle might not like it."

"He would not mind; but they are not suitable for Phebe. Some of the dresses you are done with would be more useful, if they can be made over to fit her," answered Aunt Peace in the prudent, moderate tone which is so trying to our feelings when we indulge in little fits of charitable enthusiasm.

"I'd rather give her new ones, for I think she is a little bit proud and might not like old things. If she was my sister it would do, because sisters don't mind, but she isn't, and that makes it bad, you see. I know how I can manage beautifully; I'll adopt her!" and Rose looked quite radiant with this new idea.

"I'm afraid you could not do it legally till you are older, but you might see if she likes the plan, and at any rate you can be very kind to her, for in one sense we are all sisters and should help one another."

The sweet old face looked at her so kindly that Rose was fired with a desire to settle the matter at once and rushed away to the kitchen just as she was. Phebe was there, polishing up the antique andirons so busily that she started when a voice cried out: "Smell that, taste this, and look at me!"

Phebe sniffed attar of rose, crunched the Lump of Delight tucked into her mouth, and stared with all her eyes at little Morgiana prancing about the room like a brilliant parakeet.

"My stars, ain't you splendid!" was all she could say, holding up two dusty hands.

"I've got heaps of lovely things upstairs, and I'll show them all to you, and I'd go halves, only Auntie thinks they wouldn't be useful, so I shall give you something else; and you won't mind, will you?

Because I want to adopt you as Arabella was in the story. Won't that be nice?"

"Why, Miss Rose, have you lost your wits?"

No wonder Phebe asked, for Rose talked very fast, and looked so odd in her new costume, and was so eager she could not stop to explain. Seeing Phebe's bewilderment, she quieted down and said, with a pretty air of earnestness, "It isn't fair that I should have so much and you so little, and I want to be as good to you as if you were my sister, for Aunt Peace says we are all sisters really. I thought if I adopted you as much as I can now, it would be nicer. Will you let me, please?"

To Rose's great surprise, Phebe sat down on the floor and hid her face in her apron for a minute without answering a word.

"Oh dear, now she's offended, and I don't know what to do," thought Rose, much discouraged by this reception of her offer.

"Please, forgive me; I didn't mean to hurt your feelings, and hope you won't think—" she faltered presently, feeling that she must undo the mischief if possible.

But Phebe gave her another surprise by dropping the apron and showing a face all smiles, in spite of tears in the eyes, as she put both arms round Rose and said with a laugh and sob, "I think you are the dearest girl in the world, and I'll let you do anything you like with me."

"Then you do like the plan? You didn't cry because I seemed to be kind of patronizing? I truly didn't mean to be," cried Rose, delighted.

"I guess I do like it! and cried because no one was ever so good to me before, and I couldn't help it. As for patronizing, you may walk on me if you want to, and I won't mind," said Phebe in a burst of gratitude, for the words, "we are all sisters," went straight to her lonely heart and nestled there.

"Well, now, we can play I'm a good sprite out of the box, or, what is better, a fairy godmother come down the chimney, and you are Cinderella and must say what you want," said Rose, trying to put the question delicately.

Phebe understood that, for she had a good deal of natural refine-
ment, though she did come from the poorhouse.

"I don't feel as if I wanted anything now, Miss Rose, but to find
some way of thanking you for all you've done," she said, rubbing off
a tear that went rolling down the bridge of her nose in the most
unromantic way.

"Why, I haven't done anything but given you a bit of candy! Here,
have some more, and eat 'em while you work, and think what I *can*
do. I must go and clear up, so good-bye, and don't forget I've
adopted you."

"You've given me sweeter things than candy, and I'm not likely to
forget it." And carefully wiping off the brick dust, Phebe pressed the
little hand Rose offered warmly in both her hard ones, while the
black eyes followed the departing visitor with a grateful look that
made them very soft and bright.

CHAPTER 6

UNCLE ALEC'S ROOM

Soon after dinner, and before she had got acquainted with half her new possessions, Dr. Alec proposed a drive, to carry round the first installment of gifts to the aunts and cousins. Rose was quite ready to go, being anxious to try a certain soft burnoose from the box, which not only possessed a most engaging little hood, but had funny tassels bobbing in all directions.

The big carriage was full of parcels, and even Ben's seat was loaded with Indian war clubs, a Chinese kite of immense size, and a pair of polished oxhorns from Africa. Uncle Alec, very blue as to his clothes, and very brown as to his face, sat bolt upright, surveying well-known places with interest, while Rose, feeling unusually elegant and comfortable, leaned back folded in her soft mantle and played she was an Eastern princess making a royal progress among her subjects.

At three of the places their calls were brief, for Aunt Myra's catarrh was unusually bad; Aunt Clara had a room full of company; and Aunt Jane showed such a tendency to discuss the population, productions, and politics of Europe, Asia, and Africa that even Dr. Alec was dismayed and got away as soon as possible.

"Now we will have a good time! I do hope the boys will be at home," said Rose with a sigh of relief as they wound yet higher up the hill to Aunt Jessie's.

"I left this for the last call so that we might find the lads just in from school. Yes, there is Jamie on the gate watching for us; now you'll see the clan gather; they are always swarming about together."

The instant Jamie saw the approaching guests he gave a shrill whistle, which was answered by echoes from meadow, house, and barn as the cousins came running from all directions shouting, "Hooray for Uncle Alec!" They went at the carriage like highwaymen, robbed it of every parcel, took the occupants prisoners, and marched them into the house with great exultation.

"Little Mum! Little Mum! Here they are with lots of goodies! Come down and see the fun right away! Quick!" bawled Will and Geordie amid a general ripping off of papers and a reckless cutting of strings that soon turned the tidy room into a chaos.

Down came Aunt Jessie with her pretty cap half on, but such a beaming face below it that one rather thought the flyaway headgear an improvement than otherwise. She had hardly time to greet Rose and the doctor before the boys were about her, each clamoring for her to see his gift and rejoice over it with him, for "little Mum" went halves in everything. The great horns skirmished about her as if to toss her to the ceiling; the warclubs hurtled over her head as if to annihilate her; an amazing medley from the four quarters of the globe filled her lap, and seven excited boys all talked to her at once.

But she liked it; oh dear, yes! and sat smiling, admiring, and explaining, quite untroubled by the din, which made Rose cover up her ears and Dr. Alec threaten instant flight if the riot were not quelled. That threat produced a lull, and while the uncle received thanks in one corner, the aunt had some little confidences made to her in the other.

"Well, dear, and how are things going with you now? Better, I hope, than they were a week ago."

"Aunt Jessie, I think I'm going to be very happy, now Uncle has come. He does the queerest things, but he is *so* good to me I can't help loving him"; and, nestling closer to little Mum, Rose told all that had happened, ending with a rapturous account of the splendid box.

"I am very glad, dear. But, Rose, I must warn you of one thing; don't let Uncle spoil you."

"But I like to be spoiled, Auntie."

"I don't doubt it; but if you turn out badly when the year is over he will be blamed, and his experiment prove a failure. That would be a pity, wouldn't it? When he wants to do so much for you, and can do it if his kind heart does not get in the way of his good judgment."

"I never thought of that, and I'll try not to be spoiled. But how *can* I help it?" asked Rose anxiously.

"By not complaining of the wholesome things he wants you to do; by giving him cheerful obedience as well as love; and even making some small sacrifices for his sake."

"I will, I truly will! And when I get in a worry about things, may I come to you? Uncle told me to, and I feel as if I shouldn't be afraid."

"You may, darling; this is the place where little troubles are best cured, and this is what mothers are for, I fancy"; and Aunt Jessie drew the curly head to her shoulder with a tender look that proved how well she knew what medicine the child most needed.

It was so sweet and comfortable that Rose sat still enjoying it till a little voice said, "Mamma, don't you think Pokey would like some of my shells? Rose gave Phebe some of her nice things, and it was very good of her. Can I?"

"Who is Pokey?" asked Rose, popping up her head, attracted by the odd name.

"My dolly; do you want to see her?" asked Jamie, who had been much impressed by the tale of adoption he had overheard.

"Yes; I'm fond of dollies, only don't tell the boys, or they will laugh at me."

"They don't laugh at me, and they play with my dolly a great deal; but she likes me best"; and Jamie ran away to produce his pet.

"I brought my old doll, but I keep her hidden because I am too big to play with her, and yet I can't bear to throw her away, I'm so fond of her," said Rose, continuing her confidences in a whisper.

"You can come and play with Jamie's whenever you like, for we believe in dollies up here," began Aunt Jessie, smiling to herself as if something amused her.

Just then Jamie came back, and Rose understood the smile, for his dolly proved to be a pretty four-year-old little girl, who trotted in as fast as her fat legs would carry her and, making straight for the shells, scrambled up an armful, saying, with a laugh that showed her little white teeth, "All for Dimmy and me, for Dimmy and me!"

"That's my dolly; isn't she a nice one?" asked Jamie, proudly surveying his pet with his hands behind him and his short legs rather far apart—a manly attitude copied from his brothers.

"She is a dear dolly. But why call her Pokey?" asked Rose, charmed with the new plaything.

"She is such an inquisitive little body she is always poking that mite of a nose into everything; and as Paul Pry did not suit, the boys fell to calling her Pokey. Not a pretty name, but very expressive."

It certainly was, for having examined the shells, the busy tot laid hold of everything she could find, and continued her researches till Archie caught her sucking his carved ivory chessmen to see if they were not barley sugar. Rice-paper pictures were also discovered crumpled up in her tiny pocket, and she nearly smashed Will's ostrich egg by trying to sit upon it.

"Here, Jim, take her away; she's worse than the puppies, and we can't have her round," commanded the elder brother, picking her up and handing her over to the little fellow, who received her with open arms and the warning remark, "You'd better mind what you do, for I'm going to 'dopt Pokey like Rose did Phebe, and then you'll have to be very good to her, you big fellows."

"'Dopt away, baby, and I'll give you a cage to keep her in, or you won't have her long, for she is getting worse than a monkey"; and Archie went back to his mates, while Aunt Jessie, foreseeing a crisis, proposed that Jamie should take his dolly home, as she was borrowed and it was time her visit ended.

"*My* dolly is better than yours, isn't she? 'Cause she can walk and talk and sing and dance, and yours can't do anything, can she?" asked Jamie with pride as he regarded his Pokey, who just then had been moved to execute a funny little jig and warble the well-known couplet

"Puss-tat, puss-tat, where you been?
I been Lunnin, to saw a Tween."

After which superb display she retired, escorted by Jamie, both making a fearful din blowing on conch shells.

"We must tear ourselves away, Rose, because I want to get you home before sunset. Will you come for a drive, Jessie?" said Dr. Alec as the music died away in the distance.

"No, thank you, but I see the boys want a scamper, so if you don't mind, they may escort you home, but not go in. That is only allowed on holidays."

The words were hardly out of Aunt Jessie's mouth when Archie said, in a tone of command, "Pass the word, lads. Boot and saddle, and be quick about it."

"All right!" And in a moment not a vestige of boy remained but the litter on the floor.

The cavalcade went down the hill at a pace that made Rose cling to her uncle's arm, for the fat old horses got excited by the antics of the ponies careering all about them, and went as fast as they could pelt, with the gay dogcart rattling in front, for Archie and Charlie scorned shelties since this magnificent equipage had been set up. Ben enjoyed the fun, and the lads cut up capers till Rose declared that "circus" was the proper name for them after all.

When they reached the house they dismounted and stood, three on each side of the steps, in martial attitudes, while her ladyship was handed out with great elegance by Uncle Alec. Then the clan saluted, mounted at word of command, and with a wild whoop tore down the avenue in what they considered the true Arab style.

"That was splendid, now it is safely ended," said Rose, skipping up the steps with her head over her shoulder to watch the dear tassels bob about.

"I shall get you a pony as soon as you are a little stronger," said Dr. Alec, watching her with a smile.

"Oh, I couldn't ride one of those horrid, frisky little beasts! They roll their eyes and bounce about so, I should die of fright," cried Rose, clasping her hands tragically.

"Are you a coward?"

"About horses I am."

"Never mind, then; come and see my new room"; and he led the way upstairs without another word.

As Rose followed she remembered her promise to Aunt Jessie and was sorry she had objected so decidedly. She was a great deal more sorry five minutes later, and well she might be.

"Now take a good look, and tell me what you think of it," said Dr. Alec, opening the door and letting her enter before him, while Phebe was seen whisking down the backstairs with a dustpan.

Rose walked to the middle of the room, stood still, and gazed about her with eyes that brightened as they looked, for all was changed.

This chamber had been built out over the library to suit some fancy, and had been unused for years, except at Christmas times, when the old house overflowed. It had three windows—one to the east, that overlooked the bay; one to the south, where the horse chestnuts waved their green fans; and one to the west, toward the hills and the evening sky. A ruddy sunset burned there now, filling the room with an enchanted glow; the soft murmur of the sea was heard, and a robin chirped "Good night!" among the budding trees.

Rose saw and heard these things first, and felt their beauty with a child's quick instinct; then her eye took in the altered aspect of the room, once so shrouded, still, and solitary, now so full of light and warmth and simple luxury.

India matting covered the floor, with a gay rug here and there; the antique andirons shone on the wide hearth, where a cheery blaze dispelled the dampness of the long-closed room. Bamboo lounges and chairs stood about, and quaint little tables in cozy corners; one bearing a pretty basket, one a desk, and on a third lay several familiar-looking books. In a recess stood a narrow white bed, with a lovely Madonna hanging over it. The Japanese screen half folded back showed a delicate toilet-service of blue and white set forth on a marble slab, and nearby was the great bathpan, with Turkish towels and a sponge as big as Rose's head.

"Uncle must love cold water like a duck," she thought with a shiver.

Then her eyes went on to the tall cabinet, where a half-open door revealed a tempting array of the drawers, shelves, and "cubby holes," which so delight the hearts of children.

"What a grand place for my new things," she thought, wondering what her uncle kept in that cedar retreat.

"Oh me, what a sweet toilet-table!" was her next mental exclamation, as she approached this inviting spot.

A round old-fashioned mirror hung over it, with a gilt eagle atop, holding in his beak the knot of blue ribbon that tied up a curtain of muslin falling on either side of the table, where appeared little ivory-handled brushes, two slender silver candlesticks, a porcelain matchbox, several pretty trays for small matters, and, most imposing of all, a plump blue silk cushion, coquettishly trimmed with lace, and pink rosebuds at the corners.

That cushion rather astonished Rose; in fact, the whole table did, and she was just thinking, with a sly smile, "Uncle is a dandy, but I never should have guessed it," when he opened the door of a large closet, saying, with a careless wave of the hand—

"Men like plenty of room for their rattletraps; don't you think that ought to satisfy me?"

Rose peeped in and gave a start, though all she saw was what one usually finds in closets—clothes and boots, boxes and bags. Ah! but you see these clothes were small black and white frocks; the row of little boots that stood below had never been on Dr. Alec's feet; the green bandbox had a gray veil straying out of it, and—yes! the bag hanging on the door was certainly her own piece bag, with a hole in one corner. She gave a quick look round the room and understood now why it had seemed too dainty for a man, why *her* Testament and Prayerbook were on the table by the bed, and what those rosebuds meant on the blue cushion. It came upon her in one delicious burst that this little paradise was all for her, and not knowing how else to express her gratitude, she caught Dr. Alec round the neck, saying impetuously, "O Uncle, you are *too* good to me! I'll do anything you ask me; ride wild horses and take freezing baths and eat bad-tasting messes, and let my clothes hang on me, to show how much I thank you for this dear, sweet, lovely room!"

"You like it, then? But why do you think it is yours, my lass?" asked Dr. Alec as he sat down looking well pleased and drew his excited little niece to his knee.

"I don't *think,* I *know* it is for me; I see it in your face, and I feel as if I didn't half deserve it. Aunt Jessie said you would spoil me, and I must not let you. I'm afraid this looks like it, and perhaps—oh me!— perhaps I ought not to have this beautiful room after all!" And Rose tried to look as if she could be heroic enough to give it up if it was best.

"I owe Mrs. Jessie one for that," said Dr. Alec, trying to frown, though in his secret soul he felt that she was quite right. Then he smiled that cordial smile, which was like sunshine on his brown face, as he said, "This is part of the cure, Rose, and I put you here that you might take my three great remedies in the best and easiest way. Plenty of sun, fresh air, and cold water; also cheerful surroundings and some work; for Phebe is to show you how to take care of this room, and be your little maid as well as friend and teacher. Does that sound hard and disagreeable to you, dear?"

"No, sir; very, very pleasant, and I'll do my best to be a good patient. But I really don't think anyone *could* be sick in this delightful room," she said, with a long sigh of happiness as her eye went from one pleasant object to another.

"Then you like my sort of medicine better than Aunt Myra's, and don't want to throw it out of the window, hey?"

CHAPTER 7

A TRIP TO CHINA

"COME, LITTLE GIRL, I've got another dose for you. I fancy you won't take it as well as you did the last, but you will like it better after a while," said Dr. Alec about a week after the grand surprise.

Rose was sitting in her pretty room, where she would gladly have spent all her time if it had been allowed; but she looked up with a smile, for she had ceased to fear her uncle's remedies and was always ready to try a new one. The last had been a set of light gardening tools, with which she had helped him put the flower beds in order, learning all sorts of new and pleasant things about the plants as she worked, for though she had studied botany at school, it seemed very dry stuff compared with Uncle Alec's lively lesson.

"What is it now?" she asked, shutting her workbox without a murmur.

"Salt water."

"How must I take it?"

"Put on the new suit Miss Hemming sent home yesterday, and come down to the beach; then I'll show you."

"Yes, sir," answered Rose obediently, adding to herself, with a shiver, as he went off: "It is too early for bathing, so I *know* it is something to do with a dreadful boat."

Putting on the new suit of blue flannel, prettily trimmed with white, and the little sailor hat with long streamers, diverted her mind from the approaching trial, till a shrill whistle reminded her that her uncle was waiting. Away she ran through the garden, down the sandy path, out upon the strip of beach that belonged to the house, and here she found Dr. Alec busy with a slender red-and-white boat that lay rocking on the rising tide.

"That is a dear little boat; and *Bonnie Belle* is a pretty name," she said, trying not to show how nervous she felt.

"It is for you; so sit in the stern and learn to steer, till you are ready to learn to row."

"Do all boats wiggle about in that way?" she asked, lingering as if to tie her hat more firmly.

"Oh, yes, pitch about like nutshells when the sea is a bit rough," answered her sailor uncle, never guessing her secret woe.

"Is it rough today?"

"Not very; it looks a trifle squally to the eastward, but we are all right till the wind changes. Come."

"Can you swim, Uncle?" asked Rose, clutching at his arm as he took her hand.

"Like a fish. Now then."

"Oh, please hold me *very* tight till I get there! Why *do* you have the stern so far away?" And stifling several squeaks of alarm in her passage, Rose crept to the distant seat and sat there holding on with both hands and looking as if she expected every wave to bring a sudden shipwreck.

Uncle Alec took no notice of her fear, but patiently instructed her in the art of steering, till she was so absorbed in remembering which was starboard and which larboard that she forgot to say "Ow!" every time a big wave slapped against the boat.

"Now where shall we go?" she asked, as the wind blew freshly in her face and a few long, swift strokes sent them half across the little bay.

"Suppose we go to China?"

"Isn't that rather a long voyage?"

"Not as I go. Steer round the Point into the harbor, and I'll give you a glimpse of China in twenty minutes or so."

"I should like that!" And Rose sat wondering what he meant, while she enjoyed the new sights all about her.

Behind them the green Aunt Hill sloped gently upward to the grove at the top, and all along the seaward side stood familiar houses, stately, cozy, or picturesque. As they rounded the Point, the great bay opened before them full of shipping, and the city lay beyond, its spires rising above the tall masts with their gay streamers.

"Are we going there?" she asked, for she had never seen this aspect of the rich and busy old city before.

"Yes. Uncle Mac has a ship just in from Hong Kong, and I thought you would like to go and see it."

"Oh, I should! I love dearly to go poking about in the warehouses with Uncle Mac; everything is so curious and new to me; and I'm specially interested in China because you have been there."

"I'll show you two genuine Chinamen who have just arrived. You will like to welcome Whang Lo and Fun See, I'm sure."

"Don't ask me to speak to them, Uncle; I shall be sure to laugh at the odd names and the pigtails and the slanting eyes. Please let me just trot round after you; I like that best."

"Very well; now steer toward the wharf where the big ship with the queer flag is. That's the *Rajah,* and we will go aboard if we can."

In among the ships they went, by the wharves where the water was green and still, and queer barnacles grew on the slippery piles. Odd smells saluted her nose, and odd sights met her eyes, but Rose liked it all, and played she was really landing in Hong Kong when they glided up to the steps in the shadow of the tall *Rajah.* Boxes and bales were rising out of the hold and being carried into the warehouse by stout porters, who tugged and bawled and clattered about with small trucks, or worked cranes with iron claws that came down and clutched heavy weights, whisking them aloft to where wide doors like mouths swallowed them up.

Dr. Alec took her aboard the ship, and she had the satisfaction of poking her inquisitive little nose into every available corner, at the risk of being crushed, lost, or drowned.

"Well, child, how would you like to take a voyage round the world with me in a jolly old craft like this?" asked her uncle as they rested a minute in the captain's cabin.

"I should like to see the world, but not in such a small, untidy, smelly place as this. We would go in a yacht all clean and comfortable. Charlie says that is the proper way," answered Rose, surveying the close quarters with little favor.

"You are not a true Campbell if you don't like the smell of tar and salt water, nor Charlie either, with his luxurious yacht. Now come ashore and chin-chin with the Celestials."

After a delightful progress through the great warehouse, peeping and picking as they went, they found Uncle Mac and the yellow gentlemen in his private room, where samples, gifts, curiosities, and newly arrived treasures of all sorts were piled up in pleasing profusion and con-fusion.

As soon as possible Rose retired to a corner, with a porcelain god on one side, a green dragon on the other, and what was still more embarrassing, Fun See sat on a tea chest in front, and stared at her with his beady black eyes till she did not know where to look.

Mr. Whang Lo was an elderly gentleman in American costume, with his pigtail neatly wound round his head. He spoke English, and was talking busily with Uncle Mac in the most commonplace way— so Rose considered *him* a failure. But Fun See was delightfully Chinese from his junklike shoes to the button on his pagoda hat; for he had got himself up in style and was a mass of silk jackets and slouchy trousers. He was short and fat, and waddled comically; his eyes were very "slanting," as Rose said; his queue was long, so were his nails; his yellow face was plump and shiny, and he was altogether a highly satisfactory Chinaman.

Uncle Alec told her that Fun See had come out to be educated, and could only speak a little pidgin English; so she must be kind to the poor fellow, for he was only a lad, though he looked nearly as old as Mr. Whang Lo. Rose said she would be kind but had not the least idea how to entertain the queer guest, who looked as if he had walked out of one of the rice-paper landscapes on the wall, and sat nodding at her so like a toy Mandarin that she could hardly keep sober.

In the midst of her polite perplexity, Uncle Mac saw the two young people gazing wistfully at one another, and seemed to enjoy the joke of this making acquaintance under difficulties. Taking a box from his table, he gave it to Fun See with an order that seemed to please him very much.

Descending from his perch, he fell to unpacking it with great neatness and dispatch while Rose watched him, wondering what was going to happen. Presently, out from the wrappings came a teapot, which caused her to clasp her hands with delight, for it was made in the likeness of a plump little Chinaman. His hat was the cover, his queue the handle, and his pipe the nose. It stood upon feet in shoes turned up at the toes, and the smile on the fat, sleepy face was so like that on Fun's when he displayed the teapot that Rose couldn't help laughing, which pleased him much.

Two pretty cups with covers, and a fine scarlet tray, completed the set, and made one long to have a "dish of tea," even in Chinese style, without cream or sugar.

When he had arranged them on a little table before her, Fun signified in pantomime that they were hers, from her uncle. She returned her thanks in the same way, whereupon he returned to his tea chest, and having no other means of communication, they sat smiling and nodding at one another in an absurd sort of way till a new idea seemed to strike Fun. Tumbling off his seat, he waddled away as fast as his petticoats permitted, leaving Rose hoping that he had not gone to get a roasted rat, a stewed puppy, or any other foreign mess which civility would oblige her to eat.

While she waited for her funny new friend, she improved her mind in a way that would have charmed Aunt Jane. The gentlemen were talking over all sorts of things, and she listened attentively, storing up much of what she heard, for she had an excellent memory and

longed to distinguish herself by being able to produce some useful
information when reproached with her ignorance.

She was just trying to impress upon her mind that Amoy was two
hundred and eighty miles from Hong Kong, when Fun came scuffling
back, bearing what she thought was a small sword, till he unfurled an
immense fan and presented it with a string of Chinese compliments,
the meaning of which would have amused her even more than the
sound if she could have understood it.

She had never seen such an astonishing fan and at once became
absorbed in examining it. Of course, there was no perspective whatever, which only gave it a peculiar charm to Rose, for in one place a
lovely lady, with blue knitting-needles in her hair, sat directly upon
the spire of a stately pagoda. In another charming view a brook
appeared to flow in at the front door of a stout gentleman's house,
and out at his chimney. In a third a zigzag wall went up into the sky
like a flash of lightning, and a bird with two tails was apparently
brooding over a fisherman whose boat was just going aground upon
the moon.

It was altogether a fascinating thing, and she would have sat waft-
ing it to and fro all the afternoon, to Fun's great satisfaction, if Dr.
Alec's attention had not suddenly been called to her by a breeze
from the big fan that blew his hair into his eyes and reminded him
that they must go. So the pretty china was repacked, Rose furled her
fan, and with several parcels of choice teas for the old ladies stowed
away in Dr. Alec's pockets they took their leave, after Fun had saluted them with the "three bendings and the nine knockings," as
they salute the Emperor, or "Son of Heaven," at home.

"I feel as if I had really been to China, and I'm sure I look so,"
said Rose as they glided out of the shadow of the *Rajah*.

She certainly did, for Mr. Whang Lo had given her a Chinese
umbrella; Uncle Alec had got some lanterns to light up her balcony;
the great fan lay in her lap, and the tea set reposed at her feet.

"This is not a bad way to study geography, is it?" asked her uncle,
who had observed her attention to the talk.

"It is a very pleasant way, and I really think I have learned more about China today than in all the lessons I had at school, though I used to rattle off the answers as fast as I could go. No one explained anything to us, so all I remember is that tea and silk come from there, and the women have little bits of feet. I saw Fun looking at mine, and he must have thought them perfectly immense," answered Rose, surveying her stout boots with sudden contempt.

"We will have out the maps and the globe, and I'll show you some of my journeys, telling stories as we go. That will be next best to doing it actually."

"You are so fond of traveling, I should think it would be very dull for you here, Uncle. Do you know, Aunt Plenty says she is sure you will be off in a year or two."

"Very likely."

"Oh me! what *shall* I do then?" sighed Rose in a tone of despair that made Uncle Alec's face brighten with a look of genuine pleasure as he said significantly, "Next time I go I shall take my little anchor with me. How will that suit?"

"Really, Uncle?"

"Really, Niece."

Rose gave a little bounce of rapture which caused the boat to "wiggle" in a way that speedily quieted her down. But she sat beaming joyfully and trying to think which of some hundred questions she would ask first, when Dr. Alec said, pointing to a boat that was coming up behind them in great style, "How well those fellows row! Look at them, and take notes for your own use by and by."

The *Stormy Petrel* was manned by half a dozen jaunty-looking sailors, who made a fine display of blue shirts and shiny hats, with stars and anchors in every direction.

"How beautifully they go, and they are only boys. Why, I do believe they are *our* boys! Yes, I see Charlie laughing over his shoulder. Row, Uncle, row! Oh, please do, and not let them catch up with us!" cried Rose in such a state of excitement that the new umbrella nearly went overboard.

"All right, here we go!" And away they did go with a long steady sweep of the oars that carried the *Bonnie Belle* through the water with a rush.

The lads pulled their prettiest, but Dr. Alec would have reached the Point first, if Rose, in her flurry, had not retarded him by jerking the rudder ropes in a most unseamanlike way, and just as she got right again her hat blew off. That put an end to the race, and while they were still fishing for the hat, the other boat came alongside, with all the oars in the air and the jolly young tars ready for a frolic.

"Did you catch a crab, Uncle?"

"No, a bluefish," he answered as the dripping hat was landed on a seat to dry.

"What have you been doing?"

"Seeing Fun."

"Good for you, Rose! I know what you mean. We are going to have him up to show us how to fly the big kite, for we can't get the hang of it. Isn't he great fun, though?"

"No, little Fun."

"Come, stop joking, and show us what you've got."

"You'd better hoist that fan for a sail."

"Lend Dandy your umbrella; he hates to burn his pretty nose."

"I say, Uncle, are you going to have a Feast of Lanterns?"

"No, I'm going to have a feast of bread and butter, for it's teatime. If that black cloud doesn't lie, we shall have a guest before long, so you had better get home as soon as you can, or your mother will be anxious, Archie."

"Ay, ay, skipper. Good night, Rose; come out often, and we'll teach you all there is to know about rowing," was Charlie's modest invitation.

Then the boats parted company, and across the water from the *Petrel*'s crew came a verse from one of the Nonsense Songs in which the boys delighted.

> Oh, Timballoo! how happy we are,
> We live in a sieve and a crockery jar!
> And all night long, in the starlight pale,

We sail away, with a pea-green sail,
And whistle and warble a moony song
To the echoing sound of a coppery gong.
   Far and few, far and few
Are the lands where the Jumblies live;
Their heads are green, and their hands are blue,
   And they went to sea in a sieve."

CHAPTER 8

AND WHAT CAME OF IT

"Uncle, could you lend me a ninepence? I'll return it as soon as I get my pocket money," said Rose, coming into the library in a great hurry that evening.

"I think I could, and I won't charge any interest for it, so you need not be in any hurry to repay me. Come back here and help me settle these books if you have nothing pleasanter to do," answered Dr. Alec, handing out the money with that readiness which is so delightful when we ask small loans.

"I'll come in a minute; I've been longing to fix my books, but didn't dare to touch them, because you always shake your head when I read."

"I shall shake my head when you write, if you don't do it better than you did in making out this catalogue."

"I know it's bad, but I was in a hurry when I did it, and I am in one now." And away went Rose, glad to escape a lecture.

But she got it when she came back, for Uncle Alec was still knitting his brows over the list of books, and sternly demanded, pointing to a tipsy-looking title staggering down the page, "Is that meant for 'Pulverized Bones,' ma'am?"

"No, sir; it's *Paradise Lost.*"

"Well, I'm glad to know it, for I began to think you were planning to study surgery or farming. And what is this, if you please? 'Babies' Aprons' is all *I* can make of it."

Rose looked hard at the scrawl, and presently announced, with an air of superior wisdom, "Oh, that's *Bacon's Essays.*"

"Miss Power did not teach anything so old-fashioned as writing, I see. Now look at this little memorandum Aunt Plenty gave me, and see what a handsome plain hand that is. She went to a dame school and learned a few useful things well; that is better than a smattering of half a dozen so-called higher branches, I take the liberty of thinking."

"Well, I'm sure I was considered a bright girl at school and learned everything I was taught. Luly and me were the first in all our classes, and 'specially praised for our French and music and those sort of things," said Rose, rather offended at Uncle Alec's criticism.

"I dare say; but if your French grammar was no better than your English, I think the praise was not deserved, my dear."

"Why, Uncle, we *did* study English grammar, and I could parse beautifully. Miss Power used to have us up to show off when people came. I don't see but I talk as right as most girls."

"I dare say you do, but we are all too careless about our English. Now, think a minute and tell me if these expressions are correct— 'Luly and me,' 'those sort of things,' and 'as right as most girls.' "

Rose pulled her pet curl and put up her lip, but had to own that she was wrong, and said meekly, after a pause which threatened to be sulky, "I suppose I should have said 'Luly and I,' in that case, and 'that sort of things' and 'rightly,' though 'correctly' would have been a better word, I guess."

"Thank you; and if you will kindly drop 'I guess,' I shall like my little Yankee all the better. Now, see here, Rosy, I don't pretend to set myself up for a model in anything, and you may come down on my grammar, manners, or morals as often as you think I'm wrong, and I'll thank you. I've been knocking about the world for years, and have got careless, but I want my girl to be what *I* call well educated, even if she studies nothing but the 'three R's' for a year to come. Let us be thorough, no matter how slowly we go."

He spoke so earnestly and looked so sorry to have ruffled her that Rose went and sat on the arm of his chair, saying, with a pretty air of penitence, "I'm sorry I was cross, Uncle, when I ought to thank you for taking so much interest in me. I guess—no, I think you are right about being thorough, for I used to understand a great deal better when Papa taught me a few lessons than when Miss Power hurried me through so many. I declare my head used to be such a jumble of French and German, history and arithmetic, grammar and music, I used to feel sometimes as if it would split. I'm sure I don't wonder it ached." And she held on to it as if the mere memory of the "jumble" made it swim.

"Yet that is considered an excellent school, I find, and I dare say it would be if the benighted lady did not think it necessary to cram her pupils like Thanksgiving turkeys, instead of feeding them in a natural and wholesome way. It is the fault with most American schools, and the poor little heads will go on aching till we learn better."

This was one of Dr. Alec's hobbies, and Rose was afraid he was off for a gallop, but he reined himself in and gave her thoughts a new turn by saying suddenly, as he pulled out a fat pocketbook, "Uncle Mac has put all your affairs into my hands now, and here is your month's pocket money. You keep your own little accounts, I suppose?"

"Thank you. Yes, Uncle Mac gave me an account book when I went to school, and I used to put down my expenses, but I couldn't make them go very well, for figures are the one thing I am not at all clever about," said Rose, rummaging in her desk for a dilapidated little book, which she was ashamed to show when she found it.

"Well, as figures are rather important things to most of us, and you may have a good many accounts to keep someday, wouldn't it be wise to begin at once and learn to manage your pennies before the pounds come to perplex you?"

"I thought you would do all that fussy part and take care of the pounds, as you call them. Need I worry about it? I do hate sums so!"

"I shall take care of things till you are of age, but I mean that you shall know how your property is managed and do as much of it as you can by and by; then you won't be dependent on the honesty of other people."

"Gracious me! As if I wouldn't trust you with millions of billions if I had them," cried Rose, scandalized at the mere suggestion.

"Ah, but I might be tempted; guardians are sometimes; so you'd better keep your eye on me, and in order to do that you must learn all about these affairs," answered Dr. Alec as he made an entry in his own very neat account book.

Rose peeped over his shoulder at it, and then turned to the arithmetical puzzle in her hand with a sigh of despair.

"Uncle, when you add up your expenses do you ever find you have got more money than you had in the beginning?"

"No; I usually find that I have a good deal less than I had in the beginning. Are you troubled in the peculiar way you mention?"

"Yes; it is very curious, but I never *can* make things come out square."

"Perhaps I can help you," began Uncle Alec in the most respectful tone.

"I think you had better, for if I have got to keep accounts I may as well begin in the right way. But please don't laugh! I know I'm very stupid, and my book is a disgrace, but I never *could* get it straight." And with great trepidation Rose gave up her funny little accounts.

It really *was* good in Dr. Alec not to laugh, and Rose felt deeply grateful when he said, in a mildly suggestive tone, "The dollars and cents seem to be rather mixed; perhaps if I just straighten them out a bit we should find things all right."

"Please do, and then show me on a fresh leaf how to make mine look nice and shipshape as yours do."

As Rose stood by him watching the ease with which he quickly brought order out of chaos, she privately resolved to hunt up her old arithmetic and perfect herself in the first four rules, with a good tug at fractions, before she read any more fairy tales.

"Am I a rich girl, Uncle?" she asked suddenly, as he was copying a column of figures.

"Rather a poor one, I should say, since you had to borrow a ninepence."

"That was your fault, because you forgot my pocket money. But, really, shall I be rich by and by?"

"I am afraid you will."

"Why afraid, Uncle?"

"Too much money is a bad thing."

"But I can give it away, you know; that is always the pleasantest part of having it, *I* think."

"I'm glad you feel so, for you *can* do much good with your fortune if you know how to use it well."

"You shall teach me, and when I am a woman we will set up a school where nothing but the three R's shall be taught, and all the children live on oatmeal, and the girls have waists a yard round," said Rose with a sudden saucy smile dimpling her cheeks.

"You are an impertinent little baggage, to turn on me in that way right in the midst of my first attempt at teaching. Never mind, I'll have an extra bitter dose for you next time, miss."

"I knew you wanted to laugh, so I gave you a chance. Now I will be good, master, and do my lesson nicely."

So Dr. Alec had his laugh, and then Rose sat down and took a lesson in accounts which she never forgot.

"Now come and read aloud to me; my eyes are tired, and it is pleasant to sit here by the fire while the rain pours outside and Aunt Jane lectures upstairs," said Uncle Alec when last month's accounts had been put in good order and a fresh page neatly begun.

Rose liked to read aloud and gladly gave him the chapter in *Nicholas Nickleby* where the Miss Kenwigses take their French lesson. She did her very best, feeling that she was being criticized and hoping that she might not be found wanting in this as in other things.

"Shall I go on, sir?" she asked very meekly when the chapter ended.

"If you are not tired, dear. It is a pleasure to hear you, for you read remarkably well," was the answer that filled her heart with pride and pleasure.

"Do you really think so, Uncle? I'm so glad! Papa taught me, and I read for hours to him, but I thought, perhaps, he liked it because he was fond of me."

"So am I; but you really do read unusually well, and I am very glad of it, for it is a rare accomplishment, and one I value highly. Come here in this cozy, low chair; the light is better, and I can pull these curls if you go too fast. I see you are going to be a great comfort as well as a great credit to your old uncle, Rosy." And Dr. Alec drew her close beside him with such a fatherly look and tone that she felt it would be very easy to love and obey him since he knew how to mix praise and blame so pleasantly together.

Another chapter was just finished when the sound of a carriage warned them that Aunt Jane was about to depart. Before they could go to meet her, however, she appeared in the doorway looking like an unusually tall mummy in her waterproof, with her glasses shining like cat's eyes from the depths of the hood.

"Just as I thought! Petting that child to death and letting her sit up late reading trash. I do hope you feel the weight of the responsibility you have taken upon yourself, Alec," she said with a certain grim sort of satisfaction at seeing things go wrong.

"I think I have a very realizing sense of it, sister Jane," answered Dr. Alec with a comical shrug of the shoulders and a glance at Rose's bright face.

"It is sad to see a great girl wasting these precious hours so. Now, my boys have studied all day, and Mac is still at his books, I've no doubt, while you have not had a lesson since you came, I suspect."

"I have had five today, ma'am," was Rose's very unexpected answer.

"I'm glad to hear it; and what were they, pray?"

Rose looked very demure as she replied, "Navigation, geography, grammar, arithmetic, and keeping my temper."

"Queer lessons, I fancy; and what have you learned from this remarkable mixture, I should like to know?"

A naughty sparkle came into Rose's eyes as she answered, with a droll look at her uncle, "I can't tell you all, ma'am, but I have collected some useful information about China, which you may like, especially the teas. The best are Lapsing souchong, Assam pekoe, rare ankoe, Flowery pekoe, Howqua's mixture, scented caper, Padral tea, black Congou, and green Twankey. Shanghai is on the Woosung River. Hong Kong means 'Island of sweet waters.' Singapore is 'Lion's Town.' 'Chops' are the boats they live in; and they drink tea out of little saucers. Principal productions are porcelain, tea, cinnamon, shawls, tin, tamarinds, and opium. They have beautiful temples and queer gods; and in Canton is the Dwelling of the Holy Pigs, fourteen of them, very big, and all blind."

The effect of this remarkable burst was immense, especially the fact last mentioned. It entirely took the wind out of Aunt Jane's sails; it was so sudden, so varied and unexpected, that she had not a word to say. The glasses remained fixed full upon Rose for a moment, and then, with a hasty "Oh, indeed!" the excellent lady bundled into her carriage and drove away, somewhat bewildered and very much disturbed.

She would have been more so if she had seen her reprehensible brother-in-law dancing a triumphal polka down the hall with Rose in honor of having silenced the enemy's battery for once.

CHAPTER 9

PHEBE'S SECRET

"WHY DO YOU KEEP SMILING to yourself, Phebe?" asked Rose as they were working together one morning, for Dr. Alec considered house-work the best sort of gymnastics for girls; so Rose took lessons of Phebe in sweeping, dusting, and bed making.

"I was thinking about a nice little secret I know, and couldn't help smiling."

"Shall I know it sometime?"

"Guess you will."

"Shall I like it?"

"Oh, won't you, though!"

"Will it happen soon?"

"Sometime this week."

"I know what it is! The boys are going to have fireworks on the Fourth and have got some surprise for me. Haven't they?"

"That's telling."

"Well, I can wait; only tell me one thing—is uncle in it?"

"Of course he is; there's never any fun without him."

"Then it is all right, and sure to be nice."

Rose went out on the balcony to shake the rugs and, having given

75

them a vigorous beating, hung them on the balustrade to air, while she took a look at her plants. Several tall vases and jars stood there, and a month of June sun and rain had worked wonders with the seeds and slips she had planted. Morning glories and nasturtiums ran all over the bars, making haste to bloom. Scarlet beans and honeysuckles were climbing up from below to meet their pretty neighbors, and the woodbine was hanging its green festoons wherever it could cling.

The waters of the bay were dancing in the sunshine, a fresh wind stirred the chestnut trees with a pleasant sound, and the garden below was full of roses, butterflies, and bees. A great chirping and twittering went on among the birds, busy with their summer housekeeping, and far away, the white-winged gulls were dipping and diving in the sea, where ships, like larger birds, went sailing to and fro.

"Oh, Phebe, it's such a lovely day, I do wish your fine secret was going to happen right away! I feel just like having a good time, don't you?" said Rose, waving her arms as if she were going to fly.

"I often feel that way, but I have to wait for my good times, and don't stop working to wish for 'em. There, now you can finish as soon as the dust settles; I must go do my stairs," and Phebe trudged away with the broom, singing as she went.

Rose leaned where she was, and fell to thinking how many good times she had had lately, for the gardening had prospered finely, and she was learning to swim and row, and there were drives and walks, and quiet hours of reading and talk with Uncle Alec, and, best of all, the old pain and ennui seldom troubled her now. She could work and play all day, sleep sweetly all night, and enjoy life with the zest of a healthy, happy child. She was far from being as strong and hearty as Phebe, but she was getting on; the once pale cheeks had color in them now, the hands were growing plump and brown, and the belt was not much too loose. No one talked to her about her health, and she forgot that she had "no constitution." She took no medicine but Dr. Alec's three great remedies, and they seemed to suit her excellently. Aunt Plenty said it was the pills; but, as no second batch ever followed the first, I think the old lady was mistaken.

Rose looked worthy of her name as she stood smiling to herself over a happier secret than any Phebe had—a secret which she did not know herself till she found out, some years later, the magic of good health.

"Look only," said the brownie,
    "At the pretty gown of blue,
At the kerchief pinned about her head,
    And at her little shoe,"

said a voice from below, as a great cabbage rose came flying against her cheek.

"What is the princess dreaming about up there in her hanging garden?" added Dr. Alec as she flung back a morning glory.

"I was wishing I could do something pleasant this fine day; something very new and interesting, for the wind makes me feel frisky and gay."

"Suppose we take a pull over to the Island? I intended to go this afternoon; but if you feel more like it now, we can be off at once."

"I do! I do! I'll come in fifteen minutes, Uncle. I *must* just scrabble my room to rights, for Phebe has got a great deal to do."

Rose caught up the rugs and vanished as she spoke, while Dr. Alec went in, saying to himself, with an indulgent smile, "It may upset things a trifle, but half a child's pleasure consists in having their fun *when* they want it."

Never did duster flap more briskly than the one Rose used that day, and never was a room "scrabbled" to rights in such haste as hers. Tables and chairs flew into their places as if alive; curtains shook as if a gale were blowing; china rattled and small articles tumbled about as if a young earthquake were playing with them. The boating suit went on in a twinkling, and Rose was off with a hop and a skip, little dreaming how many hours it would be before she saw her pretty room again.

Uncle Alec was putting a large basket into the boat when she arrived, and before they were off Phebe came running down with a queer, knobby bundle done up in a waterproof.

"We can't eat half that luncheon, and I know we shall not need so many wraps. I wouldn't lumber the boat up so," said Rose, who still had secret scares when on the water.

"Couldn't you make a smaller parcel, Phebe?" asked Dr. Alec, eyeing the bundle suspiciously.

"No, sir, not in such a hurry," and Phebe laughed as she gave a particularly large knob a good poke.

"Well, it will do for ballast. Don't forget the note to Mrs. Jessie, I beg of you."

"No, sir. I'll send it right off," and Phebe ran up the bank as if she had wings to her feet.

"We'll take a look at the lighthouse first, for you have not been there yet and it is worth seeing. By the time we have done that it will be pretty warm, and we will have lunch under the trees on the Island."

Rose was ready for anything, and enjoyed her visit to the lighthouse on the Point very much, especially climbing up the narrow stairs and going inside the great lantern. They made a long stay, for Dr. Alec seemed in no hurry to go and kept looking through his spyglass as if he expected to discover something remarkable on sea or land. It was past twelve before they reached the Island, and Rose was ready for her lunch long before she got it.

"Now this *is* lovely! I do wish the boys were here. Won't it be nice to have them with us all their vacation? Why, it begins today, doesn't it? Oh, I wish I'd remembered it sooner, and perhaps they would have come with us," she said as they lay luxuriously eating sandwiches under the old apple tree.

"So we might. Next time we won't be in such a hurry. I expect the lads will take our heads off when they find us out," answered Dr. Alec, placidly drinking cold tea.

"Uncle, I smell a frying sort of a smell," Rose said, pausing suddenly as she was putting away the remains of the lunch half an hour later.

"So do I; it is fish, I think."

For a moment they both sat with their noses in the air, sniffing like hounds; then Dr. Alec sprang up, saying with great decision, "Now this won't do! No one is permitted on this island without asking leave. I must see who dares to fry fish on my private property."

Taking the basket on one arm and the bundle on the other, he strode away toward the traitorous smell, looking as fierce as a lion, while Rose marched behind under her umbrella.

"We are Robinson Crusoe and his man Friday going to see if the savages have come," she said presently, for her fancy was full of the dear old stories that all children love so well.

"And there they are! Two tents and two boats, as I live! These rascals mean to enjoy themselves, that's evident."

"There ought to be more boats and no tents. I wonder where the prisoners are?"

"There are traces of them," and Dr. Alec pointed to the heads and tails of fishes strewn on the grass.

"And there are more," said Rose, laughing, as she pointed to a scarlet heap of what looked like lobsters.

"The savages are probably eating their victims now; don't you hear the knives rattle in that tent?"

"We ought to creep up and peep; Crusoe was cautious, you know, and Friday scared out of his wits," added Rose, still keeping up the joke.

"But this Crusoe is going to pounce upon them regardless of consequences. If I am killed and eaten, you seize the basket and run for the boat; there are provisions enough for your voyage home."

With that Uncle Alec slipped round to the front of the tent and, casting in the big bundle like a bombshell, roared out in a voice of thunder, "Pirates, surrender!"

A crash, a shout, a laugh, and out came the savages, brandishing knives and forks, chicken bones, and tin mugs, and all fell upon the intruder, pommeling him unmercifully as they cried, "You came too soon! We are not half ready! You've spoiled it all! Where is Rose?"

"Here I am," answered a half-stifled voice, and Rose was discovered sitting on the pile of red flannel bathing clothes, which she had mistaken for lobsters, and where she had fallen in a fit of merriment when she discovered that the cannibals were her merry cousins.

"You good-for-nothing boys! You are always bursting out upon me in some ridiculous way, and I always get taken in because I'm not used to such pranks. Uncle is as bad as the rest, and it's great fun," she said as the lads came round her, half scolding, half welcoming, and wholly enjoying the double surprise.

"You were not to come till afternoon, and Mamma was to be here to receive you. Everything is in a mess now, except your tent; we got that in order the first thing, and you can sit there and see us work," said Archie, doing the honors as usual.

"Rose felt it in her bones, as Debby says, that something was in the wind, and wanted to be off at once. So I let her come and should have kept her away an hour longer if your fish had not betrayed you," explained Uncle Alec, subsiding from a ferocious Crusoe into his good-natured self again.

"As this seat is rather damp, I think I'll rise," said Rose as the excitement lessened a little.

Several fishy hands helped her up, and Charlie said, as he scattered the scarlet garments over the grass with an oar, "We had a jolly good swim before dinner, and I told the Brats to spread these to dry. Hope you brought *your* things, Rose, for you belong to the Lobsters, you know, and we can have no end of fun teaching you to dive and float and tread water."

"I didn't bring anything—" began Rose, but was interrupted by the Brats (otherwise Will and Geordie), who appeared bearing the big bundle, so much demoralized by its fall that a red flannel tunic trailed out at one end and a little blue dressing-gown at the other, while the knobs proved to be a toilet case, rubbers, and a silver mug.

"Oh, that sly Phebe! This was the secret, and she bundled up those things after I went down to the boat," cried Rose with sparkling eyes.

"Guess something is smashed inside, for a bit of glass fell out," observed Will as they deposited the bundle at her feet.

"Catch a girl going anywhere without a looking glass. We haven't got one among the whole lot of us," added Mac with masculine scorn.

"Dandy has; I caught him touching up his wig behind the trees after our swim," cut in Geordie, wagging a derisive finger at Steve, who promptly silenced him by a smart rap on the head with the drumstick he had just polished off.

"Come, come, you lazy lubbers, fall to work, or we shall not be ready for Mamma. Take Rose's things to her tent, and tell her all about it, Prince. Mac and Steve, you cut away and bring up the rest of the straw; and you small chaps clear off the table, if you have stuffed all you can. Please, Uncle, I'd like your advice about the boundary lines and the best place for the kitchen."

Everyone obeyed the Chief, and Rose was escorted to her tent by Charlie, who devoted himself to her service. She was charmed with her quarters, and still more so with the program which he unfolded before her as they worked.

"We always camp out somewhere in vacation, and this year we thought we'd try the Island. It is handy, and our fireworks will show off well from here."

"Shall we stay over the Fourth? Three whole days! Oh, me! What a frolic it will be!"

"Bless your heart, we often camp for a week, we big fellows; but this year the small chaps wanted to come, so we let them. We have great larks, as you'll see; for we have a cave and play Captain Kidd, and have shipwrecks, and races, and all sorts of games. Arch and I are rather past that kind of thing now, but we do it to please the children," added Charlie with a sudden recollection of his sixteen years.

"I had no idea boys had such good times. Their plays never seemed a bit interesting before. But I suppose that was because I never knew any boys very well, or perhaps you are unusually nice ones," observed Rose with an artless air of appreciation that was very flattering.

"We are a pretty clever set, I fancy; but we have a good many advantages, you see. There are a tribe of us, to begin with; then our family has been here for ages, and we have plenty of 'spondulics,' so we can rather lord it over the other fellows and do as we like. There, ma'am, you can hang your smashed glass on that nail and do up your back hair as fine as you please. You can have a blue blanket or a red one, and a straw pillow or an air cushion for your head, whichever you like. You can trim up to any extent, and be as free and easy as squaws in a wigwam, for this corner is set apart for you ladies, and we never cross the line Uncle is drawing until we ask leave. Anything more I can do for you, cousin?"

"No, thank you. I think I'll leave the rest till Auntie comes, and go and help you somewhere else, if I may."

"Yes, indeed, come on and see to the kitchen. Can you cook?" asked Charlie as he led the way to the rocky nook where Archie was putting up a sailcloth awning.

"I can make tea and toast bread."

"Well, we'll show you how to fry fish and make chowder. Now you just set these pots and pans round tastefully, and sort of tidy up a bit, for Aunt Jessie insists on doing some of the work, and I want it to be decent here."

By four o'clock the camp was in order, and the weary workers settled down on Lookout Rock to watch for Mrs. Jessie and Jamie, who was never far from Mamma's apron string. They looked like a flock of bluebirds, all being in sailor rig, with blue ribbon enough flying from the seven hats to have set up a milliner. Very tuneful bluebirds they were, too, for all the lads sang, and the echo of their happy voices reached Mrs. Jessie long before she saw them.

The moment the boat hove in sight, up went the Island flag, and the bluejackets cheered lustily, as they did on every possible occasion, like true young Americans. This welcome was answered by the flapping of a handkerchief and the shrill "Rah! Rah! Rah!" of the one small tar who stood in the stern waving his hat manfully while a maternal hand clutched him firmly in the rear.

Cleopatra landing from her golden galley never received a heartier greeting than "little Mum" as she was borne to her tent by the young folk, for love of whom she smilingly resigned herself to three days of discomfort; while Jamie immediately attached himself to Rose, assuring her of his protection from the manifold perils which might assail them.

Taught by long experience that boys are *always* hungry, Aunt Jessie soon proposed supper, and proceeded to get it, enveloped in an immense apron, with an old hat of Archie's stuck atop of her cap. Rose helped, and tried to be as handy as Phebe, though the peculiar style of table she had to set made it no easy task. It was accomplished at last, and a very happy party lay about under the trees, eating and drinking out of anyone's plate and cup, and quite untroubled by the frequent appearance of ants and spiders in places which these interesting insects are not expected to adorn.

"I never thought I should like to wash dishes, but I do," said Rose as she sat in a boat after supper lazily rinsing plates in the sea, and rocking luxuriously as she wiped them.

"Mum is mighty particular; *we* just give 'em a scrub with sand, and dust 'em off with a bit of paper. It's much the best way, *I* think," replied Geordie, who reposed in another boat alongside.

"How Phebe would like this! I wonder Uncle did not have her come."

"I believe he tried to, but Debby was as cross as two sticks and said she couldn't spare her. I'm sorry, for we all like the Phebe bird, and she'd chirp like a good one out here, wouldn't she?"

"She ought to have a holiday like the rest of us. It's too bad to leave her out."

This thought came back to Rose several times that evening, for Phebe would have added much to the little concert they had in the moonlight, would have enjoyed the stories told, been quick at guessing the conundrums, and laughed with all her heart at the fun. The merry going to bed would have been best of all, for Rose wanted someone to cuddle under the blue blanket with her, there to whisper and giggle and tell secrets, as girls delight to do.

Long after the rest were asleep, Rose lay wide awake, excited by the novelty of all about her, and a thought that had come into her mind. Far away she heard a city clock strike twelve; a large star like a mild eye peeped in at the opening of the tent, and the soft plash of the waves seemed calling her to come out. Aunt Jessie lay fast asleep, with Jamie rolled up like a kitten at her feet, and neither stirred as Rose in her wrapper crept out to see how the world looked at midnight.

She found it very lovely, and sat down on a cracker keg to enjoy it with a heart full of the innocent sentiment of her years. Fortunately, Dr. Alec saw her before she had time to catch cold, for coming out to tie back the door flap of his tent for more air, he beheld the small figure perched in the moonlight. Having no fear of ghosts, he quietly approached and, seeing that she was wide awake, said, with a hand on her shining hair, "What is my girl doing here?"

"Having a good time," answered Rose, not at all startled.

"I wonder what she was thinking about with such a sober look?"

"The story you told of the brave sailor who gave up his place on the raft to the woman, and the last drop of water to the poor baby. People who make sacrifices are very much loved and admired, aren't they?" she asked earnestly.

"If the sacrifice is a true one. But many of the bravest never are known, and get no praise. That does not lessen their beauty, though perhaps it makes them harder, for we all like sympathy," and Dr. Alec sighed a patient sort of sigh.

"I suppose you have made a great many? Would you mind telling me one of them?" asked Rose, arrested by the sigh.

"My last was to give up smoking," was the very unromantic answer to her pensive question.

"Why did you?"

"Bad example for the boys."

"That was very good of you, Uncle! Was it hard?"

"I'm ashamed to say it was. But as a wise old fellow once said, 'It is necessary to do right; it is not necessary to be happy.' "

Rose pondered over the saying as if it pleased her, and then said, with a clear, bright look, "A real sacrifice is giving up something you want to enjoy very much, isn't it?"

"Yes."

"Doing it one's own self because one loves another person very much and wants her to be happy?"

"Yes."

"And doing it pleasantly, and being glad about it, and not minding the praise if it doesn't come?"

"Yes, dear, that is the true spirit of self-sacrifice; you seem to understand it, and I dare say you will have many chances in your life to try the real thing. I hope they won't be very hard ones."

"I think they will," began Rose, and there stopped short.

"Well, make one now, and go to sleep, or my girl will be ill tomorrow, and then the aunts will say camping out was bad for her."

"I'll go—good night!" And throwing him a kiss, the little ghost vanished, leaving Uncle Alec to pace the shore and think about some of the unsuspected sacrifices that had made him what he was.

CHAPTER 10

ROSE'S SACRIFICE

THERE CERTAINLY WERE "LARKS" on Campbell's Island next day, as Charlie had foretold, and Rose took her part in them like one intent on enjoying every minute to the utmost. There was a merry breakfast, a successful fishing expedition, and then the lobsters came out in full force, for even Aunt Jessie appeared in red flannel. There was nothing Uncle Alec could not do in the water, and the boys tried their best to equal him in strength and skill, so there was a great diving and ducking, for everyone was bent on distinguishing himself.

Rose swam far out beyond her depth, with Uncle to float her back; Aunt Jessie splashed placidly in the shallow pools, with Jamie paddling nearby like a little whale beside its mother; while the lads careered about, looking like a flock of distracted flamingoes and acting like the famous dancing party in *Alice's Adventures in Wonderland.*

Nothing but chowder would have lured them from their gambols in the briny deep; that time-honored dish demanded the concentrated action of several mighty minds; so the "Water Babies" came ashore and fell to cooking.

It is unnecessary to say that, when done, it was the most

remarkable chowder ever cooked, and the quantity eaten would have amazed the world if the secret had been divulged. After this exertion a siesta was considered the thing, and people lay about in tents or out as they pleased, the boys looking like warriors slumbering where they fell.

The elders had just settled to a comfortable nap when the youngsters rose, refreshed and ready for further exploits. A hint sent them all off to the cave, and there were discovered bows and arrows, battle clubs, old swords, and various relics of an interesting nature. Perched upon a commanding rock, with Jamie to "splain" things to her, Rose beheld a series of stirring scenes enacted with great vigor and historical accuracy by her gifted relatives.

Captain Cook was murdered by the natives of Owhyhee in the most thrilling manner. Captain Kidd buried untold wealth in the chowder kettle at the dead of night and shot both the trusting villains who shared the secret of the hiding place. Sinbad came ashore there and had manifold adventures, and numberless wrecks bestrewed the sands.

Rose considered them by far the most exciting dramas she had ever witnessed; and when the performance closed with a grand ballet of Feejee Islanders, whose barbaric yells alarmed the gulls, she had no words in which to express her gratification.

Another swim at sunset, another merry evening on the rocks watching the lighted steamers pass seaward and the pleasure boats come into port, ended the second day of the camping out and sent everyone to bed early that they might be ready for the festivities of the morrow.

"Archie, didn't I hear Uncle ask you to row home in the morning for fresh milk and things?"

"Yes; why?"

"Please, may I go too? I have something of *great* importance to arrange; you know I was carried off in a hurry," Rose said in a confidential whisper as she was bidding her cousins good-night.

"I'm willing, and I guess Charlie won't mind."

"Thank you; be sure you stand by me when I ask leave in

the morning, and don't say anything till then, except to Charlie. Promise," urged Rose, so eagerly that Archie struck an attitude and cried dramatically, "By yonder moon I swear!"

"Hush! It's all right, go along"; and Rose departed as if satisfied.

"She's a queer little thing, isn't she, Prince?"

"Rather a nice little thing, *I* think. I'm quite fond of her."

Rose's quick ears caught both remarks, and she retired to her tent, saying to herself with sleepy dignity, "Little thing, indeed! Those boys talk as if I was a baby. They will treat me with more respect after tomorrow, I guess."

Archie did stand by her in the morning, and her request was readily granted, as the lads were coming directly back. Off they went, and Rose waved her hand to the islanders with a somewhat pensive air, for a heroic purpose glowed within her, and the spirit of self-sacrifice was about to be illustrated in a new and touching manner.

While the boys got the milk Rose ran to Phebe, ordered her to leave her dishes, to put on her hat, and take a note back to Uncle Alec, which would explain this somewhat mysterious performance. Phebe obeyed, and when she went to the boat Rose accompanied her, telling the boys she was not ready to go yet, but they could some of them come for her when she hung a white signal on her balcony.

"But why not come now? What are you about, miss? Uncle won't like it," protested Charlie in great amazement.

"Just do as I tell you, little boy; Uncle will understand and explain. Obey, as Phebe does, and ask no questions. *I* can have secrets as well as other people"; and Rose walked off with an air of lofty independence that impressed her friends immensely.

"It's some plot between uncle and herself, so we won't meddle. All right, Phebe? Pull away, Prince"; and off they went, to be received with much surprise by the islanders.

This was the note Phebe bore:

DEAR UNCLE—I am going to take Phebe's place today, and let her have all the fun she can. Please don't mind what she says, but keep her, and tell the boys to be very good to her for my sake. Don't think it is easy to do this; it is very hard to give up the best day of all, but I feel so selfish to have all the pleasure, and Phebe none, that I wish to make this sacrifice. Do let me, and don't laugh at it; I truly do not wish to be praised, and I truly want to do it. Love to all from ROSE

"Bless the little dear, what a generous heart she has! Shall we go after her, Jessie, or let her have her way?" said Dr. Alec after the first mingled amusement and astonishment had subsided.

"Let her alone, and don't spoil her little sacrifice. She means it, I know, and the best way in which we can show our respect for her effort is to give Phebe a pleasant day. I'm sure she has earned it"; and Mrs. Jessie made a sign to the boys to suppress their disappointment and exert themselves to please Rose's guest.

Phebe was with difficulty kept from going straight home and declared that she should not enjoy herself one bit without Miss Rose.

"She won't hold out all day, and we shall see her paddling back before noon, I'll wager anything," said Charlie; and the rest so strongly inclined to his opinion that they resigned themselves to the loss of the little queen of the revels, sure that it would be only a temporary one.

But hour after hour passed, and no signal appeared on the balcony, though Phebe watched it hopefully. No passing boat brought the truant back, though more than one pair of eyes looked out for the bright hair under the round hat; and sunset came, bringing no Rose but the lovely color in the western sky.

"I really did not think the child had it in her. I fancied it was a bit of sentiment, but I see she *was* in earnest and means that her sacrifice shall be a true one. Dear little soul! I'll make it up to her a thousand times over and beg her pardon for thinking it might be done for effect," Dr. Alec said remorsefully as he strained his eyes through the dusk, fancying he saw a small figure sitting in the garden as it had sat on the keg the night before, laying the generous little plot that had cost more than he could guess.

"Well, she can't help seeing the fireworks anyway, unless she is goose enough to think she must hide in a dark closet and not look," said Archie, who was rather disgusted at Rose's seeming ingratitude.

"She will see ours capitally, but miss the big ones on the hill, unless Papa has forgotten all about them," added Steve, cutting short the harangue Mac had begun upon the festivals of the ancients.

"I'm sure the sight of her will be better than the finest fireworks that ever went off," said Phebe, meditating an elopement with one of the boats if she could get a chance.

"Let things work; if she resists the brilliant invitation we give her she will be a heroine," added Uncle Alec, secretly hoping that she would not.

Meanwhile Rose had spent a quiet, busy day helping Debby, waiting on Aunt Peace, and steadily resisting Aunt Plenty's attempts to send her back to the happy island. It had been hard in the morning to come in from the bright world outside, with flags flying, cannon booming, crackers popping, and everyone making ready for a holiday, and go to washing cups while Debby grumbled and the aunts lamented. It was very hard to see the day go by, knowing how gay each hour must have been across the water, and how a word from her would take her where she longed to be with all her heart. But it was hardest of all when evening came and Aunt Peace was asleep, Aunt Plenty seeing a gossip in the parlor, Debby established in the porch to enjoy the show, and nothing left for the little maid to do but sit alone in her balcony and watch the gay rockets whizz up from island, hill, and city while bands played and boats laden with happy people went to and fro in the fitful light.

Then it must be confessed that a tear or two dimmed the blue eyes, and once, when a very brilliant display illuminated the island for a moment, and she fancied she saw the tents, the curly head went down on the railing, and a wide-awake nasturtium heard a little whisper, "I hope some one wishes I was there!"

The tears were all gone, however, and she was watching the hill and island answer each other with what Jamie called "whizzers, whirligigs, and busters," and smiling as she thought how hard the boys must be working to keep up such a steady fire, when Uncle Mac came walking in upon her, saying hurriedly, "Come, child, put on your tippet, pelisse, or whatever you call it, and run off with me. I came to get Phebe, but aunt says she is gone, so I want you. I've got Fun down in the boat, and I want you to go with us and see my fireworks. Got them up for you, and you mustn't miss them, or I shall be disappointed."

"But, Uncle," began Rose, feeling as if she ought to refuse even a glimpse of bliss, "perhaps—"

"I know, my dear, I know; Aunt told me; but no one needs you now so much as I do, and I insist on your coming," said Uncle Mac, who seemed in a great hurry to be off, yet was unusually kind.

So Rose went and found the little Chinaman with a funny lantern waiting to help her in and convulse her with laughter trying to express his emotions in pidgin English. The city clocks were striking nine as they got out into the bay, and the island fireworks seemed to be over, for no rocket answered the last Roman candle that shone on the Aunthill.

"Ours are done, I see, but they are going up all round the city, and how pretty they are," said Rose, folding her mantle about her and surveying the scene with a pensive interest.

"Hope my fellows have not got into trouble up there," muttered Uncle Mac, adding, with a satisfied chuckle, as a spark shone out, "No; there it goes! Look, Rosy, and see how you like this one; it was ordered especially in honor of your coming."

Rose looked with all her eyes and saw the spark grow into the likeness of a golden vase, then green leaves came out, and then a crimson flower glowing on the darkness with a splendid luster.

"Is it a rose, Uncle?" she asked, clasping her hands with delight as she recognized the handsome flower.

"Of course it is! Look again, and guess what those are," answered Uncle Mac, chuckling and enjoying it all like a boy.

A wreath of what looked at first like purple brooms appeared below the vase, but Rose guessed what they were meant for and stood straight up, holding by his shoulder, and crying excitedly, "Thistles, Uncle, Scotch thistles! There are seven of them—one for each boy! Oh, what a joke!" and she laughed so that she plumped into the bottom of the boat and stayed there till the brilliant spectacle was quite gone.

"That was rather a neat thing, I flatter myself," said Uncle Mac in high glee at the success of his illumination. "Now, shall I leave you on the Island or take you home again, my good little girl?" he added, lifting her up with such a tone of approbation in his voice that Rose kissed him on the spot.

"Home, please, Uncle; and I thank you very, very much for the beautiful fireworks you got up for me. I'm so glad I saw it; and I know I shall dream about it," answered Rose steadily, though a wistful glance went toward the Island, now so near that she could smell powder and see shadowy figures flitting about.

Home they went; and Rose fell asleep saying to herself, "It was harder than I thought, but I'm glad I did it, and I truly don't want any reward but Phebe's pleasure."

CHAPTER 11

POOR MAC

ROSE'S SACRIFICE WAS A FAILURE in one respect, for, though the elders loved her the better for it and showed that they did, the boys were not inspired with the sudden respect which she had hoped for. In fact, her feelings were much hurt by overhearing Archie say that he couldn't see any sense in it; and the Prince added another blow by pronouncing her "the queerest chicken ever seen."

It is apt to be so, and it is hard to bear; for though we do not want trumpets blown, we do like to have our little virtues appreciated and cannot help feeling disappointed if they are not.

A time soon came, however, when Rose, quite unconsciously, won not only the respect of her cousins, but their gratitude and affection likewise.

Soon after the Island episode, Mac had a sunstroke and was very ill for some time. It was so sudden that everyone was startled, and for some days the boy's life was in danger. He pulled through, however; and then, just as the family were rejoicing, a new trouble appeared which cast a gloom over them all.

Poor Mac's eyes gave out; and well they might, for he had abused them, and never being very strong, they suffered doubly now.

No one dared to tell him the dark predictions of the great oculist who came to look at them, and the boy tried to be patient, thinking that a few weeks of rest would repair the overwork of several years.

He was forbidden to look at a book, and as that was the one thing he most delighted in, it was a terrible affliction to the Worm. Everyone was very ready to read to him, and at first the lads contended for this honor. But as week after week went by, and Mac was still condemned to idleness and a darkened room, their zeal abated, and one after the other fell off. It *was* hard for the active fellows, right in the midst of their vacation; and nobody blamed them when they contented themselves with brief calls, running of errands, and warm expressions of sympathy.

The elders did their best, but Uncle Mac was a busy man. Aunt Jane's reading was of a funereal sort, impossible to listen to long, and the other aunties were all absorbed in their own cares, though they supplied the boy with every delicacy they could invent.

Uncle Alec was a host in himself, but he could not give all his time to the invalid; and if it had not been for Rose, the afflicted Worm would have fared ill. Her pleasant voice suited him, her patience was unfailing, her time of no apparent value, and her eager goodwill was very comforting.

The womanly power of self-devotion was strong in the child, and she remained faithfully at her post when all the rest dropped away. Hour after hour she sat in the dusky room, with one ray of light on her book, reading to the boy, who lay with shaded eyes silently enjoying the only pleasure that lightened the weary days. Sometimes he was peevish and hard to please, sometimes he growled because his reader could not manage the dry books he wished to hear, and sometimes he was so despondent that her heart ached to see him. Through all these trials Rose persevered, using all her little arts to please him. When he fretted, she was patient; when he growled, she plowed bravely through the hard pages—not dry to her in one sense, for quiet tears dropped on them now and then; and when Mac fell into a despairing mood, she comforted him with every hopeful word she dared to offer.

He said little, but she knew he was grateful, for she suited him better than anyone else. If she was late, he was impatient; when she had to go, he seemed forlorn; and when the tired head ached worst, she could always soothe him to sleep, crooning the old songs her father used to love.

"I don't know what I *should* do without that child," Aunt Jane often said.

"She's worth all those racketing fellows put together," Mac would add, fumbling about to discover if the little chair was ready for her coming.

That was the sort of reward Rose liked, the thanks that cheered her; and whenever she grew very tired, one look at the green shade, the curly head so restless on the pillow, and the poor groping hands, touched her tender heart and put new spirit into the weary voice.

She did not know how much she was learning, both from the books she read and the daily sacrifices she made. Stories and poetry were her delight, but Mac did not care for them; and since his favorite Greeks and Romans were forbidden, he satisfied himself with travels, biographies, and the history of great inventions or discoveries. Rose despised this taste at first, but soon got interested in Livingston's adventures, Hobson's stirring life in India, and the brave trials and triumphs of Watt and Arkwright, Fulton, and *Palissy, the Potter*. The true, strong books helped the dreamy girl; her faithful service and sweet patience touched and won the boy; and long afterward both learned to see how useful those seemingly hard and weary hours had been to them.

One bright morning, as Rose sat down to begin a fat volume entitled *History of the French Revolution*, expecting to come to great grief over the long names, Mac, who was lumbering about the room like a blind bear, stopped her by asking abruptly, "What day of the month is it?"

"The seventh of August, I believe."

"More than half my vacation gone, and I've only had a week of it! I call that hard," and he groaned dismally.

"So it is; but there is more to come, and you may be able to enjoy that."

"*May* be able! I *will* be able! Does that old noodle think I'm going to stay stived up here much longer?"

"I guess he does, unless your eyes get on faster than they have yet."

"Has he said anything more lately?"

"I haven't seen him, you know. Shall I begin?—this looks rather nice."

"Read away; it's all one to me." And Mac cast himself down upon the old lounge, where his heavy head felt easiest.

Rose began with great spirit and kept on gallantly for a couple of chapters, getting over the unpronounceable names with unexpected success, she thought, for her listener did not correct her once, and lay so still she fancied he was deeply interested. All of a sudden she was arrested in the middle of a fine paragraph by Mac, who sat bolt upright, brought both feet down with a thump, and said, in a rough, excited tone, "Stop! I don't hear a word, and you may as well save your breath to answer my question."

"What is it?" asked Rose, looking uneasy, for she had something on her mind and feared that he suspected what it was. His next words proved that she was right.

"Now look here, I want to know something, and you've *got* to tell me."

"Please, don't—" began Rose beseechingly.

"You *must,* or I'll pull off this shade and stare at the sun as hard as ever I can stare. Come now!" and he half rose, as if ready to execute the threat.

"I will! Oh, I will tell, if I know! But don't be reckless and do anything so crazy as that," cried Rose in great distress.

"Very well; then listen, and don't dodge, as everyone else does. Didn't the doctor think my eyes worse the last time he came? Mother won't say, but you *shall.*"

"I believe he did," faltered Rose.

"I thought so! Did he say I should be able to go to school when it begins?"

"No, Mac," very low.

"Ah!"

That was all, but Rose saw her cousin set his lips together and take a long breath, as if she had hit him hard. He bore the disappointment bravely, however, and asked quite steadily in a minute, "How soon does he think I *can* study again?"

It was so hard to answer that! Yet Rose knew she must, for Aunt Jane had declared she *could* not do it, and Uncle Mac had begged her to break the truth to the poor lad.

"Not for a good many months."

"How many?" he asked with a pathetic sort of gruffness.

"A year, perhaps."

"A whole year! Why, I expected to be ready for college by that time." And pushing up the shade, Mac stared at her with startled eyes that soon blinked and fell before the one ray of light.

"Plenty of time for that; you must be patient now, and get them thoroughly well, or they will trouble you again when it will be harder to spare them," she said with tears in her own eyes.

"I won't do it! I *will* study and get through somehow. It's all humbug about taking care so long. These doctors like to keep hold of a fellow if they can. But I won't stand it—I vow I won't!" and he banged his fist down on the unoffending pillow as if he were pommeling the hardhearted doctor.

"Now, Mac, listen to me," Rose said very earnestly, though her voice shook a little and her heart ached. "You know you have hurt your eyes reading by firelight and in the dusk, and sitting up late, and now you'll have to pay for it; the doctor said so. You *must* be careful and do as he tells you, or you will be—blind."

"No!"

"Yes, it is true, and he wanted us to tell you that nothing but entire rest would cure you. I know it's dreadfully hard, but we'll all help you; I'll read all day long, and lead you, and wait upon you, and try to make it easier—"

She stopped there, for it was evident that he did not hear a sound; the word *blind* seemed to have knocked him down, for he had buried his face in the pillow and lay so still that Rose was frightened. She sat motionless for many minutes, longing to comfort him but not knowing how, and wishing Uncle Alec would come, for he had promised to tell Mac.

Presently, a sort of choking sound came out of the pillow and went straight to her heart—the most pathetic sob she ever heard, for though it was the most natural means of relief, the poor fellow must not indulge in it because of the afflicted eyes. The *French Revolution* tumbled out of her lap, and running to the sofa, she knelt down by it, saying, with the motherly sort of tenderness girls feel for any sorrowing creature, "Oh, my dear, you mustn't cry! It is so bad for your poor eyes. Take your head out of that hot pillow, and let me cool it. I don't wonder you feel so, but please don't cry. I'll cry for you; it won't hurt *me.*"

As she spoke, she pulled away the cushion with gentle force and saw the green shade all crushed and stained with the few hot tears that told how bitter the disappointment had been. Mac felt her sympathy but, being a boy, did not thank her for it; only sat up with a jerk, saying, as he tried to rub away the telltale drops with the sleeve of his jacket: "Don't bother; weak eyes always water. I'm all right."

But Rose cried out and caught his arm: "Don't touch them with that rough woolen stuff! Lie down and let me bathe them, there's a dear boy; then there will be no harm done."

"They do smart confoundedly. I say, don't you tell the other fellows that I made a baby of myself, will you?" he added, yielding with a sigh to the orders of his nurse, who had flown for the eyewash and linen cambric handkerchief.

"Of course I won't; but anyone would be upset at the idea of being —well—troubled in this way. I'm sure you bear it splendidly, and you know it isn't half so bad when you get used to it. Besides, it is only for a time, and you can do lots of pleasant things if you can't study. You'll have to wear blue goggles, perhaps; won't that be funny?"

And while she was pouring out all the comfortable words she

could think of, Rose was softly bathing the eyes and dabbing the hot forehead with lavender water, as her patient lay quiet with a look on his face that grieved her sadly.

"Homer was blind, and so was Milton, and they did something to be remembered by, in spite of it," he said, as if to himself, in a solemn tone, for even the blue goggles did not bring a smile.

"Papa had a picture of Milton and his daughters writing for him. It was a very sweet picture, I thought," observed Rose in a serious voice, trying to meet the sufferer on his own ground.

"Perhaps I could study if someone read and did the eye part. Do you suppose I could, by and by?" he asked with a sudden ray of hope.

"I daresay, if your head is strong enough. This sunstroke, you know, is what upset you, and your brains need rest, the doctor says."

"I'll have a talk with the old fellow next time he comes, and find out just what I *may* do; then I shall know where I am. What a fool I was that day to be stewing my brains and letting the sun glare on my book till the letters danced before me! I see 'em now when I shut my eyes; black balls bobbing round, and stars and all sorts of queer things. Wonder if all blind people do?"

"Don't think about them; I'll go on reading, shall I? We shall come to the exciting part soon, and then you'll forget all this," suggested Rose.

"No, I never shall forget. Hang the old *Revolution!* I don't want to hear another word of it. My head aches, and I'm hot. Oh, wouldn't I like to go for a pull in the *Stormy Petrel!*" And poor Mac tossed about as if he did not know what to do with himself.

"Let me sing, and perhaps you'll drop off; then the day will seem shorter," said Rose, taking up a fan and sitting down beside him.

"Perhaps I shall; I didn't sleep much last night, and when I did I dreamed like fun. See here, you tell the people that I know, and it's all right, and I don't want them to talk about it or howl over me. That's all; now drone away, and I'll try to sleep. Wish I could for a year, and wake up cured."

"Oh, I wish, I wish you could!"

Rose said it so fervently that Mac was moved to grope for her apron and hold on to a corner of it, as if it was comfortable to feel her near him. But all he said was, "You are a good little soul, Rosy. Give us 'The Birks'; that is a drowsy one that always sends me off."

Quite contended with this small return for all her sympathy, Rose waved her fan and sang, in a dreamy tone, the pretty Scotch air, the burden of which is

> Bonny lassie, will ye gang, will ye gang
> To the Birks of Aberfeldie?

Whether the lassie went or not I cannot say, but the laddie was off to the land of Nod in about ten minutes, quite worn out with hearing the bad tidings and the effort to bear them manfully.

CHAPTER 12

"THE OTHER FELLOWS"

ROSE DID TELL "the people" what had passed, and no one "howled" over Mac or said a word to trouble him. He had his talk with the doctor and got very little comfort out of it, for he found that "just what he might do" was nothing at all; though the prospect of some study by and by, if all went well, gave him courage to bear the woes of the present. Having made up his mind to this, he behaved so well that everyone was astonished, never having suspected so much manliness in the quiet Worm.

The boys were much impressed, both by the greatness of the afflic-tion which hung over him and by his way of bearing it. They were very good to him, but not always particularly wise in their attempts to cheer and amuse; and Rose often found him much downcast after a visit of condolence from the clan. She still kept her place as head nurse and chief reader, though the boys did their best in an irregular sort of way. They were rather taken aback sometimes at finding Rose's services preferred to theirs, and privately confided to one another that "Old Mac was getting fond of being mollycoddled." But they could not help seeing how useful she was and owning that she

103

alone had remained faithful—a fact which caused some of them much secret compunction now and then.

Rose felt that she ruled in that room, if nowhere else, for Aunt Jane left a great deal to her, finding that her experience with her invalid father fitted her for a nurse, and in a case like this her youth was an advantage rather than a drawback. Mac soon came to think that no one could take care of him so well as Rose, and Rose soon grew fond of her patient, though at first she had considered this cousin the least attractive of the seven. He was not polite and sensible like Archie, nor gay and handsome like Prince Charlie, nor neat and obliging like Steve, nor amusing like the "Brats," nor confiding and affectionate like little Jamie. He was rough, absentminded, careless, and awkward, rather priggish, and not at all agreeable to a dainty, beauty-loving girl like Rose.

But when his trouble came upon him, she discovered many good things in this cousin of hers and learned not only to pity but to respect and love the poor Worm, who tried to be patient, brave, and cheerful and found it a harder task than anyone guessed, except the little nurse, who saw him in his gloomiest moods. She soon came to think that his friends did not appreciate him, and upon one occasion was moved to free her mind in a way that made a deep impression on the boys.

Vacation was almost over, and the time drawing near when Mac would be left outside the happy school world which he so much enjoyed. This made him rather low in his mind, and his cousins exerted themselves to cheer him up, especially one afternoon when a spasm of devotion seemed to seize them all. Jamie trudged down the hill with a basket of blackberries which he had "picked all his ownself," as his scratched fingers and stained lips plainly testified. Will and Geordie brought their puppies to beguile the weary hours, and the three elder lads called to discuss baseball, cricket, and kindred subjects, eminently fitted to remind the invalid of his privations.

Rose had gone to drive with Uncle Alec, who declared she was getting as pale as a potato sprout, living so much in a dark room. But her thoughts were with her boy all the while, and she ran up to him the moment she returned, to find things in a fine state of confusion.

With the best intentions in life, the lads had done more harm than good, and the spectacle that met Nurse Rose's eye was a trying one. The puppies were yelping, the small boys romping, and the big boys all talking at once; the curtains were up, the room close, berries scattered freely about, Mac's shade half off, his cheeks flushed, his temper ruffled, and his voice loudest of all as he disputed hotly with Steve about lending certain treasured books which he could no longer use.

Now Rose considered this her special kingdom, and came down upon the invaders with an energy which amazed them and quelled the riot at once. They had never seen her roused before, and the effect was tremendous; also comical, for she drove the whole flock of boys out of the room like an indignant little hen defending her brood. They all went as meekly as sheep; the small lads fled from the house precipitately, but the three elder ones only retired to the next room, and remained there hoping for a chance to explain and apologize, and so appease the irate young lady who had suddenly turned the tables and clattered them about their ears.

As they waited, they observed her proceedings through the half-open door and commented upon them briefly but expressively, feeling quite bowed down with remorse at the harm they had innocently done.

"She's put the room to rights in a jiffy. What jacks we were to let those dogs in and kick up such a row," observed Steve after a prolonged peep.

"The poor old Worm turns as if she was treading on him instead of cuddling him like a pussycat. Isn't he cross, though?" added Charlie as Mac was heard growling about his "confounded head."

"She will manage him; but it's mean in us to rumple him up and then leave her to smooth him down. I'd go and help, but I don't know how," said Archie, looking much depressed, for he was a conscientious fellow and blamed himself for his want of thought.

"No more do I. Odd, isn't it, what a knack women have for taking care of sick folks?" and Charlie fell a-musing over this undeniable fact.

"She has been ever so good to Mac," began Steve, in a self-reproachful tone.

"Better than his own brother, hey?" cut in Archie, finding relief for his own regret in the delinquencies of another.

"Well, you needn't preach; you didn't any of you do any more, and you might have, for Mac likes you better than he does me. I always fret him, he says, and it isn't my fault if I am a quiddle," protested Steve in self-defence.

"We have all been selfish and neglected him, so we won't fight about it, but try and do better," said Archie, generously taking more than his share of blame, for he had been less inattentive than either of the others.

"Rose has stood by him like a good one, and it's no wonder he likes to have her round best. I should myself if I was down on my luck as he is," put in Charlie, feeling that he really had not done "the little thing" justice.

"I'll tell you what it is, boys—we haven't been half good enough to Rose, and we've got to make it up to her somehow," said Archie, who had a very manly sense of honor about paying his debts, even to a girl.

"I'm awfully sorry I made fun of her doll when Jamie lugged it out; and I called her 'baby bunting' when she cried over the dead kitten. Girls *are* such geese sometimes, I can't help it," said Steve, confessing his transgressions handsomely and feeling quite ready to atone for them if he only knew how.

"I'll go down on my knees and beg her pardon for treating her as if she was a child. Don't it make her mad, though? Come to think of it, she's only two years or so younger than I am. But she is so small and pretty, she always seems like a dolly to me," and the Prince looked down from his lofty height of five feet five as if Rose were indeed a pygmy beside him.

"That dolly has got a real good little heart, and a bright mind of her own, you'd better believe. Mac says she understands some things quicker than he can, and Mother thinks she is an uncommonly nice girl, though she don't know all creation. You needn't put on airs, Charlie, though you *are* a tall one, for Rose likes Archie better than you; she said she did because he treated her respectfully."

"Steve looks as fierce as a gamecock; but don't you get excited, my son, for it won't do a bit of good. Of course, everybody likes the Chief best; they ought to, and I'll punch their heads if they don't. So calm yourself, Dandy, and mend your own manners before you come down on other people's."

Thus the Prince with great dignity and perfect good nature, while Archie looked modestly gratified with the flattering opinions of his kinsfolk, and Steve subsided, feeling he had done his duty as a cousin and a brother. A pause ensued, during which Aunt Jane appeared in the other room, accompanied by a tea tray sumptuously spread, and prepared to feed her big nestling, as that was a task she allowed no one to share with her.

"If you have a minute to spare before you go, child, I wish you'd just make Mac a fresh shade; this has got a berry stain on it, and he must be tidy, for he is to go out tomorrow if it is a cloudy day," said Mrs. Jane, spreading toast in a stately manner while Mac slopped his tea about without receiving a word of reproof.

"Yes, Aunt," answered Rose so meekly that the boys could hardly believe it could be the same voice which had issued the stern command, "Out of this room, every one of you!" not very long ago.

They had not time to retire, without unseemly haste, before she walked into the parlor and sat down at the worktable without a word. It was funny to see the look the three tall lads cast at the little person sedately threading a needle with green silk. They all wanted to say something expressive of repentance, but no one knew how to begin, and it was evident, from the prim expression of Rose's face, that she intended to stand upon her dignity till they had properly abased themselves. The pause was becoming very awkward when Charlie, who possessed all the persuasive arts of a born scapegrace, went slowly down upon his knees before her, beat his breast, and said, in a heartbroken tone, "Please forgive me this time, and I'll never do so anymore."

It was very hard to keep sober, but Rose managed it, and answered gravely, "It is Mac's pardon you should ask, not mine, for you haven't hurt me, and I shouldn't wonder if you had him a great deal, with all that light and racket, and talk about things that only worry him."

"Do you really think we've hurt him, cousin?" asked Archie with a troubled look while Charlie settled down in a remorseful heap among the table legs.

"Yes, I do, for he has got a raging headache, and his eyes are as red as—as this emery bag," answered Rose, solemnly plunging her needle into a fat flannel strawberry.

Steve tore his hair, metaphorically speaking, for he clutched his cherished topknot and wildly disheveled it, as if that was the heaviest penance he could inflict upon himself at such short notice. Charlie laid himself out flat, melodramatically begging someone to take him away and hang him; but Archie, who felt worst of all, said nothing except to vow within himself that he would read to Mac till his own eyes were as red as a dozen emery bags combined.

Seeing the wholesome effects of her treatment upon these culprits, Rose felt that she might relent and allow them a gleam of hope. She found it impossible to help trampling upon the prostrate Prince a little, in words at least, for he had hurt her feelings oftener than he knew; so she gave him a thimble pie on the top of his head, and said, with the air of an infinitely superior being, "Don't be silly, but get up, and I'll tell you something much better to do than sprawling on the floor and getting all over lint."

Charlie obediently sat himself upon a hassock at her feet; the other sinners drew near to catch the words of wisdom about to fall from her lips, and Rose, softened by this gratifying humility, addressed them in her most maternal tone.

"Now, boys, if you really want to be good to Mac, you can do it in this way. Don't keep talking about things he can't do, or go and tell what fun you have had batting your ridiculous balls about. Get some nice book and read quietly; cheer him up about school and offer to help him study by and by; *you* can do that better than I, because I'm only a girl and don't learn Greek and Latin and all sorts of headachy stuff."

"Yes, but you can do heaps of things better than we can; you've proved that," said Archie with an approving look that delighted Rose, though she could not resist giving Charlie one more rebuke by saying, with a little bridling up of the head and a curl of the lip that wanted to smile instead, "I'm glad you think so, though I *am* a 'queer chicken.' "

This scathing remark caused the Prince to hide his face for shame, and Steve to erect his head in the proud consciousness that this shot was not meant for him. Archie laughed, and Rose, seeing a merry blue eye winking at her from behind two brown hands, gave Charlie's ear a friendly tweak and extended the olive branch of peace.

"Now we'll all be good and plan nice things for poor Mac," she said, smiling so graciously that the boys felt as if the sun had suddenly burst out from behind a heavy cloud and was shining with great brilliancy.

The storm had cleared the air, and quite a heavenly calm succeeded, during which plans of a most varied and surprising sort were laid, for everyone burned to make noble sacrifices upon the shrine of "poor Mac," and Rose was the guiding star to whom the others looked with most gratifying submission. Of course, this elevated state of things could not endure long, but it was *very* nice while it lasted, and left an excellent effect upon the minds of all when the first ardor had subsided.

"There, that's ready for tomorrow, and I do hope it will be cloudy," said Rose as she finished off the new shade, the progress of which the boys had watched with interest.

"I'd bespoken an extra sunny day, but I'll tell the clerk of the weather to change it. He's an obliging fellow, and he'll attend to it; so make yourself easy," said Charlie, who had become quite perky again.

"It is very easy for you to joke, but how would you like to wear a blinder like that for weeks and weeks, sir?" And Rose quenched his rising spirits by slipping the shade over his eyes as he still sat on the cushion at her feet.

"It's horrid! Take it off, take it off! I don't wonder the poor old boy has the blues with a thing like that on"; and Charlie sat looking at what seemed to him an instrument of torture, with such a sober face that Rose took it gently away and went in to bid Mac good night.

"I shall go home with her, for it is getting darkish and she is rather timid," said Archie, forgetting that he had often laughed at this very timidity.

"I think *I* might, for she's taking care of my brother," put in Steve, asserting his rights.

"Let's all go; that will please her," proposed Charlie with a burst of gallantry which electrified his mates.

"We will!" they said with one voice, and they did, to Rose's great surprise and secret contentment; though Archie had all the care of her, for the other two were leaping fences, running races, and having wrestling matches all the way down.

They composed themselves on reaching the door, however; shook hands cordially all round, made their best bows, and retired with great elegance and dignity, leaving Rose to say to herself, with girlish satisfaction, as she went in, "Now, *that* is the way I like to be treated."

CHAPTER 13

COZY CORNER

VACATION WAS OVER, the boys went back to school, and poor Mac was left lamenting. He was out of the darkened room now and promoted to blue goggles, through which he took a gloomy view of life, as might have been expected; for there was nothing he could do but wander about and try to amuse himself without using his eyes. Anyone who has ever been condemned to that sort of idleness knows how irksome it is and can understand the state of mind which caused Mac to say to Rose in a desperate tone one day, "Look here, if you don't invent some new employment or amusement for me, I shall knock myself on the head as sure as you live."

Rose flew to Uncle Alec for advice, and he ordered both patient and nurse to the mountains for a month, with Aunt Jessie and Jamie as escort. Pokey and her mother joined the party, and one bright September morning six very happy-looking people were aboard the express train for Portland—two smiling mammas, laden with luncheon baskets and wraps; a pretty young girl with a bag of books on her arm; a tall, thin lad with his hat over his eyes; and two small children, who sat with their short legs straight out before them and their chubby faces beaming with the first speechless delight of "truly traveling."

An especially splendid sunset seemed to have been prepared to welcome them when, after a long day's journey, they drove into a wide, green dooryard, where a white colt, a red cow, two cats, four kittens, many hens, and a dozen people, old and young, were gayly disporting themselves. Everyone nodded and smiled in the friendliest manner, and a lively old lady kissed the newcomers all round as she said heartily, "Well, now, I'm proper glad to see you! Come right in and rest, and we'll have tea in less than no time, for you must be tired. Lizzie, you show the folks upstairs; Kitty, you fly round and help father in with the trunks; and Jenny and I will have the table all ready by the time you come down. Bless the dears, they want to go see the pussies, and so they shall!"

The three pretty daughters did "fly round," and everyone felt at home at once, all were so hospitable and kind. Aunt Jessie had raptures over the homemade carpets, quilts, and quaint furniture; Rose could not keep away from the windows, for each framed a lovely picture; and the little folks made friends at once with the other children, who filled their arms with chickens and kittens and did the honors handsomely.

The toot of a horn called all to supper, and a goodly party, including six children besides the Campbells, assembled in the long dining room, armed with mountain appetites and the gayest spirits. It was impossible for anyone to be shy or sober, for such gales of merriment arose they blew the starch out of the stiffest and made the saddest jolly. Mother Atkinson, as all called their hostess, was the merriest there, and the busiest; for she kept flying up to wait on the children, to bring out some new dish, or to banish the livestock, who were of such a social turn that the colt came into the entry and demanded sugar; the cats sat about in people's laps, winking suggestively at the food; and speckled hens cleared the kitchen floor of crumbs as they joined in the chat with a cheerful clucking.

Everybody turned out after tea to watch the sunset till all the lovely red was gone, and mosquitoes wound their shrill horns to sound the retreat. The music of an organ surprised the newcomers, and in the parlor they found Father Atkinson playing sweetly on the little instrument made by himself. All the children gathered about him and, led by the tuneful sisters, sang prettily till Pokey fell asleep behind the door, and Jamie gaped audibly right in the middle of his favorite

"Coo," said the little doves: "Coo," said she,
"All in the top of the old pine tree."

The older travelers, being tired, went to "bye low" at the same time and slept like tops in homespun sheets, on husk mattresses made by Mother Atkinson, who seemed to have put some soothing powder among them, so deep and sweet was the slumber that came.

Next day began the wholesome out-of-door life, which works such wonders with tired minds and feeble bodies. The weather was perfect, and the mountain air made the children as frisky as young lambs; while the elders went about smiling at one another, and saying, "Isn't it splendid?" Even Mac, the "slow coach," was seen to leap over a fence as if he really could not help it; and when Rose ran after him with his broad-brimmed hat, he made the spirited proposal to go into the woods and hunt for a catamount.

Jamie and Pokey were at once enrolled in the Cozy Corner Light Infantry—a truly superb company composed entirely of officers, all wearing cocked hats, carrying flags, waving swords, or beating drums. It was a spectacle to stir the dullest soul when this gallant band marched out of the yard in full regimentals, with Captain Dove—a solemn, big-headed boy of eleven—issuing his orders with the gravity of a general, and his Falstaffian regiment obeying them with more docility than skill. The little Snow children did very well, and Lieutenant Jack Dove was fine to see; so was Drummer Frank, the errand boy of the house, as he rub-a-dub-dubbed with all his heart and drumsticks. Jamie had "trained" before and was made a colonel at once; but Pokey was the best of all and called forth a spontaneous burst of applause from the spectators as she brought up the rear, her cocked hat all over one eye, her flag trailing over her shoulder, and her wooden sword straight up in the air; her face beaming and every curl bobbing with delight as her fat legs tottered in the vain attempt to keep step manfully.

Mac and Rose were picking blackberries in the bushes beside the road when the soldiers passed without seeing them, and they witnessed a sight that was both pretty and comical. A little farther on was one of the family burial spots so common in those parts, and just this side of it Captain Fred Dove ordered his company to halt, explaining his reason for so doing in the following words: "That's a graveyard, and it's proper to muffle the drums and lower the flags as we go by, and we'd better take off our hats, too; it's more respectable, I think."

"Isn't that cunning of the dears?" whispered Rose as the little troop marched slowly by to the muffled roll of the drums, every flag and sword held low, all the little heads uncovered, and the childish faces very sober as the leafy shadows flickered over them.

"Let's follow and see what they are after," proposed Mac, who found sitting on a wall and being fed with blackberries luxurious but tiresome.

So they followed and heard the music grow lively, saw the banners wave in the breeze again when the graveyard was passed, and watched the company file into the dilapidated old church that stood at the corner of three woodland roads. Presently the sound of singing made the outsiders quicken their steps, and stealing up, they peeped in at one of the broken windows.

Captain Dove was up in the old wooden pulpit, gazing solemnly down upon his company, who, having stacked their arms in the porch, now sat in the bare pews singing a Sunday-school hymn with great vigor and relish.

"Let us pray," said Captain Dove with as much reverence as an army chaplain; and folding his hands, he repeated a prayer which he thought all would know—an excellent little prayer, but not exactly appropriate to the morning, for it was

"Now I lay me down to sleep."

Everyone joined in saying it, and it was a pretty sight to see the little creatures bowing their curly heads and lisping out the words they knew so well. Tears came into Rose's eyes as she looked; Mac took his hat off involuntarily and then clapped it on again as if ashamed of showing any feeling.

"Now I shall preach you a short sermon, and my text is 'Little children, love one another.' I asked Mamma to give me one, and she thought that would be good; so you all sit still and I'll preach it. You mustn't whisper, Marion, but hear *me*. It means that we should be good to each other, and play fair, and not quarrel as we did this very day about the wagon. Jack can't always drive, and needn't be mad because I like to go with Frank. Annette ought to be horse sometimes and not always driver; and Willie may as well make up his mind to let Marion build her house by his, for she *will* do it, and he needn't fuss about it. Jamie seems to be a good boy, but I shall preach to him if he isn't. No, Pokey, people don't kiss in church or put their hats on. Now you must all remember what I tell you, because I'm the captain, and you should mind me."

Here Lieutenant Jack spoke right out in meeting with the rebellious remark "Don't care if you are; you'd better mind yourself, and tell how you took away my strap, and kept the biggest doughnut, and didn't draw fair when we had the truck."

"Yes, and you slapped Frank; I saw you," bawled Willie Snow, bobbing up in his pew.

"And you took my book away and hid it 'cause I wouldn't go and swing when you wanted me to," added Annette, the oldest of the Snow trio.

"I *shan't* build my house by Willie's if he don't want me to, so now!" put in little Marion, joining the mutiny.

"I *will* tiss Dimmy! And I tored up my hat 'tause a pin picked me," shouted Pokey, regardless of Jamie's efforts to restrain her.

Captain Dove looked rather taken aback at this outbreak in the ranks; but, being a dignified and calm personage, he quelled the rising rebellion with great tact and skill by saying, briefly, "We will sing the last hymn: 'Sweet, Sweet Good-bye'—you all know that, so do it nicely, and then we will go and have luncheon."

Peace was instantly restored, and a burst of melody drowned the suppressed giggles of Rose and Mac, who found it impossible to keep sober during the latter part of this somewhat remarkable service. Fifteen minutes of repose rendered it a physical impossibility for the company to march out as quietly as they had marched in. I grieve to state that the entire troop raced home as hard as they could pelt and were soon skirmishing briskly over their lunch, utterly oblivious of what Jamie (who had been much impressed by the sermon) called "the captain's beautiful teck."

It was astonishing how much they all found to do at Cozy Corner; and Mac, instead of lying in a hammock and being read to, as he had expected, was busiest of all. He was invited to survey and lay out Skeeterville, a town which the children were getting up in a huckleberry pasture; and he found much amusement in planning little roads, staking off house lots, attending to the waterworks, and consulting with the "selectmen" about the best sites for public buildings; for Mac was a boy still, in spite of his fifteen years and his love of books.

Then he went fishing with a certain jovial gentleman from the West; and though they seldom caught anything but colds, they had great fun and exercise chasing the phantom trout they were bound to have. Mac also developed a geological mania and went tapping about at rocks and stones, discoursing wisely of "strata, periods, and fossil remains"; while Rose picked up leaves and lichens and gave him lessons in botany in return for his lectures on geology.

They led a very merry life; for the Atkinson girls kept up a sort of perpetual picnic, and did it so capitally that one was never tired of it. So their visitors throve finely, and long before the month was out it was evident that Dr. Alec had prescribed the right medicine for his patients.

CHAPTER 14

A HAPPY BIRTHDAY

THE TWELFTH OF OCTOBER was Rose's birthday, but no one seemed to remember that interesting fact and she felt delicate about mentioning it, so fell asleep the night before, wondering if she would have any presents. That question was settled early the next morning, for she was awakened by a soft tap on her face, and opening her eyes she beheld a little black-and-white figure sitting on her pillow, staring at her with a pair of round eyes very like blueberries, while one downy paw patted her nose to attract her notice. It was Kitty Comet, the prettiest of all the pussies, and Comet evidently had a mission to perform, for a pink bow adorned her neck, and a bit of paper was pinned to it bearing the words "For Miss Rose, from Frank."

That pleased her extremely, and that was only the beginning of the fun, for surprises and presents kept popping out in the most delightful manner all through the day, the Atkinson girls being famous jokers and Rose a favorite. But the best gift of all came on the way to Mount Windy Top, where it was decided to picnic in honor of the great occasion. Three jolly loads set off soon after breakfast, for everybody went, and everybody seemed bound to have an extra good time, especially Mother Atkinson, who wore a hat as broad-brimmed

119

as an umbrella and took the dinner horn to keep her flock from straying away.

"I'm going to drive Aunty and a lot of the babies, so you must ride the pony. And please stay behind us a good bit when we go to the station, for a parcel is coming, and you are not to see it till dinner-time. You won't mind, will you?" said Mac in a confidential aside during the wild flurry of the start.

"Not a bit," answered Rose. "It hurts my feelings *very* much to be told to keep out of the way at any other time, but birthdays and Christmas it is part of the fun to be blind and stupid, and poked into corners. I'll be ready as soon as you are, Giglamps."

"Stop under the big maple till I call—then you can't possibly see anything," added Mac as he mounted her on the pony his father had sent up for his use. Barkis was so gentle and so "willin'," however, that Rose was ashamed to be afraid to ride him; so she had learned, that she might surprise Dr. Alec when she got home; meantime she had many a fine canter "over the hills and far away" with Mac, who preferred Mr. Atkinson's old Sorrel.

Away they went, and coming to the red maple, Rose obediently paused, but could not help stealing a glance in the forbidden direction before the call came. Yes, there was a hamper going under the seat, and then she caught sight of a tall man whom Mac seemed to be hustling into the carriage in a great hurry. One look was enough, and with a cry of delight, Rose was off down the road as fast as Barkis could go.

"Now I'll astonish Uncle," she thought. "I'll dash up in grand style, and show him that I am not a coward, after all."

Fired by this ambition, she startled Barkis by a sharp cut, and still more bewildered him by leaving him to his own guidance down the steep, stony road. The approach would have been a fine success if, just as Rose was about to pull up and salute, two or three distracted hens had not scuttled across the road with a great squawking, which caused Barkis to shy and stop so suddenly that his careless rider landed in an ignominious heap just under old Sorrel's astonished nose.

Rose was up again before Dr. Alec was out of the carryall, and threw two dusty arms about his neck, crying with a breathless voice, "Oh, Uncle, I'm *so* glad to see you! It is better than a cartload of goodies, and so dear of you to come!"

"But aren't you hurt, child? That was a rough tumble, and I'm afraid you must be damaged somewhere," answered the doctor, full of fond anxiety as he surveyed his girl with pride.

"My feelings are hurt, but my bones are all safe. It's too bad! I was going to do it so nicely, and those stupid hens spoiled it all," said Rose, quite crestfallen as well as much shaken.

"I couldn't believe my eyes when I asked 'Where is Rose?' and Mac pointed to the little Amazon pelting down the hill at such a rate. You couldn't have done anything that would please me more, and I'm delighted to see how well you ride. Now, will you mount again, or shall we turn Mac out and take you in?" asked Dr. Alec, as Aunt Jessie proposed a start, for the others were beckoning them to follow.

"Pride goeth before a fall—better not try to show off again, ma'am," said Mac, who would have been more than mortal if he had refrained from teasing when so good a chance offered.

"Pride does go before a fall, but I wonder if a sprained ankle always comes after it?" thought Rose, bravely concealing her pain as she answered, with great dignity, "I *prefer* to ride. Come on, and see who will catch up first."

She was up and away as she spoke, doing her best to efface the memory of her downfall by sitting very erect, elbows down, head well up, and taking the motion of the pony as Barkis cantered along as easily as a rocking chair.

"You ought to see her go over a fence and race when we ride together. She can scud, too, like a deer when we play follow the leader, and skip stones and bat balls almost as well as I can," said Mac in reply to his uncle's praise of his pupil.

"I'm afraid you will think her a sad tomboy, Alec; but really she seems so well and happy, I have not the heart to check her. She has broken out in the most unexpected way and frisks like a colt; for she says she feels so full of spirits she *must* run and shout whether it is proper or not," added Mrs. Jessie, who had been a pretty hoyden years ago herself.

"Good—good! That's the best news you could tell me"; and Dr. Alec rubbed his hands heartily. "Let the girl run and shout as much as she will—it is a sure sign of health and as natural to a happy child as frisking is to any young animal full of life. Tomboys make strong women usually, and I had far rather find Rose playing football with Mac than puttering over beadwork like that affected midget Ariadne Blish."

"But she cannot go on playing football very long; and we must not forget that she has a woman's work to do by and by," began Mrs. Jessie.

"Neither will Mac play football much longer, but he will be all the better fitted for business, because of the health it gives him. Polish is easily added, if the foundations are strong; but no amount of gilding will be of use if your timber is not sound. I'm sure I'm right, Jessie; and if I can do as well by my girl during the next six months as I have the last, my experiment *will* succeed."

"It certainly will; for when I contrast that bright, blooming face with the pale, listless one that made my heart ache a while ago, I can believe in almost any miracle," said Mrs. Jessie as Rose looked round to point out a lovely view, with cheeks like the ruddy apples in the orchard nearby, eyes clear as the autumn sky overhead, and vigor in every line of her girlish figure.

A general scramble among the rocks was followed by a regular gypsy lunch, which the young folks had the rapture of helping to prepare. Mother Atkinson put on her apron, turned up her sleeves, and fell to work as gayly as if in her own kitchen, boiling the kettle slung on three sticks over a fire of cones and fir boughs; while the girls spread the mossy table with a feast of country goodies, and the children tumbled about in everyone's way till the toot of the horn made them settle down like a flock of hungry birds.

As soon as the merry meal and a brief interval of repose were over, it was unanimously voted to have some charades. A smooth green spot between two stately pines was chosen for the stage; shawls hung up, properties collected, audience and actors separated, and a word quickly chosen.

The first scene discovered Mac in a despondent attitude and shabby dress, evidently much troubled in mind. To him entered a remarkable creature with a brown paper bag over its head. A little pink nose peeped through one hole in the middle, white teeth through another, and above two eyes glared fiercely. Spires of grass stuck in each side of the mouth seemed meant to represent whiskers; the upper corners of the bag were twisted like ears, and no one could doubt for a moment that the black scarf pinned on behind was a tail.

This singular animal seemed in pantomime to be comforting his master and offering advice, which was finally acted upon, for Mac pulled off his boots, helped the little beast into them, and gave him a bag; then, kissing his paw with a hopeful gesture, the creature retired, purring so successfully that there was a general cry of "Cat, puss, boots!"

"Cat is the word," replied a voice, and the curtain fell.

The next scene was a puzzler, for in came another animal, on all fours this time, with a new sort of tail and long ears. A gray shawl concealed its face, but an inquisitive sunbeam betrayed the glitter as of goggles under the fringe. On its back rode a small gentleman in Eastern costume, who appeared to find some difficulty in keeping his seat as his steed jogged along. Suddenly a spirit appeared, all in white, with long newspaper wings upon its back and golden locks about its face. Singularly enough, the beast beheld this apparition and backed instantly, but the rider evidently saw nothing and whipped up unmercifully, also unsuccessfully, for the spirit stood directly in the path, and the amiable beast would not budge a foot. A lively skirmish followed, which ended in the Eastern gentleman's being upset into a sweet-fern bush while the better-bred animal abased itself before the shining one.

The children were all in the dark till Mother Atkinson said, in an inquiring tone, "If that isn't Balaam and the ass, I'd like to know what it is. Rose makes a sweet angel, don't she?"

Ass was evidently the word, and the angel retired, smiling with mundane satisfaction over the compliment that reached her ears.

The next was a pretty little scene from the immortal story of "Babes in the Wood." Jamie and Pokey came trotting in, hand in hand, and, having been through the parts many times before, acted with great ease and much fluency, audibly directing each other from time to time as they went along. The berries were picked, the way lost, tears shed, baby consolation administered, and then the little pair lay down among the brakes and died with their eyes wide open and the toes of their four little boots turned up to the daisies in the most pathetic manner.

"Now the wobins tum. You be twite dead, Dimmy, and I'll peep and see 'em," one defunct innocent was heard to say.

"I hope they'll be quick, for I'm lying on a stone, and ants are walking up my leg like fury," murmured the other.

Here the robins came flapping in with red scarfs over their breasts and leaves in their mouths, which they carefully laid upon the babes wherever they would show best. A prickly blackberry leaf placed directly over Pokey's nose caused her to sneeze so violently that her little legs flew into the air; Jamie gave a startled "Ow!" and the pitying fowls fled giggling.

After some discussion it was decided that the syllable must be *strew* or *strow,* and then they waited to see if it was a good guess.

This scene discovered Annette Snow in bed, evidently very ill; Miss Jenny was her anxious mamma, and her merry conversation amused the audience till Mac came in as a physician and made great fun with his big watch, pompous manner, and absurd questions. He prescribed one pellet with an unpronounceable name and left after demanding twenty dollars for his brief visit.

The pellet was administered, and such awful agonies immediately set in that the distracted mamma bade a sympathetic neighbor run for Mother Know-all. The neighbor ran, and in came a brisk little old lady in cap and specs, with a bundle of herbs under her arm, which she at once applied in all sorts of funny ways, explaining their virtues as she clapped a plantain poultice here, put a pounded catnip plaster there, or tied a couple of mullein leaves round the sufferer's throat. Instant relief ensued, the dying child sat up and demanded baked beans, the grateful parent offered fifty dollars; but Mother Know-all indignantly refused it and went smiling away, declaring that a neighborly turn needed no reward, and a doctor's *fee* was all a humbug.

The audience were in fits of laughter over this scene, for Rose imitated Mrs. Atkinson capitally, and the herb cure was a good hit at the excellent lady's belief that "yarbs" would save mankind if properly applied. No one enjoyed it more than herself, and the saucy children prepared for the grand finale in high feather.

This closing scene was brief but striking, for two trains of cars whizzed in from opposite sides, met with a terrible collision in the middle of the stage, and a general smash-up completed the word *catastrophe.*

"Now, let us act a proverb. I've got one all ready," said Rose, who was dying to distinguish herself in some way before Uncle Alec.

So everyone but Mac, the gay westerner, and Rose took their places on the rocky seats and discussed the late beautiful and varied charade, in which Pokey frankly pronounced her own scene the "bestest of all."

In five minutes the curtain was lifted; nothing appeared but a very large sheet of brown paper pinned to a tree, and on it was drawn a clock face, the hands pointing to four. A small note below informed the public that 4 A.M. was the time. Hardly had the audience grasped this important fact when a long waterproof serpent was seen uncoiling itself from behind a stump. An inchworm, perhaps, would be a better description, for it traveled in the same humpy way as that pleasing reptile. Suddenly a very wide-awake and active fowl advanced, pecking, chirping, and scratching vigorously. A tuft of green leaves waved upon his crest, a larger tuft of brakes made an umbrageous tail, and a shawl of many colors formed his flapping wings. A truly noble bird, whose legs had the genuine strut, whose eyes shone watchfully, and whose voice had a ring that evidently struck terror into the caterpillar's soul, if it was a caterpillar. He squirmed, he wriggled, he humped as fast as he could, trying to escape; but all in vain. The tufted bird espied him, gave one warbling sort of crow, pounced upon him, and flapped triumphantly away.

"That early bird got such a big worm he could hardly carry him off," laughed Aunt Jessie as the children shouted over the joke suggested by Mac's nickname.

"That is one of Uncle's favorite proverbs, so I got it up for his especial benefit," said Rose, coming up with the two-legged worm beside her.

"Very clever; what next?" asked Dr. Alec as she sat down beside him.

"The Dove boys are going to give us an 'Incident in the Life of Napoleon,' as they call it; the children think it very splendid, and the little fellows do it rather nicely," answered Mac with condescension.

A tent appeared, and pacing to and fro before it was a little sentinel, who, in a brief soliloquy, informed the observers that the elements were in a great state of confusion, that he had marched some hundred miles or so that day, and that he was dying for want of sleep. Then he paused, leaned upon his gun, and seemed to doze; dropped slowly down, overpowered with slumber, and finally lay flat, with his gun beside him, a faithless little sentinel. Enter Napoleon, cocked hat, gray coat, high boots, folded arms, grim mouth, and a melodramatic stride. Freddy Dove always covered himself with glory in this part, and "took the stage" with a Napoleonic attitude that brought down the house; for the big-headed boy, with solemn, dark eyes and square brow, was "the very moral of that rascal, Boneyparty," Mother Atkinson said.

Some great scheme was evidently brewing in his mighty mind—a trip across the Alps, a bonfire at Moscow, or a little skirmish at Waterloo, perhaps, for he marched in silent majesty till suddenly a gentle snore disturbed the imperial reverie. He saw the sleeping soldier and glared upon him, saying in an awful tone, "Ha! Asleep at his post! Death is the penalty—he must die!"

Picking up the musket, he is about to execute summary justice, as emperors are in the habit of doing, when something in the face of the weary sentinel appears to touch him. And well it might, for a most engaging little warrior was Jack as he lay with his shako half off, his childish face trying to keep sober, and a great black mustache over his rosy mouth. It would have softened the heart of any Napoleon, and the Little Corporal proved himself a man by relenting, and saying, with a lofty gesture of forgiveness, "Brave fellow, he is worn out; I will let him sleep, and mount guard in his place."

Then, shouldering the gun, this noble being strode to and fro with a dignity which thrilled the younger spectators. The sentinel awakes, sees what has happened, and gives himself up for lost. But the Emperor restores his weapon and, with that smile which won all hearts, says, pointing to a high rock whereon a crow happens to be sitting: "Be brave, be vigilant, and remember that from yonder Pyramid generations are beholding you," and with these memorable words he vanishes, leaving the grateful soldier bolt upright, with his hand at his temple and deathless devotion stamped upon his youthful countenance.

The applause which followed this superb piece had hardly subsided when a sudden splash and a shrill cry caused a general rush toward the waterfall that went gamboling down the rocks, singing sweetly as it ran. Pokey had tried to gambol also, and had tumbled into a shallow pool, whither Jamie had gallantly followed in a vain attempt to fish her out, and both were paddling about half frightened, half pleased with the unexpected bath.

This mishap made it necessary to get the dripping infants home as soon as possible; so the wagons were loaded up, and away they went, as merry as if the mountain air had really been "Oxygenated Sweets Not Bitters," as Dr. Alec suggested when Mac said he felt as jolly as if he had been drinking champagne instead of the currant wine that came with a great frosted cake wreathed with sugar roses in Aunt Plenty's hamper of goodies.

Rose took part in all the fun and never betrayed by look or word the twinges of pain she suffered in her ankle. She excused herself from the games in the evening, however, and sat talking to Uncle Alec in a lively way that both amazed and delighted him; for she confided to him that she played horse with the children, drilled with the light infantry, climbed trees, and did other dreadful things that would have caused the aunts to cry aloud if they knew of them.

"I don't care a pin what they say if you don't mind, Uncle," she answered when he pictured the dismay of the good ladies.

"Ah, it's all very well to defy *them,* but you are getting so rampant, I'm afraid you will defy me next, and then where are we?"

"No, I won't! I shouldn't dare; because you are my guardian and can put me in a straitjacket if you like"; and Rose laughed in his face, even while she nestled closer with a confiding gesture pleasant to see.

"Upon my word, Rosy, I begin to feel like the man who bought an elephant and then didn't know what to do with him. I thought I had got a pet and plaything for years to come; but here you are growing up like a beanstalk, and I shall find I've got a strong-minded little woman on my hands before I can turn round. There's a predicament for a man and an uncle!"

Dr. Alec's comic distress was mercifully relieved for the time being by a dance of goblins on the lawn, where the children, with pumpkin lanterns on their heads, frisked about like will-o'-the-wisps as a parting surprise.

When Rose went to bed, she found that Uncle Alec had not forgotten her; for on the table stood a delicate little easel, holding two miniatures set in velvet. She knew them both and stood looking at them till her eyes brimmed over with tears that were both sweet and sad; for they were the faces of her father and mother, beautifully copied from portraits fast fading away.

Presently she knelt down and, putting her arms round the little shrine, kissed one after the other, saying with an earnest voice, "I'll truly try to make them glad to see me by and by."

And that was Rose's little prayer on the night of her fourteenth birthday.

Two days later, the Campbells went home, a larger party than when they came; for Dr. Alec was escort, and Kitty Comet was borne in state in a basket, with a bottle of milk, some tiny sandwiches, and a doll's dish to drink out of, as well as a bit of carpet to lie on in her palace car, out of which she kept popping her head in the most fascinating manner.

There was a great kissing and cuddling, waving of handkerchiefs, and last good-byes as they went; and when they had started, Mother Atkinson came running after them to tuck in some little pies, hot from the oven, "for the dears, who might get tired of bread and butter during that long day's travel."

Another start, and another halt; for the Snow children came shrieking up to demand the three kittens that Pokey was coolly carrying off in a traveling bag. The unhappy kits were rescued, half smothered, and restored to their lawful owners, amid dire lamentation from the little kidnapper, who declared that she only "tooked um 'cause they'd want to go wid their sister Tomit."

Start number three and stoppage number three, as Frank hailed them with the luncheon basket, which had been forgotten, after everyone had protested that it was safely in.

All went well after that, and the long journey was pleasantly beguiled by Pokey and Pussy, who played together so prettily that they were considered public benefactors.

"Rose doesn't want to go home, for she knows the aunts won't let her rampage as she did up at Cozy Corner," said Mac as they approached the old house.

"I *can't* rampage if I want to—for a time, at least; and I'll tell you why. I sprained my ankle when I tumbled off of Barkis, and it gets worse and worse; though I've done all I know to cure it and hide it, so it shouldn't trouble anyone," whispered Rose, knitting her brows with pain as she prepared to descend, wishing her uncle would take her instead of her bundles.

How he did it, she never knew; but Mac had her up the steps and on the parlor sofa before she could put her foot to the ground.

"There you are—right side up with care; and mind, now, if your ankle bothers you, and you are laid up with it, *I* am to be your footman. It's only fair, you know; for I don't forget how good you have been to me." And Mac went to call Phebe, so full of gratitude and goodwill that his very goggles shone.

CHAPTER 15

EARRINGS

ROSE'S SPRAIN PROVED to be a serious one, owing to neglect, and Dr. Alec ordered her to lie on the sofa for a fortnight at least; whereat she groaned dismally, but dared not openly complain, lest the boys turn upon her with some of the wise little sermons on patience which she had delivered for their benefit.

It was Mac's turn now, and honorably did he repay his debt; for as school was still forbidden, he had plenty of leisure and devoted most of it to Rose. He took many steps for her, and even allowed her to teach him to knit, after assuring himself that many a brave Scotchman knew how to "click the pricks." She was obliged to take a solemn vow of secrecy, however, before he would consent; for though he did not mind being called "Giglamps," "Granny" was more than his boyish soul could bear, and at the approach of any of the clan his knitting vanished as if by magic, which frequent "chucking" out of sight did not improve the stripe he was doing for Rose's new afghan.

She was busy with this pretty work one bright October afternoon, all nicely established on her sofa in the upper hall, while Jamie and

Pokey (lent for her amusement) were keeping house in a corner, with Comet and Rose's old doll for their "childerns."

Presently, Phebe appeared with a card. Rose read it, made a grimace, then laughed and said, "I'll see Miss Bliss," and immediately put on her company face, pulled out her locket, and settled her curls.

"You dear thing, how *do* you do? I've been trying to call every day since you got back, but I have so many engagements, I really couldn't manage it till today. So glad you are alone, for Mamma said I could sit awhile, and I brought my lacework to show you, for it's perfectly lovely," cried Miss Bliss, greeting Rose with a kiss, which was not very warmly returned, though Rose politely thanked her for coming and bid Phebe roll up the easy chair.

"How nice to have a maid!" said Annabel as she settled herself with much commotion. "Still, dear, you must be very lonely, and feel the need of a bosom friend."

"I have my cousins," began Rose, with dignity, for her visitor's patronizing manner ruffled her temper.

"Gracious, child! You don't make friends of those great boys, do you? Mamma says she really doesn't think it's proper for you to be with them so much."

"They are like brothers, and my aunts *do* think it's proper," replied Rose rather sharply, for it struck her that this was none of Miss Bliss's business.

"I was merely going to say I should be glad to have you for *my* bosom friend, for Hatty Mason and I have had an awful quarrel, and don't speak. She is too mean to live, so I gave her up. Just think, she never paid back one of the caramels I've given her and never invited me to her party. I could have forgiven the caramels, but to be left out in that rude way was more than I could bear, and I told her never to look at me again as long as she lived."

"You are very kind, but I don't think I want a bosom friend, thank you," said Rose as Annabel stopped to bridle and shake her flaxen head over the delinquent Hatty Mason.

Now, in her heart Miss Bliss thought Rose "a stuck-up puss," but the other girls wanted to know her and couldn't, the old house was a charming place to visit, the lads were considered fine fellows, and the Campbells "are one of our first families," Mamma said. So Annabel concealed her vexation at Rose's coolness and changed the subject as fast as possible.

"Studying French, I see; who is your teacher?" she asked, flirting over the leaves of *Paul and Virginia* that lay on the table.

"I don't *study* it, for I read French as well as English, and Uncle and I often speak it for hours. He talks like a native and says I have a remarkably good accent."

Rose really could not help this small display of superiority, for French was one of her strong points and she was vain of it, though she usually managed to hide this weakness. She felt that Annabel would be the better for a little crushing and could not resist the temptation to patronize in her turn.

"Oh, indeed!" said Miss Bliss rather blankly, for French was not *her* strong point by any means.

"I am to go abroad with Uncle in a year or two, and he knows how important it is to understand the languages. Half the girls who leave school can't speak decent French, and when they go abroad they are *so* mortified. I shall be very glad to help you, if you like, for of course *you* have no one to talk with at home."

Now Annabel, though she *looked* like a wax doll, had feelings within her instead of sawdust, and these feelings were hurt by Rose's lofty tone. She thought her more "stuck up" than ever, but did not know how to bring her down, yet longed to do it, for she felt as if she had received a box on the ear and involuntarily put her hand up to it. The touch of an earring consoled her and suggested a way of returning tit for tat in a telling manner.

"Thank you, dear; I don't need any help, for our teacher is from Paris, and of course *he* speaks better French than your uncle." Then she added, with a gesture of her head that set the little bells on her ears to tingling: "How do you like my new earrings? Papa gave them to me last week, and everyone says they are lovely."

Rose came down from her high horse with a rapidity that was comical, for Annabel had the upper hand now. Rose adored pretty things, longed to wear them, and the desire of her girlish soul was to have her ears bored, only Dr. Alec thought it foolish, so she never had done it. She would gladly have given all the French she could jabber for a pair of golden bells with pearl-tipped tongues like those Annabel wore; and clasping her hands, she answered, in a tone that went to the hearer's heart, "They are *too* sweet for anything! If Uncle would only let me wear some, I should be *perfectly* happy."

"I wouldn't mind what he says. Papa laughed at me at first, but he likes them now and says I shall have diamond solitaires when I am eighteen," said Annabel, quite satisfied with her shot.

"I've got a pair now that were Mamma's, and a beautiful little pair of pearl and turquoise ones that I am dying to wear," sighed Rose.

"Then do it. I'll pierce your ears, and you must wear a bit of silk in them till they are well; your curls will hide them nicely; then, some-day, slip in your smallest earrings, and see if your uncle don't like them."

"I asked him if it wouldn't do my eyes good once when they were red, and he only laughed. People do cure weak eyes that way, don't they?"

"Yes, indeed, and yours *are* sort of red. Let me see. Yes, I really think you ought to do it before they get worse," said Annabel, peer-ing into the large clear eye offered for inspection.

"Does it hurt much?" asked Rose, wavering.

"Oh dear, no! Just a prick and a pull and it's all over. I've done lots of ears and know just how. Come, push up your hair and get a big needle."

"I don't quite like to do it without asking Uncle's leave," faltered Rose when all was ready for the operation.

"Did he ever forbid it?" demanded Annabel, hovering over her prey like a vampire.

"No, never!"

"Then do it, unless you are *afraid,*" cried Miss Bliss, bent on ac-complishing the deed.

That last word settled the matter, and closing her eyes, Rose said "Punch!" in the tone of one giving the fatal order "Fire!"

Annabel punched, and the victim bore it in heroic silence, though she turned pale and her eyes were full of tears of anguish.

"There! Now pull the bits of silk often, and cold-cream your ears every night, and you'll soon be ready for the rings," said Annabel, well pleased with her job, for the girl who spoke French with "a fine accent" lay flat upon the sofa, looking as exhausted as if she had had both ears cut off.

"It does hurt dreadfully, and I know Uncle won't like it," sighed Rose as remorse began to gnaw. "Promise not to tell, or I shall be teased to death," she added anxiously, entirely forgetting the two little pitchers gifted with eyes as well as ears, who had been watching the whole performance from afar.

"Never. Mercy me, what's that?" And Annabel started as a sudden sound of steps and voices came up from below.

"It's the boys! Hide the needle. Do my ears show? Don't breathe a word!" whispered Rose, scrambling about to conceal all traces of their iniquity from the sharp eyes of the clan.

Up they came, all in good order, laden with the proceeds of a nutting expedition, for they always reported to Rose and paid tribute to their queen in the handsomest manner.

"How many, and how big! We'll have a grand roasting frolic after tea, won't we?" said Rose, plunging both hands into a bag of glossy brown nuts while the clan "stood at ease" and nodded to Annabel.

"That lot was picked especially for you, Rosy. I got every one myself, and they are extra whackers," said Mac, presenting a bushel or so.

"You should have seen Giglamps when he was after them. He pitched out of the tree and would have broken his blessed old neck if Arch had not caught him," observed Steve as he lounged gracefully in the window seat.

"You needn't talk, Dandy, when you didn't know a chestnut from a beech and kept on thrashing till I told you of it," retorted Mac, festooning himself over the back of the sofa, being a privileged boy.

"I don't make mistakes when I thrash you, old Worm, so you'd better mind what you are about," answered Steve without a ray of proper respect for his elder brother.

"It is getting dark, and I must go, or Mamma will be alarmed," said Annabel, rising in sudden haste, though she hoped to be asked to remain to the nut party.

No one invited her; and all the while she was putting on her things and chatting to Rose the boys were telegraphing to one another the sad fact that someone ought to escort the young lady home. Not a boy felt heroic enough to cast himself into the breach, however; even polite Archie shirked the duty, saying to Charlie, as they quietly slipped into an adjoining room, "I'm not going to do all the galli- vanting. Let Steve take that chit home and show his manners."

"I'll be hanged if I do!" answered Prince, who disliked Miss Bliss because she tried to be coquettish with him.

"Then I will," and to the dismay of both recreant lads, Dr. Alec walked out of the room to offer his services to the "chit."

He was too late, however, for Mac, obeying a look from Rose, had already made a victim of himself and trudged meekly away, wishing the gentle Annabel at the bottom of the Red Sea.

"Then I will take this lady down to tea, as the other one has found a *gentleman* to go home with her. I see the lamps are lighted below, and I smell a smell which tells me that Aunty has something extra nice for us tonight."

As he spoke, Dr. Alec was preparing to carry Rose downstairs as usual; but Archie and Prince rushed forward, begging with penitent eagerness for the honor of carrying her in an armchair. Rose con- sented, fearing that her uncle's keen eye would discover the fatal bits of silk; so the boys crossed hands, and taking a good grip of each curly pate, she was borne down in state while the others followed by way of the banisters.

Tea was ordered earlier than usual so that Jamie and his dolly could have a taste, at least, of the holiday fun, for they were to stay till seven and be allowed twelve roasted chestnuts apiece, which they were under bonds not to eat till next day.

Tea was dispatched rapidly, therefore, and the party gathered round the wide hearth in the dining room, where the nuts were soon dancing gayly on hot shovels or bouncing out among the company, thereby causing delightful panics among the little ones.

"Come, Rosy, tell us a story while we work, for you can't help much and must amuse us as your share," proposed Mac, who sat in the shade pricking nuts, and who knew by experience what a capital little Scheherazade his cousin was.

"Yes, we poor monkeys can't burn our paws for nothing, so tell away, Pussy," added Charlie as he threw several hot nuts into her lap and shook his fingers afterward.

"Well, I happen to have a little story with a moral to it in my mind, and I will tell it, though it is intended for younger children than you," answered Rose, who was rather fond of telling instructive tales.

"Fire away," said Geordie, and she obeyed, little thinking what a disastrous story it would prove to herself.

"Well, once upon a time, a little girl went to see a young lady who was very fond of her. Now, the young lady happened to be lame and had to have her foot bandaged up every day; so she kept a basketful of bandages, all nicely rolled and ready. The little girl liked to play with this basket, and one day, when she thought no one saw her, she took one of the rolls without asking leave, and put it in her pocket."

Here Pokey, who had been peering lovingly down at the five warm nuts that lay at the bottom of her tiny pocket, suddenly looked up and said, "Oh!" in a startled tone, as if the moral tale had become intensely interesting all at once.

Rose heard and saw the innocent betrayal of the small sinner and went on in a most impressive manner, while the boys nudged one another and winked as they caught the joke.

"But an eye did see this naughty little girl, and whose eye do you think it was?"

"Eye of Dod," murmured the conscience-stricken Pokey, spreading two chubby little hands before the round face, which they were not half big enough to hide.

Rose was rather taken aback by this reply but feeling that she was producing a good effect, she added, seriously, "Yes, God saw her, and so did the young lady, but she did not say anything; she waited to see what the little girl would do about it. She had been very happy before she took the bandage, but when it was in her pocket she seemed troubled, and pretty soon stopped playing and sat down in a corner, looking very sober. She thought a few minutes and then went and put back the roll very softly, and her face cleared up, and she was a happy child again. The young lady was glad to see that, and wondered what made the little girl put it back."

"Tonscience p'icked her," murmured a contrite voice from behind the small hands pressed tightly over Pokey's red face.

"And why did she take it, do you suppose?" asked Rose in a schoolmarmish tone, feeling that all the listeners were interested in her tale and its unexpected application.

"It was *so* nice and wound, and she wanted it deffly," answered the little voice.

"Well, I'm glad she had such a good conscience. The moral is that people who steal don't enjoy what they take and are not happy till they put it back. What makes that little girl hide her face?" asked Rose as she concluded.

"Me's so 'shamed of Pokey," sobbed the small culprit, quite overcome by remorse and confusion at this awful disclosure.

"Come, Rose, it's too bad to tell her little tricks before everyone and preach at her in that way; you wouldn't like it yourself," began Dr. Alec, taking the weeper on his knee and administering consolation in the shape of kisses and nuts.

Before Rose could express her regret, Jamie, who had been reddening and ruffling like a little turkey cock for several minutes, burst out indignantly, bent on avenging the wound given to his beloved dolly, "*I* know something bad that *you* did, and I'm going to tell right out. You thought we didn't see you, but we did, and you said Uncle wouldn't like it, and the boys would tease, and you made Annabel promise not to tell, and she punched holes in your ears to put earrings in. So now! And that's much badder than to take an old piece of rag; and I hate you for making my Pokey cry."

Jamie's somewhat incoherent explosion produced such an effect that Pokey's small sin was instantly forgotten, and Rose felt that her hour had come.

"What! What! What!" cried the boys in a chorus, dropping their shovels and knives to gather round Rose, for a guilty clutching at her ears betrayed her, and with a feeble cry of "Annabel made me!" she hid her head among the pillows like an absurd little ostrich.

"Now she'll go prancing round with birdcages and baskets and carts and pigs, for all I know, in her ears, as the other girls do, and won't she look like a goose?" asked one tormentor, tweaking a curl that strayed out from the cushions.

"I didn't think she'd be so silly," said Mac in a tone of disappointment that told Rose she had sunk in the esteem of her wise cousin.

"That Bliss girl is a nuisance and ought not to be allowed to come here with her nonsensical notions," said the Prince, feeling a strong desire to shake that young person as an angry dog might shake a mischievous kitten.

"How do *you* like it, Uncle?" asked Archie, who, being the head of a family himself, believed in preserving discipline at all costs.

"I am very much surprised; but I see she is a girl, after all, and must have her vanities like all the rest of them," answered Dr. Alec with a sigh, as if he had expected to find Rose a sort of angel, above all earthly temptation.

"What shall you do about it, sir?" inquired Geordie, wondering what punishment would be inflicted on a feminine culprit.

"As she is fond of ornaments, perhaps we had better give her a nose ring also. I have one somewhere that a Fiji belle once wore; I'll look it up." And leaving Pokey to Jamie's care, Dr. Alec rose as if to carry out his suggestion in earnest.

"Good! Good! We'll do it right away! Here's a gimlet, so you hold her, boys, while I get her dear little nose all ready," cried Charlie, whisking away the pillows as the other boys danced about the sofa in true Fiji style.

It was a dreadful moment, for Rose could not run away—she could only grasp her precious nose with one hand and extend the other, crying distractedly, "Oh, Uncle, save me, save me!"

Of course he saved her; and when she was securely barricaded by his strong arm, she confessed her folly in such humiliation of spirit that the lads, after a good laugh at her, decided to forgive her and lay all the blame on the tempter, Annabel. Even Dr. Alec relented so far as to propose two gold rings for the ears instead of one copper one for the nose; a proceeding which proved that if Rose had all the weakness of her sex for jewelry, he had all the inconsistency of his in giving a pretty penitent exactly what she wanted, spite of his better judgment.

CHAPTER 16

BREAD AND BUTTONHOLES

"WHAT IN THE WORLD is my girl thinking about all alone here, with such a solemn face?" asked Dr. Alec, coming into the study one November day to find Rose sitting there with folded hands and a very thoughtful aspect.

"Uncle, I want to have some serious conversation with you, if you have time," she said, coming out of a brown study, as if she had not heard his question.

"I'm entirely at your service and most happy to listen," he answered in his politest manner, for when Rose put on her womanly little airs he always treated her with a playful sort of respect that pleased her very much.

Now, as he sat down beside her, she said very soberly, "I've been trying to decide what trade I would learn, and I want you to advise me."

"Trade, my dear?" And Dr. Alec looked so astonished that she hastened to explain.

"I forgot that you didn't hear the talk about it up at Cozy Corner. You see, we used to sit under the pines and sew, and talk a great deal —all the ladies, I mean—and I liked it very much. Mother Atkinson thought that everyone should have a trade, or something to make a living out of, for rich people may grow poor, you know, and poor people have to work. Her girls were very clever and could do ever so many things, and Aunt Jessie thought the old lady was right; so when I saw how happy and independent those young ladies were, I wanted to have a trade, and then it wouldn't matter about money, though I like to have it well enough."

Dr. Alec listened to this explanation with a curious mixture of surprise, pleasure, and amusement in his face, and looked at his little niece as if she had suddenly changed into a young woman. She had grown a good deal in the last six months, and an amount of thinking had gone on in that young head which would have astonished him greatly could he have known it all, for Rose was one of the children who observe and meditate much, and now and then nonplus their friends by a wise or curious remark.

"I quite agree with the ladies and shall be glad to help you decide on something if I can," said the doctor seriously. "What do you incline to? A natural taste or talent is a great help in choosing, you know."

"I haven't any talent, or any especial taste that I can see, and that is why I can't decide, Uncle. So I think it would be a good plan to pick out some very *useful* business and learn it, because I don't do it for pleasure, you see, but as a part of my education, and to be ready in case I'm ever poor," answered Rose, looking as if she rather longed for a little poverty so that her useful gift might be exercised.

"Well, now, there is one very excellent, necessary, and womanly accomplishment that no girl should be without, for it is a help to rich and poor, and the comfort of families depends upon it. This fine talent is neglected nowadays and considered old-fashioned, which is a sad mistake and one that I don't mean to make in bringing up my girl. It should be a part of every girl's education, and I know of a most accomplished lady who will teach you in the best and pleasantest manner."

"Oh, what is it?" cried Rose eagerly, charmed to be met in this helpful and cordial way.

"Housekeeping!" answered Dr. Alec.

"Is that an accomplishment?" asked Rose while her face fell, for she had indulged in all sorts of vague, delightful dreams.

"Yes; it is one of the most beautiful as well as useful of all the arts a woman can learn. Not so romantic, perhaps, as singing, painting, writing, or teaching, even; but one that makes many happy and comfortable, and home the sweetest place in the world. Yes, you may open your big eyes; but it is a fact that I had rather see you a good housekeeper than the greatest belle in the city. It need not interfere with any talent you may possess, but it *is* a necessary part of your training, and I hope that you will set about it at once, now that you are well and strong."

"Who is the lady?" asked Rose, rather impressed by her uncle's earnest speech.

"Aunt Plenty."

"Is *she* accomplished?" began Rose in a wondering tone, for this great-aunt of hers had seemed the least cultivated of them all.

"In the good old-fashioned way she is very accomplished and has made this house a happy home to us all, ever since we can remember. She is not elegant, but genuinely good, and so beloved and respected that there will be universal mourning for her when her place is empty. No one can fill it, for the solid, homely virtues of the dear soul have gone out of fashion, as I say, and nothing new can be half so satisfactory, to me at least."

"I should like to have people feel so about me. Can she teach me to do what she does, and to grow as good?" asked Rose with a little prick of remorse for even thinking that Aunt Plenty was a commonplace old lady.

"Yes, if you don't despise such simple lessons as she can give. I know it would fill her dear old heart with pride and pleasure to feel that anyone cared to learn of her, for she fancies her day gone by. Let her teach you how to be what she has been—a skillful, frugal, cheerful housewife; the maker and the keeper of a happy home, and by and by you will see what a valuable lesson it is."

"I will, Uncle. But how shall I begin?"

"I'll speak to her about it, and she will make it all right with Debby, for cooking is one of the main things, you know."

"So it is! I don't mind that a bit, for I like to mess, and used to try at home; but I had no one to tell me, so I never did much but spoil my aprons. Pies are great fun, only Debby is *so* cross, I don't believe she will ever let me do a thing in the kitchen."

"Then we'll cook in the parlor. I fancy Aunt Plenty will manage her, so don't be troubled. Only mind this, I'd rather you learned how to make good bread than the best pies ever baked. When you bring me a handsome, wholesome loaf, entirely made by yourself, I shall be more pleased than if you offered me a pair of slippers embroidered in the very latest style. I don't wish to bribe you, but I'll give you my heartiest kiss, and promise to eat every crumb of the loaf myself."

"It's a bargain! It's a bargain! Come and tell Aunty all about it, for I'm in a hurry to begin," cried Rose, dancing before him toward the parlor, where Miss Plenty sat alone knitting contentedly, yet ready to run at the first call for help of any sort, from any quarter.

No need to tell how surprised and gratified she was at the invitation she received to teach the child the domestic arts which were her only accomplishments, nor to relate how energetically she set about her pleasant task. Debby dared not grumble, for Miss Plenty was the one person whom she obeyed, and Phebe openly rejoiced, for these new lessons brought Rose nearer to her and glorified the kitchen in the good girl's eyes.

To tell the truth, the elder aunts had sometimes felt that they did not have quite their share of the little niece who had won their hearts long ago and was the sunshine of the house. They talked it over together sometimes, but always ended by saying that as Alec had all the responsibility, he should have the larger share of the dear girl's love and time, and they would be contented with such crumbs of comfort as they could get.

Dr. Alec had found out this little secret and, after reproaching himself for being blind and selfish, was trying to devise some way of mending matters without troubling anyone, when Rose's new whim suggested an excellent method of weaning her a little from himself. He did not know how fond he was of her till he gave her up to the new teacher, and often could not resist peeping in at the door to see how she got on, or stealing sly looks through the slide when she was deep in dough or listening intently to some impressive lecture from Aunt Plenty. They caught him at it now and then and ordered him off the premises at the point of the rolling pin; or, if unusually successful and, therefore, in a milder mood, they lured him away with bribes of gingerbread, a stray pickle, or a tart that was not quite symmetrical enough to suit their critical eyes.

Of course he made a point of partaking copiously of all the delectable messes that now appeared at table, for both the cooks were on their mettle, and he fared sumptuously every day. But an especial relish was given to any dish when, in reply to his honest praise of it, Rose colored up with innocent pride and said modestly, "I made that, Uncle, and I'm glad you like it."

It was some time before the perfect loaf appeared, for bread making is an art not easily learned and Aunt Plenty was very thorough in her teaching; so Rose studied yeast first, and through various stages of cake and biscuit came at last to the crowning glory of the "handsome, wholesome loaf." It appeared at teatime on a silver salver, proudly borne in by Phebe, who could not refrain from whispering, with a beaming face, as she set it down before Dr. Alec, "Ain't it just lovely, sir?"

"It is a regularly splendid loaf! Did my girl make it all herself?" he asked, surveying the shapely, sweet-smelling object with real interest and pleasure.

"Every particle herself, and never asked a bit of help or advice from anyone," answered Aunt Plenty, folding her hands with an air of unmitigated satisfaction, for her pupil certainly did her great credit.

"I've had so many failures and troubles that I really thought I never should be able to do it alone. Debby let one splendid batch burn up because I forgot it. She was there and smelled it, but never did a thing, for she said, when I undertook to bake bread I must give my whole mind to it. Wasn't it hard? She might have called me at least," said Rose, recollecting with a sigh the anguish of that moment.

"She meant you should learn by experience, as Rosamond did in that little affair of the purple jar, you remember."

"I always thought it very unfair in her mother not to warn the poor thing a little bit; and she was regularly mean when Rosamond asked for a bowl to put the purple stuff in, and she said, in such a provoking way, 'I did not agree to lend you a bowl, but I will, my dear.' Ugh! I always want to shake that hateful woman, though she *was* a moral mamma."

"Never mind her now, but tell me all about my loaf," said Dr. Alec, much amused at Rose's burst of indignation.

"There's nothing to tell, Uncle, except that I did my best, gave my mind to it, and sat watching over it all the while it was in the oven till I was quite baked myself. Everything went right this time, and it came out a nice, round, crusty loaf, as you see. Now taste it, and tell me if it is good as well as handsome."

"Must I cut it? Can't I put it under a glass cover and keep it in the parlor as they do wax flowers and fine works of that sort?"

"What an idea, Uncle! It would mold and be spoiled. Besides, people would laugh at us and make fun of my old-fashioned accomplishment. You promised to eat it, and you must; not all at once, but as soon as you can, so I can make you some more."

Dr. Alec solemnly cut off his favorite crusty slice, and solemnly ate it; then wiped his lips, and brushing back Rose's hair, solemnly kissed her on the forehead, saying heartily, "My dear, it is perfect bread, and you are an honor to your teacher. When we have our model school, I shall offer a prize for the best bread, and *you* will get it."

"I've got it already, and I'm quite satisfied," said Rose, slipping into her seat and trying to hide her right hand, which had a burn on it.

But Dr. Alec saw it, guessed how it came there, and after tea insisted on easing the pain which she would hardly confess.

"Aunt Clara says I am spoiling my hands, but I don't care, for I've had *such* good times with Aunt Plenty and I think she has enjoyed it as much as I have. Only one thing troubles me, Uncle, and I want to ask you about it," said Rose as they paced up and down the hall in the twilight, the bandaged hand very carefully laid on Dr. Alec's arm.

"More little confidences? I like them immensely, so tell away, my dear."

"Well, you see, I feel as if Aunt Peace would like to do something for me, and I've found out what it can be. You know she can't go about like Aunty Plen, and we are so busy nowadays that she is rather lonely, I'm afraid. So I want to take lessons in sewing of her. She works so beautifully, and it is a useful thing, you know, and I ought to be a good needlewoman as well as housekeeper, oughtn't I?"

"Bless your kind little heart. That is what I was thinking of the other day when Aunt Peace said she saw you very seldom now, you were so busy. I wanted to speak of it, but fancied you had as much on your hands as you could manage. It would delight the dear woman to teach you all her delicate handicraft, especially button-holes, for I believe that is where young ladies fail; at least I've heard them say so. So, do you devote your mind to buttonholes; make 'em all over my clothes if you want something to practice on. I'll wear any quantity."

Rose laughed at this reckless offer, but promised to attend to that important branch, though she confessed that darning was her weak point. Whereupon Uncle Alec engaged to supply her with socks in all stages of dilapidation, and to have a new set at once, so that she could run the heels for him as a pleasant beginning.

Then they went up to make their request in due form, to the great delight of gentle Aunt Peace, who got quite excited with the fun that went on while they wound yarn, looked up darning needles, and fitted out a nice little mending basket for her pupil.

Very busy and very happy were Rose's days now, for in the morning she went about the house with Aunt Plenty, attending to linen closets and storerooms, pickling and preserving, exploring garret and cellar to see that all was right, and learning, in the good old-fashioned manner, to look well after the ways of the household.

In the afternoon, after her walk or drive, she sat with Aunt Peace plying her needle, while Aunt Plenty, whose eyes were failing, knit and chatted briskly, telling many a pleasant story of old times, till the three were moved to laugh and cry together, for the busy needles were embroidering all sorts of bright patterns on the lives of the workers, though they seemed to be only stitching cotton and darning hose.

It was a pretty sight to see the rosy-faced little maid sitting between the two old ladies, listening dutifully to their instructions, and cheering the lessons with her lively chatter and blithe laugh. If the kitchen had proved attractive to Dr. Alec when Rose was there at work, the sewing room was quite irresistible, and he made himself so agreeable that no one had the heart to drive him away, especially when he read aloud or spun yarns.

"There! I've made you a new set of warm nightgowns with four buttonholes in each. See if they are not neatly done," said Rose one day, some weeks after the new lessons began.

"Even to a thread, and nice little bars across the end so I can't tear them when I twitch the buttons out. Most superior work, ma'am, and I'm deeply grateful; so much so, that I'll sew on these buttons myself and save those tired fingers from another prick."

"You sew them on?" cried Rose with her eyes wide open in amazement.

"Wait a bit till I get my sewing tackle, and then you shall see what *I* can do."

"Can he—really?" asked Rose of Aunt Peace as Uncle Alec marched off with a comical air of importance.

"Oh, yes, I taught him years ago, before he went to sea; and I suppose he has had to do things for himself, more or less, ever since; so he has kept his hand in."

He evidently had, for he was soon back with a funny little work-bag, out of which he produced a thimble without a top; and having threaded his needle, he proceeded to sew on the buttons so handily that Rose was much impressed and amused.

"I wonder if there is anything in the world that *you* cannot do," she said in a tone of respectful admiration.

"There are one or two things that I am not up to yet," he answered, with a laugh in the corner of his eye, as he waxed his thread with a flourish.

"I should like to know what?"

"Bread and buttonholes, ma'am."

CHAPTER 17

GOOD BARGAINS

IT WAS A RAINY SUNDAY afternoon, and four boys were trying to spend it quietly in the "liberry," as Jamie called the room devoted to books and boys, at Aunt Jessie's. Will and Geordie were sprawling on the sofa, deep in the adventures of the scapegraces and ragamuffins whose histories are now the fashion. Archie lounged in the easy chair surrounded by newspapers; Charlie stood upon the rug, in an Englishman's favorite attitude, and, I regret to say, both were smoking cigars.

"It is my opinion that this day will *never* come to an end," said Prince with a yawn that nearly rent him asunder.

"Read and improve your mind, my son," answered Archie, peering solemnly over the paper behind which he had been dozing.

"Don't you preach, parson; but put on your boots and come out for a tramp, instead of mulling over the fire like a granny."

"No, thank you. Tramps in an easterly storm don't strike me as amusing." There Archie stopped and held up his hand, for a pleasant voice was heard saying outside, "Are the boys in the library, Auntie?"

151

"Yes, dear, and longing for sunshine; so run in and make it for them," answered Mrs. Jessie.

"It's Rose." And Archie threw his cigar into the fire.

"What's that for?" asked Charlie.

"Gentlemen don't smoke before ladies."

"True; but I'm not going to waste *my* weed." And Prince poked his into the empty inkstand that served them for an ash tray.

A gentle tap at the door was answered by a chorus of "Come in," and Rose appeared, looking blooming and breezy with the chilly air.

"If I disturb you, say so, and I'll go away," she began, pausing on the threshold with modest hesitation, for something in the elder boys' faces excited her curiosity.

"You never disturb us, cousin," said the smokers, while the readers tore themselves from the heroes of the barroom and gutter long enough to nod affably to their guest.

As Rose bent to warm her hands, one end of Archie's cigar stuck out of the ashes, smoking furiously and smelling strongly.

"Oh, you bad boys, how could you do it, today of all days?" she said reproachfully.

"Where's the harm?" asked Archie.

"You know as well as I do; your mother doesn't like it, and it's a bad habit, for it wastes money and does you no good."

"Fiddlesticks! Every man smokes, even Uncle Alec, whom you think so perfect," began Charlie in his teasing way.

"No, he doesn't! He has given it up, and I know why," cried Rose eagerly.

"Now I think of it, I haven't seen the old meerschaum since he came home. Did he stop it on our account?" asked Archie.

"Yes," and Rose told the little scene on the seashore in the camping-out time.

Archie seemed much impressed and said manfully, "He won't have done that in vain so far as I'm concerned. I don't care a pin about smoking, so can give it up as easy as not, and I promise you I will. I only do it now and then for fun."

"You too?" And Rose looked up at the bonny Prince, who never looked less bonny than at that moment, for he had resumed his cigar, just to torment her.

Now Charlie cared as little as Archie about smoking, but it would not do to yield too soon; so he shook his head, gave a great puff, and said loftily, "You women are always asking us to give up harmless little things, just because *you* don't approve of them. How would you like it if we did the same by you, miss?"

"If I did harmful or silly things, I'd thank you for telling me of them, and I'd try to mend my ways," answered Rose heartily.

"Well, now, we'll see if you mean what you say. I'll give up smoking to please you, if you will give up something to please me," said Prince, seeing a good chance to lord it over the weaker vessel at small cost to himself.

"I'll agree if it is as foolish as cigars."

"Oh, it's ever so much sillier."

"Then I promise; what is it?" And Rose quite trembled with anxiety to know which of her pet habits or possessions she must lose.

"Give up your earrings," and Charlie laughed wickedly, sure that she would never hold to that bargain.

Rose uttered a cry and clapped both hands to her ears where the gold rings hung.

"Oh, Charlie, wouldn't anything else do as well? I've been through so much teasing and trouble, I do want to enjoy my pretty earrings, for I can wear them now."

"Wear as many as you like, and I'll smoke in peace," returned this bad boy.

"Will *nothing* else satisfy you?" imploringly.

"Nothing," sternly.

Rose stood silent for a minute, thinking of something Aunt Jessie once said, "You have more influence over the boys than you know; use it for their good, and I shall thank you all my life." Here was a chance to do some good by sacrificing a little vanity of her own. She felt it was right to do it, yet found it very hard, and asked wistfully, "Do you mean *never* wear them, Charlie?"

"*Never*, unless you want me to smoke."

"I never do."

"Then clinch the bargain."

He had no idea she would do it, and was much surprised when she took the dear rings from her ears, with a quick gesture, and held them out to him, saying, in a tone that made the color come up to his brown cheek, it was so full of sweet goodwill, "I care more for my cousins than for my earrings, so I promise, and I'll keep my word."

"For shame, Prince! Let her wear her little danglers if she likes, and don't bargain about doing what you know is right," cried Archie, coming out of his grove of newspapers with an indignant bounce.

But Rose was bent on showing her aunt that she *could* use her influence for the boys' good, and said steadily, "It is fair, and I want it to be so, then you will believe I'm in earnest. Here, each of you wear one of these on your watch guard to remind you. *I* shall not forget, because very soon I cannot wear earrings if I want to."

As she spoke, Rose offered a little ring to each cousin, and the boys, seeing how sincere she was, obeyed her. When the pledges were safe, Rose stretched a hand to each, and the lads gave hers a hearty grip, half pleased and half ashamed of their part in the compact.

Just at that moment Dr. Alec and Mrs. Jessie came in.

"What's this? Dancing Ladies Triumph on Sunday?" exclaimed Uncle Alec, surveying the trio with surprise.

"No, sir, it is the Anti-Tobacco League. Will you join?" said Charlie, while Rose slipped away to her aunt, and Archie buried both cigars behind the back log.

When the mystery was explained, the elders were well pleased and Rose received a vote of thanks, which made her feel as if she had done a service to her country, as she had, for every boy who grows up free from bad habits bids fair to make a good citizen.

"I wish Rose would drive a bargain with Will and Geordie also, for I think these books are as bad for the small boys as cigars for the large ones," said Mrs. Jessie, sitting down on the sofa between the readers, who politely curled up their legs to make room for her.

"I thought they were all the fashion," answered Dr. Alec, settling in the big chair with Rose.

"So is smoking, but it is harmful. The writers of these popular stories intend to do good, I have no doubt, but it seems to me they fail because their motto is 'Be smart, and you will be rich,' instead of 'Be honest, and you will be happy.' I do not judge hastily, Alec, for I have read a dozen, at least, of these stories, and, with much that is attractive to boys, I find a great deal to condemn in them, and other parents say the same when I ask them."

"Now, Mum, that's too bad! I like 'em tiptop. This one is a regular screamer," cried Will.

"They're bully books, and I'd like to know where's the harm," added Geordie.

"You have just shown us one of the chief evils, and that is slang," answered their mother quickly.

"Must have it, ma'am. If these chaps talked all right, there'd be no fun in 'em," protested Will.

"A bootblack *mustn't* use good grammar, and a newsboy *must* swear a little, or he wouldn't be natural," explained Geordie, both boys ready to fight gallantly for their favorites.

"But my sons are neither bootblacks nor newsboys, and I object to hearing them use such words as *screamer, bully,* and *buster.* In fact, I fail to see the advantage of writing books about such people unless it is done in a very different way. I cannot think they will help to refine the ragamuffins, if they read them, and I'm sure they can do no good to the better class of boys, who through these books are introduced to police courts, counterfeiters' dens, gambling houses, drinking saloons, and all sorts of low life."

"Some of them are about first-rate boys, Mother; and they go to sea and study, and sail round the world, having great larks all the way."

"I have read about them, Geordie, and though they *are* better than the others, I am not satisfied with these *optical* delusions, as I call them. Now, I put it to you, boys, is it natural for lads from fifteen to eighteen to command ships, defeat pirates, outwit smugglers, and so cover themselves with glory that Admiral Farragut invites them to dinner, saying: 'Noble boy, you are an honor to your country!' Or, if the hero is in the army, he has hairbreadth escapes and adventures enough in one small volume to turn his hair white, and in the end he goes to Washington at the express desire of the President or Commander-in-Chief to be promoted to no end of stars and bars. Even if the hero is merely an honest boy trying to get his living, he is not permitted to do so in a natural way, by hard work and years of patient effort, but is suddenly adopted by a millionaire whose pocketbook he has returned; or a rich uncle appears from sea, just in the nick of time; or the remarkable boy earns a few dollars, speculates in peanuts or neckties, and grows rich so rapidly that Sinbad in the diamond valley is a pauper compared to him. Isn't it so, boys?"

"Well, the fellows in these books *are* mighty lucky, and very smart, I must say," answered Will, surveying an illustration on the open page before him, where a small but virtuous youth is upsetting a tipsy giant in a barroom, and under it the elegant inscription: "Dick Dauntless punches the head of Sam Soaker."

"It gives boys such wrong ideas of life and business; shows them so much evil and vulgarity that they need not know about, and makes the one success worth having a fortune, a lord's daughter, or some worldly honor, often not worth the time it takes to win. It does seem to me that someone might write stories that should be lively, natural, and helpful—tales in which the English should be good, the morals pure, and the characters such as we can love in spite of the faults that all may have. I can't bear to see such crowds of eager little fellows at the libraries reading such trash; weak, when it is not wicked, and totally unfit to feed the hungry minds that feast on it for want of something better. There! My lecture is done; now I should like to hear what you gentlemen have to say." And Aunt Jessie subsided with a pretty flush on the face that was full of motherly anxiety for her boys.

"*Tom Brown* just suits Mother, and me too, so I wish Mr. Hughes would write another story as good," said Archie.

"You don't find things of this sort in *Tom Brown;* yet these books are all in the Sunday-school libraries"—and Mrs. Jessie read the following paragraph from the book she had taken from Will's hand: " 'In this place we saw a tooth of John the Baptist. Ben said he could see locust and wild honey sticking to it. I couldn't. Perhaps John used a piece of the true cross for a toothpick.' "

"A larky sort of a boy says that, Mum, and we skip the parts where they describe what they saw in the different countries," cried Will.

"And those descriptions, taken mostly from guidebooks, I fancy, are the only parts of any real worth. The scrapes of the bad boys make up the rest of the story, and it is for those you read these books, I think," answered his mother, stroking back the hair off the honest little face that looked rather abashed at this true statement of the case.

"Anyway, Mother, the ship part is useful, for we learn how to sail her, and by and by that will all come handy when we go to sea," put in Geordie.

"Indeed; then you can explain this maneuver to me, of course—" and Mrs. Jessie read from another page the following nautical paragraph: "The wind is south-south-west, and we can have her up four points closer to the wind, and still be six points off the wind. As she luffs up we shall man the fore and main sheets, slack on the weather, and haul on the lee braces."

"I guess I could, if I wasn't afraid of Uncle. He knows so much more than I do, he'd laugh," began Geordie, evidently puzzled by the question.

"Ho, you know you can't, so why make believe? We don't understand half of the sea lingo, Mum, and I daresay it's all wrong," cried Will, suddenly going over to the enemy, to Geordie's great disgust.

"I do wish the boys wouldn't talk to me as if I was a ship," said Rose, bringing forward a private grievance. "Coming home from church this morning, the wind blew me about, and Will called out, right in the street, 'Brail up the foresail, and take in the flying jib, that will ease her.' "

The boys shouted at the plaintive tone in which Rose repeated the words that offended her, and Will vainly endeavored to explain that he only meant to tell her to wrap her cloak closer and tie a veil over the tempest-tossed feathers in her hat.

"To tell the truth, if the boys *must* have slang, I can bear the 'sea lingo,' as Will calls it, better than the other. It afflicts me less to hear my sons talk about 'brailing up the foresail' than doing as they 'darn please,' and 'cut your cable' is decidedly preferable to 'let her rip.' I once made a rule that I would have no slang in the house. I give it up now, for I cannot keep it; but I will *not* have rubbishy books; so, Archie, please send these two after your cigars."

Mrs. Jessie held both the small boys fast with an arm round each neck, and when she took this base advantage of them they could only squirm with dismay. "Yes, right behind the back log," she continued energetically. "There, my hearties—(you like sea slang, so I'll give you a bit)—now, I want you to promise not to read any more stuff for a month, and I'll agree to supply you with wholesome fare."

"O Mother! Not a single one?" cried Will.

"Couldn't we just finish those?" pleaded Geordie.

"The boys threw away half-smoked cigars; and your books must go after them. Surely you would not be outdone by the 'old fellows,' as you call them, or be less obedient to little Mum than they were to Rose."

"Course not! Come on, Geordie." And Will took the vow like a hero. His brother sighed, and obeyed, but privately resolved to finish his story the minute the month was over.

"You have laid out a hard task for yourself, Jessie, in trying to provide good reading for boys who have been living on sensation stories. It will be like going from raspberry tarts to plain bread and butter; but you will probably save them from a bilious fever," said Dr. Alec, much amused at the proceedings.

"I remember hearing Grandpa say that a love for good books was one of the best safeguards a man could have," began Archie, staring thoughtfully at the fine library before him.

"Yes, but there's no time to read nowadays; a fellow has to keep scratching round to make money or he's nobody," cut in Charlie, trying to look worldly-wise.

"This love of money is the curse of America, and for the sake of it men will sell honor and honesty, till we don't know whom to trust, and it is only a genius like Agassiz who dares to say, 'I cannot waste my time in getting rich,' " said Mrs. Jessie sadly.

"Do you want us to be poor, Mother?" asked Archie, wondering.

"No, dear, and you never need be while you can use your hands; but I *am* afraid of this thirst for wealth, and the temptations it brings. Oh, my boys! I tremble for the time when I must let you go, because I think it would break my heart to have you fail as so many fail. It would be far easier to see you dead if it could be said of you as of Sumner, 'No man dared offer him a bribe.' "

Mrs. Jessie was so earnest in her motherly anxiety that her voice faltered over the last words, and she hugged the yellow heads closer in her arms, as if she feared to let them leave that safe harbor for the great sea where so many little boats go down. The younger lads nestled closer to her, and Archie said, in his quiet, resolute way, "I cannot promise to be an Agassiz or a Sumner, Mother; but I do promise to be an honest man, please God."

"Then I'm satisfied!" And holding fast the hand he gave her, she sealed his promise with a kiss that had all a mother's hope and faith in it.

"I don't see how they ever *can* be bad, she is so fond and proud of them," whispered Rose, quite touched by the little scene.

"You must help her make them what they should be. You have begun already, and when I see those rings where they are, my girl is prettier in my sight than if the biggest diamonds that ever twinkled shone in her ears," answered Dr. Alec, looking at her with approving eyes.

"I'm so glad you think I can do anything, for I perfectly *ache* to be useful; everyone is *so* good to me, especially Aunt Jessie."

"I think you are in a fair way to pay your debts, Rosy, for when girls give up their little vanities, and boys their small vices, and try to strengthen each other in well-doing, matters are going as they ought. Work away, my dear, and help their mother keep these sons fit friends for an innocent creature like yourself; they will be the manlier men for it, I can assure you."

CHAPTER 18

FASHION AND PHYSIOLOGY

"PLEASE, SIR, I guess you'd better step up right away, or it will be too late, for I heard Miss Rose say she knew you wouldn't like it, and she'd never dare to let you see her."

Phebe said this as she popped her head into the study, where Dr. Alec sat reading a new book.

"They are at it, are they?" he said, looking up quickly and giving himself a shake, as if ready for a battle of some sort.

"Yes, sir, as hard as they can talk, and Miss Rose don't seem to know what to do, for the things are ever so stylish, and she looks elegant in 'em; though I like her best in the old ones," answered Phebe.

"You are a girl of sense. I'll settle matters for Rosy, and you'll lend a hand. Is everything ready in her room, and are you sure you understand how they go?"

"Oh, yes, sir; but they are so funny! I know Miss Rose will think it's a joke." And Phebe laughed as if something tickled her immensely.

"Never mind what she thinks so long as she obeys. Tell her to do it for my sake, and she will find it the best joke she ever saw. I expect

161

to have a tough time of it, but we'll win yet," said the doctor as he marched upstairs with the book in his hand and an odd smile on his face.

There was such a clatter of tongues in the sewing room that no one heard his tap at the door, so he pushed it open and took an observation. Aunt Plenty, Aunt Clara, and Aunt Jessie were all absorbed in gazing at Rose, who slowly revolved between them and the great mirror, in a full winter costume of the latest fashion.

"Bless my heart! Worse even than I expected," thought the doctor with an inward groan, for to his benighted eyes, the girl looked like a trussed fowl, and the fine new dress had neither grace, beauty, nor fitness to recommend it.

The suit was of two peculiar shades of blue, so arranged that patches of light and dark distracted the eye. The upper skirt was tied so tightly back that it was impossible to take a long step, and the under one was so loaded with plaited frills that it "wobbled"—no other word will express it—ungracefully, both fore and aft. A bunch of folds was gathered up just below the waist behind, and a great bow rode atop. A small jacket of the same material was adorned with a high ruff at the back, and laid well open over the breast, to display some lace and a locket. Heavy fringes, bows, puffs, ruffles, and revers finished off the dress, making one's head ache to think of the amount of work wasted, for not a single graceful line struck the eye, and the beauty of the material was quite lost in the profusion of ornament.

A high velvet hat, audaciously turned up in front, with a bunch of pink roses and a sweeping plume, was cocked over one ear, and with her curls braided into a club at the back of her neck, Rose's head looked more like that of a dashing young cavalier than a modest little girl's. High-heeled boots tilted her well forward, a tiny muff pinioned her arms, and a spotted veil tied so closely over her face that her eyelashes were rumpled by it, gave the last touch of absurdity to her appearance.

"Now she looks like other girls, and as *I* like to see her," Mrs. Clara was saying with an air of great satisfaction.

"She does look like a fashionable young lady, but somehow I miss my little Rose, for children dressed like children in my day," answered Aunt Plenty, peering through her glasses with a troubled look, for she could not imagine the creature before her ever sitting in her lap, running to wait upon her, or making the house gay with a child's blithe presence.

"Things have changed since your day, Aunt, and it takes time to get used to new ways. But you, Jessie, surely like this costume better than the dowdy things Rose has been wearing all summer. Now, be honest, and own you do," said Mrs. Clara, bent on being praised for her work.

"Well, dear, to be *quite* honest, then, I think it is frightful," answered Mrs. Jessie with a candor that caused revolving Rose to stop in dismay.

"Hear, hear," cried a deep voice, and with a general start the ladies became aware that the enemy was among them.

Rose blushed up to her hat brim, and stood looking, as she felt, like a fool, while Mrs. Clara hastened to explain.

"Of course I don't expect *you* to like it, Alec, but I don't consider you a judge of what is proper and becoming for a young lady. Therefore I have taken the liberty of providing a pretty street suit for Rose. She need not wear it if you object, for I know we promised to let you do what you liked with the poor dear for a year."

"It is a street costume, is it?" asked the doctor mildly. "Do you know, I never should have guessed that it was meant for winter weather and brisk locomotion. Take a turn, Rosy, and let me see all its beauties and advantages."

Rose tried to walk off with her usual free tread, but the underskirt got in her way, the overskirt was so tight she could not take a long step, and her boots made it impossible to carry herself perfectly erect.

"I haven't got used to it yet," she said petulantly, kicking at her train as she turned to toddle back again.

"Suppose a mad dog or a runaway horse was after you, could you get out of the way without upsetting, Colonel?" asked the doctor with a twinkle in the eyes that were fixed on the rakish hat.

"Don't think I could, but I'll try." And Rose made a rush across the room. Her bootheels caught on a rug, several strings broke, her hat tipped over her eyes, and she plunged promiscuously into a chair, where she sat laughing so infectiously that all but Mrs. Clara joined in her mirth.

"I should say that a walking suit in which one could not walk, and a winter suit which exposes the throat, head, and feet to cold and damp, was rather a failure, Clara; especially as it has no beauty to reconcile one to its utter unfitness," said Dr. Alec as he helped Rose undo her veil, adding, in a low tone, "Nice thing for the eyes; you'll soon see spots when it is off as well as when it is on and, by and by, be a case for an oculist."

"No beauty!" cried Mrs. Clara warmly. "Now that is just a man's blindness. This is the best of silk and camel's hair, real ostrich feathers, and an expensive ermine muff. What *could* be in better taste, or more proper for a young girl?"

"I'll show you, if Rose will go to her room and oblige me by putting on what she finds there," answered the doctor with unexpected readiness.

"Alec, if it is a Bloomer, I shall protest. I've been expecting it, but I know I *cannot* bear to see that pretty child sacrificed to your wild ideas of health. Tell me it *isn't* a Bloomer!" and Mrs. Clara clasped her hands imploringly.

"It is not."

"Thank Heaven!" And she resigned herself with a sigh of relief, adding plaintively, "I did hope you'd accept my suit, for poor Rose has been afflicted with frightful clothes long enough to spoil the taste of any girl."

"You talk of *my* afflicting the child, and then make a helpless guy like that of her!" answered the doctor, pointing to the little fashion plate that was scuttling out of sight as fast as it could go.

He closed the door with a shrug, but before anyone could speak, his quick eye fell upon an object which caused him to frown and demand in an indignant tone, "After all I have said, were you really going to tempt my girl with those abominable things?"

"I thought we put them away when she wouldn't wear them," murmured Mrs. Clara, whisking a little pair of corsets out of sight with guilty haste. "I only brought them to try, for Rose is growing stout and will have no figure if it is not attended to soon," she added, with an air of calm conviction that roused the doctor still more, for this was one of his special abominations.

"Growing stout! Yes, thank Heaven, she is, and shall continue to do it, for Nature knows how to mold a woman better than any corset maker, and I won't have her interfered with. My dear Clara, *have* you lost your senses that you can for a moment dream of putting a growing girl into an instrument of torture like this?" And with a sudden gesture he plucked forth the offending corsets from under the sofa cushion and held them out with the expression one would wear on beholding the thumbscrews or the rack of ancient times.

"Don't be absurd, Alec. There is no torture about it, for tight lacing is out of fashion, and we have nice, sensible things nowadays. Everyone wears them; even babies have stiffened waists to support their weak little backs," began Mrs. Clara, rushing to the defense of the pet delusion of most women.

"I know it, and so the poor little souls have weak backs all their days, as their mothers had before them. It is vain to argue the matter, and I won't try, but I wish to state, once for all, that if I ever see a pair of corsets near Rose, I'll put them in the fire, and you may send the bill to me."

As he spoke, the corsets were on their way to destruction, but Mrs. Jessie caught his arm, exclaiming merrily, "Don't burn them, for mercy sake, Alec; they are full of whalebones and will make a dreadful odor. Give them to me. I'll see that they do no harm."

"Whalebones indeed! A regular fence of them, and metal gateposts in front. As if our own bones were not enough, if we'd give them a chance to do their duty," growled the doctor, yielding up the bone of contention with a last shake of contempt. Then his face cleared suddenly, and he held up his finger, saying, with a smile,

"Hear those girls laugh; cramped lungs could not make hearty music like that."

Peals of laughter issued from Rose's room, and smiles involuntarily touched the lips of those who listened to the happy sound.

"Some new prank of yours, Alec?" asked Aunt Plenty indulgently, for she had come to believe in most of her nephew's odd notions because they seemed to work so well.

"Yes, ma'am, my last, and I hope you will like it. I discovered what Clara was at, and got my rival suit ready for today. I'm not going to 'afflict' Rose, but let her choose, and if I'm not entirely mistaken, she will like my rig best. While we wait I'll explain, and then you will appreciate the general effect better. I got hold of this little book and was struck with its good sense and good taste, for it suggests a way to clothe women both healthfully and handsomely, and that is a great point. It begins at the foundations, as you will see if you will look at these pictures, and I should think women would rejoice at this lightening of their burdens."

As he spoke, the doctor laid the book before Aunt Plenty, who obediently brought her spectacles to bear upon the illustrations, and after a long look exclaimed with a scandalized face, "Mercy on us, these things are like the nightdrawers Jamie wears! You don't mean to say you want Rose to come out in this costume? It's not proper, and I won't consent to it!"

"I do mean it, and I'm sure my sensible aunt *will* consent when she understands that these—well, I'll call them by an Indian name, and say *pajamas*—are for underwear, and Rose can have as pretty frocks as she likes outside. These two suits of flannel, each in one piece from head to foot, with a skirt or so hung on this easily fitting waist, will keep the child warm without burdening her with belts, and gathers, and buckles, and bunches round the waist, and leave free the muscles that need plenty of room to work in. She shall never have the backache if *I* can help it, nor the long list of ills you dear women think you cannot escape."

"*I* don't consider it modest, and I'm sure Rose will be shocked at it," began Mrs. Clara, but stopped suddenly as Rose appeared in the doorway, not looking shocked a bit.

"Come on, my hygienic model, and let us see you," said her uncle with an approving glance, as she walked in looking so mischievously merry that it was evident she enjoyed the joke.

"Well, I don't see anything remarkable. That is a neat, plain suit; the materials are good, and it's not unbecoming if you want her to look like a little schoolgirl; but it has not a particle of style, and no one would ever give it a second glance," said Mrs. Clara, feeling that her last remark condemned the whole thing.

"Exactly what I want," answered the provoking doctor, rubbing his hands with a satisfied air. "Rosy looks now like what she is, a modest little girl who does not want to be stared at. I think she would get a glance of approval, though, from people who liked sense and simplicity, rather than fuss and feathers. Revolve, my Hebe, and let me refresh my eyes by the sight of you."

There was very little to see, however, only a pretty Gabrielle dress of a soft, warm shade of brown, coming to the tops of a trim pair of boots with low heels. A sealskin sack, cap, and mittens, with a glimpse of scarlet at the throat, and the pretty curls tied up with a bright velvet of the same color, completed the external adornment, making her look like a robin redbreast—wintry, yet warm.

"How do you like it, Rosy?" asked the doctor, feeling that *her* opinion was more important to the success of his new idea than that of all the aunts on the hill.

"I feel very odd and light, but I'm warm as a toast, and nothing seems to be in my way," answered Rose, with a skip which displayed shapely gaiters on legs that now might be as free and active as a boy's under the modest skirts of the girl.

"You can run away from the mad dogs and walk off at a smart pace without tumbling on your nose now, I fancy?"

"Yes, Uncle! Suppose the dog coming, I just hop over a wall so— and when I walk of a cold day, I go like this—"

Entering fully into the spirit of the thing, Rose swung herself over the high back of the sofa as easily as one of her cousins, and then went down the long hall as if her stout boots were related to the famous seven-leaguers.

"There! You see how it will be; dress her in that boyish way and she will act like a boy. I do hate all these inventions of strong-minded women!" exclaimed Mrs. Clara as Rose came back at a run.

"Ah, but you see some of these sensible inventions come from the brain of a fashionable *modiste,* who will make you lovely, or what you value more—'stylish' outside and comfortable within. Mrs. Van Tassel has been to Madame Stone and is wearing a full suit of this sort. Van himself told me, when I asked how she was, that she had given up lying on the sofa and was going about in a most astonishing way, considering her feeble health."

"You don't say so! Let me see that book a moment." And Aunt Clara examined the new patterns with a more respectful air, for if the elegant Mrs. Van Tassel wore these "dreadful things" it would never do to be left behind, in spite of her prejudices.

Dr. Alec looked at Mrs. Jessie, and both smiled, for "little Mum" had been in the secret, and enjoyed it mightily.

"I thought that would settle it," he said with a nod.

"I didn't wait for Mrs. Van to lead the way, and for once in my life I have adopted a new fashion before Clara. My freedom suit is ordered, and you *may* see me playing tag with Rose and the boys before long," answered Mrs. Jessie, nodding back at him.

Meantime Aunt Plenty was examining Rose's costume, for the hat and sack were off, and the girl was eagerly explaining the new undergarments.

"See, Auntie, all nice scarlet flannel, and a gay little petticoat, and long stockings, oh, so warm! Phebe and I nearly died laughing when I put this rig on, but I like it ever so much. The dress is so comfortable, and doesn't need any belt or sash, and I can sit without rumpling any trimming, that's *such* a comfort! I like to be tidy, and so, when I wear fussed-up things, I'm thinking of my clothes all the time, and that's tiresome. Do say you like it. I resolved *I* would, just to please Uncle, for he does know more about health than anyone else, I'm sure, and I'd wear a bag if he asked me to do it."

"I don't ask that, Rose, but I wish you'd weigh and compare the two suits, and then choose which seems best. I leave it to your own common sense," answered Dr. Alec, feeling pretty sure he had won.

"Why, I take this one, of course, Uncle. The other is fashionable, and—yes—I must say I think it's pretty—but it's very heavy, and I should have to go round like a walking doll if I wore it. I'm much obliged to Auntie, but I'll keep this, please."

Rose spoke gently but decidedly, though there was a look of regret when her eye fell on the other suit which Phebe had brought in; and it was very natural to like to look as other girls did. Aunt Clara sighed; Uncle Alec smiled and said heartily, "Thank you, dear; now read this book and you will understand why I ask it of you. Then, if you like, I'll give you a new lesson; you asked for one yesterday, and this is more necessary than French or housekeeping."

"Oh, what?" And Rose caught up the book which Mrs. Clara had thrown down with a disgusted look.

Though Dr. Alec was forty, the boyish love of teasing was not yet dead in him, and being much elated at his victory, he could not resist the temptation of shocking Mrs. Clara by suggesting dreadful possibilities, so he answered, half in earnest, half in jest: "Physiology, Rose. Wouldn't you like to be a little medical student with Uncle Doctor for teacher, and be ready to take up his practice when he has to stop? If you agree, I'll hunt up my old skeleton tomorrow."

That was *too* much for Aunt Clara, and she hastily departed with her mind in a sad state of perturbation about Mrs. Van Tassel's new costume and Rose's new study.

CHAPTER 19

BROTHER BONES

Rose accepted her uncle's offer, as Aunt Myra discovered two or three days later. Coming in for an early call, and hearing voices in the study, she opened the door, gave a cry, and shut it quickly, looking a good deal startled. The doctor appeared in a moment and begged to know what the matter was.

"How *can* you ask when that long box looks so like a coffin I thought it was one, and that dreadful thing stared me in the face as I opened the door," answered Mrs. Myra, pointing to the skeleton that hung from the chandelier cheerfully grinning at all beholders.

"This is a medical college where women are freely admitted, so walk in, madam, and join the class if you'll do me the honor," said the doctor, waving her forward with his politest bow.

"Do, Auntie; it's perfectly splendid," cried Rose's voice, and Rose's blooming face was seen behind the ribs of the skeleton, smiling and nodding in the gayest possible manner.

"What *are* you doing, child?" demanded Aunt Myra, dropping into a chair and staring about her.

"Oh, I'm learning bones today, and I like it so much. There are twelve ribs, you know, and the two lower ones are called floating

171

ribs, because they are not fastened to the breastbone. That's why they go in so easily if you lace tight and squeeze the lungs and heart in the—let me see, what was that big word—oh, I know—thoracic cavity," and Rose beamed with pride as she aired her little bit of knowledge.

"Do you think that is a good sort of thing for her to be poking over? She is a nervous child, and I'm afraid it will be bad for her," said Aunt Myra, watching Rose as she counted vertebrae and waggled a hip joint in its socket with an inquiring expression.

"An excellent study, for she enjoys it, and I mean to teach her how to manage her nerves so that they won't be a curse to her, as many a woman's become through ignorance or want of thought. To make a mystery or a terror of these things is a mistake, and I mean Rose shall understand and respect her body so well that she won't dare to trifle with it as most women do."

"And she really likes it?"

"Very much, Auntie! It's all so wonderful, and so nicely planned, you can hardly believe what you see. Just think, there are six hundred million air cells in one pair of lungs, and two thousand pores to a square inch of surface; so you see what quantities of air we *must* have, and what care we should take of our skin so all the little doors will open and shut right. And brains, Auntie, you've no idea how curious they are; I haven't got to them yet, but I long to, and Uncle is going to show me a manikin that you can take to pieces. Just think how nice it will be to see all the organs in their places; I only wish they could be made to work as ours do."

It was funny to see Aunt Myra's face as Rose stood before her talking rapidly with one hand laid in the friendliest manner on the skeleton's shoulder. Every word both the doctor and Rose uttered hit the good lady in her weakest spot, and as she looked and listened a long array of bottles and pillboxes rose up before her, reproaching her with the "ignorance and want of thought" that made her what she was, a nervous, dyspeptic, unhappy old woman.

"Well, I don't know but you may be right, Alec, only I wouldn't carry it too far. Women don't need much of this sort of knowledge and are not fit for it. I couldn't bear to touch that ugly thing, and it gives me the creeps to hear about 'organs,' " said Aunt Myra with a sigh and her hand on her side.

"Wouldn't it be a comfort to know that your liver was on the right side, Auntie, and not on the left?" asked Rose with a naughty laugh in her eyes, for she had lately learned that Aunt Myra's liver complaint was not in the proper place.

"It's a dying world, child, and it don't much matter where the pain is, for sooner or later we all drop off and are seen no more" was Aunt Myra's cheerful reply.

"Well, I intend to know what kills me if I can, and meantime I'm going to enjoy myself in spite of a dying world. I wish you'd do so too, and come and study with Uncle; it would do you good, I'm sure." And Rose went back to counting vertebrae with such a happy face that Aunt Myra had not the heart to say a word to dampen her ardor.

"Perhaps it's as well to let her do what she likes the little while she is with us. But pray be careful of her, Alec, and not allow her to overwork," she whispered as she went out.

"That's exactly what I'm trying to do, ma'am, and rather a hard job I find it," he added as he shut the door, for the dear aunts were dreadfully in his way sometimes.

Half an hour later came another interruption in the shape of Mac, who announced his arrival by the brief but elegant remark, "Hullo! What new game is this?"

Rose explained, and Mac gave a long whistle of surprise, and then took a promenade round the skeleton, observing gravely, "Brother Bones looks very jolly, but I can't say much for his beauty."

"You mustn't make fun of him, for he's a good old fellow, and you'd be just as ugly if your flesh was off," said Rose, defending her new friend with warmth.

"I daresay, so I'll keep my flesh on, thank you. You are so busy you can't read to a fellow, I suppose?" asked Mac, whose eyes were better but still too weak for books.

"Don't you want to come and join my class? Uncle explains it all to us, and you can take a look at the plates as they come along. We'll give up bones today and have eyes instead; that will be more interesting to *you*," added Rose, seeing no ardent thirst for physiological information in his face.

"Rose, we must not fly about from one thing to another in this way," began Dr. Alec; but she whispered quickly, with a nod toward Mac, whose goggles were turned wistfully in the direction of the forbidden books, "He's blue today, and we must amuse him; give a little lecture on eyes, and it will do him good. No matter about me, Uncle."

"Very well; the class will please be seated." And the Doctor gave a sounding rap on the table.

"Come, sit by me, dear, then we can both see the pictures; and if your head gets tired you can lie down," said Rose, generously opening her little college to a brother, and kindly providing for the weaknesses that all humanity is subject to.

Side by side they sat and listened to a very simple explanation of the mechanism of the eye, finding it as wonderful as a fairy tale, for fine plates illustrated it and a very willing teacher did his best to make the lesson pleasant.

"Jove! If I'd known what mischief I was doing to that mighty delicate machine of mine, you wouldn't have caught me reading by firelight, or studying with a glare of sunshine on my book," said Mac, peering solemnly at a magnified eyeball; then, pushing it away, he added indignantly: "Why isn't a fellow taught all about his works, and how to manage 'em, and not left to go blundering into all sorts of worries? Telling him after he's down isn't much use, for then he's found it out himself and won't thank you."

"Ah, Mac, that's just what I keep lecturing about, and people *won't* listen. You lads need that sort of knowledge so much, and fathers and mothers ought to be able to give it to you. Few of them *are* able and so we all go blundering, as you say. Less Greek and Latin and more knowledge of the laws of health for *my* boys, if I had them. Mathematics are all very well, but morals are better, and I wish, *how* I wish, I could help teachers and parents to feel it as they ought."

"Some do; Aunt Jessie and her boys have capital talks, and I wish we could; but Mother's so busy with her housekeeping, and Father with his business, there never seems to be any time for that sort of thing; even if there was, it don't seem as if it would be easy to talk to them, because we've never got into the way of it, you know."

Poor Mac was right there and expressed a want that many a boy and girl feels. Fathers and mothers *are* too absorbed in business and housekeeping to study their children and cherish that sweet and natural confidence which is a child's surest safeguard and a parent's subtlest power. So the young hearts hide trouble or temptation till the harm is done, and mutual regret comes too late. Happy the boys and girls who tell all things freely to father or mother, sure of pity, help, and pardon; and thrice happy the parents who, out of their own experience and by their own virtues, can teach and uplift the souls for which they are responsible.

This longing stirred in the hearts of Rose and Mac, and by a natural impulse both turned to Dr. Alec, for in this queer world of ours, fatherly and motherly hearts often beat warm and wise in the breasts of bachelor uncles and maiden aunts; and it is my private opinion that these worthy creatures are a beautiful provision of nature for the cherishing of other people's children. They certainly get great comfort out of it and receive much innocent affection that otherwise would be lost.

Dr. Alec was one of these, and his big heart had room for every one of the eight cousins, especially orphaned Rose and afflicted Mac; so, when the boy uttered that unconscious reproach to his parents, and Rose added with a sigh, "It must be beautiful to have a mother!"—the good Doctor yearned over them and, shutting his book with a decided slam, said in that cordial voice of his, "Now, look here, children, you just come and tell *me* all your worries, and with God's help I'll settle them for you. That is what I'm here for, I believe, and it will be a great happiness to me if you can trust me."

"We can, Uncle, and we will!" both answered with a heartiness that gratified him much.

"Good! Now school is dismissed, and I advise you to go and refresh your six hundred million air cells by a brisk run in the garden. Come again whenever you like, Mac, and we'll teach you all we can about your 'works,' as you call them, so you can keep them running smoothly."

"We'll come, sir, much obliged." And the class in physiology went out to walk.

Mac did come again, glad to find something he could study in spite of his weak eyes, and learned much that was of more value than anything his school had ever taught him.

Of course, the other lads made great fun of the whole thing and plagued Dr. Alec's students half out of their lives. But they kept on persistently, and one day something happened which made the other fellows behave themselves forever after.

It was a holiday, and Rose up in her room thought she heard the voices of her cousins, so she ran down to welcome them, but found no one there.

"Never mind, they will be here soon, and then we'll have a frolic," she said to herself, and thinking she had been mistaken she went into the study to wait. She was lounging over the table looking at a map when an odd noise caught her ear. A gentle tapping somewhere, and following the sound it seemed to come from the inside of the long case in which the skeleton lived when not professionally engaged. This case stood upright in a niche between two bookcases at the back of the room, a darkish corner, where Brother Bones, as the boys *would* call him, was out of the way.

As Rose stood looking in that direction, and wondering if a rat had got shut in, the door of the case swung slowly open, and with a great start she saw a bony arm lifted, and a bony finger beckon to her. For a minute she was frightened and ran to the study door with a fluttering heart, but just as she touched the handle, a queer, stifled sort of giggle made her stop short and turn red with anger. She paused an instant to collect herself and then went softly toward the bony beckoner. A nearer look revealed black threads tied to the arm and fingers, the ends of threads disappearing through holes bored in the back of the case. Peeping into the deep recess, she also caught sight of the tip of an elbow covered with a rough gray cloth which she knew very well.

Quick as a flash she understood the joke, her fear vanished, and with a wicked smile, she whipped out her scissors, cut the threads, and the bony arm dropped with a rattle. Before she could say, "Come out, Charlie, and let my skeleton alone," a sudden irruption of boys all in a high state of tickle proclaimed to the hidden rogue that his joke was a failure.

"I told him not to do it, because it might give you a start," explained Archie, emerging from the closet.

"I had a smelling bottle all ready if she fainted away," added Steve, popping up from behind the great chair.

"It's too bad of you not to squawk and run; we depended on it, it's such fun to howl after you," said Will and Geordie, rolling out from under the sofa in a promiscuous heap.

"You are getting altogether too strong-minded, Rose; most girls would have been in a jolly twitter to see this old fellow waggling his finger at them," complained Charlie, squeezing out from his tight quarters, dusty and disgusted.

"I'm used to your pranks now, so I'm always on the watch and prepared. But I won't have Brother Bones made fun of. I know Uncle wouldn't like it, so please don't," began Rose just as Dr. Alec came in, and seeing the state of the case at a glance, he said quietly, "Hear how I got that skeleton, and then I'm sure you will treat it with respect."

The boys settled down at once on any article of furniture that was nearest and listened dutifully.

"Years ago, when I was in the hospital, a poor fellow was brought there with a rare and very painful disease. There was no hope for him, but we did our best, and he was so grateful that when he died he left us his body that we might discover the mysteries of his complaint and so be able to help others afflicted in the same way. It did do good, and his brave patience made us remember him long after he was gone. He thought I had been kind to him, and said to a fellow student of mine: 'Tell the doctor I lave him me bones, for I've nothing else in the wide world, and I'll not be wanting 'em at all, at all, when the great pain has kilt me entirely.' So that is how they came to be mine, and why I've kept them carefully; for though only a poor, ignorant fellow, Mike Nolan did what he could to help others and prove his gratitude to those who tried to help him."

As Dr. Alec paused, Archie closed the door of the case as respectfully as if the mummy of an Egyptian king were inside; Will and Geordie looked solemnly at one another, evidently much impressed, and Charlie pensively remarked from the coal hod where he sat, "I've often heard of a skeleton in the house, but I think few people have one as useful and as interesting as ours."

CHAPTER 20

UNDER THE MISTLETOE

ROSE MADE PHEBE PROMISE that she would bring her stocking into the "Bower," as she called her pretty room, on Christmas morning, because that first delicious rummage loses half its charm if two little nightcaps at least do not meet over the treasures, and two happy voices *oh* and *ah* together.

So when Rose opened her eyes that day they fell upon faithful Phebe, rolled up in a shawl, sitting on the rug before a blazing fire, with her untouched stocking laid beside her.

"Merry Christmas!" cried the little mistress, smiling gayly.

"Merry Christmas!" answered the little maid, so heartily that it did one good to hear her.

"Bring the stockings right away, Phebe, and let's see what we've got," said Rose, sitting up among the pillows and looking as eager as a child.

A pair of long knobby hose were laid out upon the coverlet and their contents examined with delight, though each knew every blessed thing that had been put into the other's stocking.

Never mind what they were; it is evident that they were quite satisfactory, for as Rose leaned back, she said, with a luxurious sigh of satisfaction: "Now, I believe I've got everything in the world that I want," and Phebe answered, smiling over a lapful of treasures: "This is the most splendid Christmas I ever had since I was born." Then she added with an important air, "Do wish for something else, because I happen to know of two more presents outside the door this minute."

"Oh, me, what richness!" cried Rose, much excited. "I used to wish for a pair of glass slippers like Cinderella's, but as I can't have them, I really don't know what to ask for."

Phebe clapped her hands as she skipped off the bed and ran to the door, saying merrily: "One of them *is* for your feet anyway. I don't know what you'll say to the other, but *I* think it's elegant."

So did Rose when a shining pair of skates and a fine sled appeared.

"Uncle sent those; I know he did; and now I see them, I remember that I did want to skate and coast. Isn't it a beauty? See! They fit nicely." And sitting on the new sled, Rose tried to skate on her little bare foot while Phebe stood by admiring the pretty tableau.

"Now we must hurry and get dressed, for there is a deal to do today, and I want to get through in time to try my sled before dinner."

"Gracious me, and I ought to be dusting my parlors this blessed minute!" And mistress and maid separated with such happy faces that anyone would have known what day it was without being told.

"Birnam Wood has come to Dunsinane, Rosy," said Dr. Alec as he left the breakfast table to open the door for a procession of holly, hemlock, and cedar boughs that came marching up the steps.

Snowballs and "Merry Christmases!" flew about pretty briskly for several minutes; then all fell to work trimming up the old house, for the family always dined together there on that day.

"I rode miles and mileses, as Ben says, to get this fine bit, and I'm going to hang it there as the last touch to the rig-a-madooning," said Charlie as he fastened a dull green branch to the chandelier in the front parlor.

"It isn't very pretty," said Rose, who was trimming the chimney piece with glossy holly sprays.

"Never mind that, it's mistletoe, and anyone who stands under it will get kissed whether they like it or not. Now's your time, ladies," answered the saucy Prince, keeping his place and looking sentimentally at the girls, who retired precipitately from the dangerous spot.

"You won't catch me," said Rose with great dignity.

"See if I don't!"

"I've got my eye on Phebe," observed Will in a patronizing tone that made them all laugh.

"Bless the dear; I sha'n't mind it a bit," answered Phebe with such a maternal air that Will's budding gallantry was chilled to death.

"Oh, the mistletoe bough!" sang Rose.

"Oh, the mistletoe bough!" echoed all the boys, and the teasing ended in the plaintive ballad they all liked so well.

There was plenty of time to try the new skates before dinner, and then Rose took her first lesson on the little bay, which seemed to have frozen over for that express purpose. She found tumbling down and getting up again warm work for a time, but with six boys to teach her, she managed at last to stand alone; and satisfied with that success, she refreshed herself with a dozen grand coasts on the Amazon, as her sled was called.

"Ah, that fatal color! It breaks my heart to see it," croaked Aunt Myra as Rose came down a little late, with cheeks almost as ruddy as the holly berries on the wall, and every curl as smooth as Phebe's careful hands could make it.

"I'm glad to see that Alec allows the poor child to make herself pretty in spite of his absurd notions," added Aunt Clara, taking infinite satisfaction in the fact that Rose's blue silk dress had three frills on it.

"She is a very intelligent child and has a nice little manner of her own," observed Aunt Jane with unusual affability; for Rose had just handed Mac a screen to guard his eyes from the brilliant fire.

"If I had a daughter like that to show my Jem when he gets home, I should be a very proud and happy woman," thought Aunt Jessie, and then reproached herself for not being perfectly satisfied with her four brave lads.

Aunt Plenty was too absorbed in the dinner to have an eye for anything else; if she had not been, she would have seen what an effect her new cap produced upon the boys. The good lady owned that she did "love a dressy cap," and on this occasion her headgear was magnificent; for the towering structure of lace was adorned with buff ribbons to such an extent that it looked as if a flock of yellow butterflies had settled on her dear old head. When she trotted about the rooms the ruches quivered, the little bows all stood erect, and the streamers waved in the breeze so comically that it was absolutely necessary for Archie to smother the Brats in the curtains till they had had their first laugh out.

Uncle Mac had brought Fun See to dinner, and it was a mercy he did, for the elder lads found a vent for their merriment in joking the young Chinaman on his improved appearance. He was in American costume now, with a cropped head, and spoke remarkably good English after six months at school; but for all that, his yellow face and beady eyes made a curious contrast to the blond Campbells all about him. Will called him the "Typhoon," meaning Tycoon, and the name stuck to him to his great disgust.

Aunt Peace was brought down and set in the chair of state at table, for she never failed to join the family on this day, and sat smiling at them all "like an embodiment of Peace on earth," Uncle Alec said as he took his place beside her, while Uncle Mac supported Aunt Plenty at the other end.

"I ate hardly any breakfast, and I've done everything I know to make myself extra hungry, but I really don't think I *can* eat straight through, unless I burst my buttons off," whispered Geordie to Will as he surveyed the bounteous stores before him with a hopeless sigh.

"A fellow never knows what he can do till he tries," answered Will, attacking his heaped-up plate with the evident intention of doing his duty like a man.

Everybody knows what a Christmas dinner is, so we need waste no words in describing this one, but hasten at once to tell what happened at the end of it. The end, by the way, was so long in coming that the gas was lighted before dessert was over, for a snow flurry had come on and the wintry daylight faded fast. But that only made it all the jollier in the warm, bright rooms full of happy souls. Everyone was very merry, but Archie seemed particularly uplifted—so much so that Charlie confided to Rose that he was afraid the Chief had been at the decanters.

Rose indignantly denied the insinuation, for when healths were drunk in the good old-fashioned way to suit the elders, she had observed that Aunt Jessie's boys had filled their glasses with water, and had done the same herself in spite of the Prince's jokes about "the rosy."

But Archie certainly *was* unusually excited, and when someone remembered that it was the anniversary of Uncle Jem's wedding, and wished he were there to make a speech, his son electrified the family by trying to do it for him. It was rather incoherent and flowery, as maiden speeches are apt to be, but the end was considered superb; for turning to his mother with a queer little choke in his voice, he said that she "deserved to be blessed with peace and plenty, to be crowned with roses and lad's-love, and to receive the cargo of happiness sailing home to her in spite of wind or tide to add another Jem to the family jewels."

That allusion to the Captain, now on his return trip, made Mrs. Jessie sob in her napkin and set the boys cheering. Then, as if that were not sensation enough, Archie suddenly dashed out of the room as if he had lost his wits.

"Too bashful to stay and be praised," began Charlie, excusing the peculiarities of his Chief as in duty bound.

"Phebe beckoned to him; I saw her," cried Rose, staring hard at the door.

"Is it more presents coming?" asked Jamie, just as his brother reappeared looking more excited than ever.

"Yes; a present for Mother, and here it is!" roared Archie, flinging wide the door to let in a tall man who cried out, "Where's my little woman? The first kiss for her, then the rest may come on as fast as they like."

Before the words were out of his mouth, Mrs. Jessie was half hidden under his rough greatcoat, and four boys were prancing about him clamoring for their turn.

Of course, there was a joyful tumult for a time, during which Rose slipped into the window recess and watched what went on as if it were a chapter in a Christmas story. It was good to see bluff Uncle Jem look proudly at his tall son and fondly hug the little ones. It was better still to see him shake his brothers' hands as if he would never leave off, and kiss all the sisters in a way that made even solemn Aunt Myra brighten up for a minute. But it was best of all to see him finally established in grandfather's chair, with his "little woman" beside him, his three youngest boys in his lap, and Archie hovering over him like a large-sized cherub. That really was, as Charlie said, "a landscape to do one's heart good."

"All hearty and all here, thank God!" said Captain Jem in the first pause that came, as he looked about him with a grateful face.

"All but Rose," answered loyal little Jamie, remembering the absent.

"Faith, I forgot the child! Where is George's little girl?" asked the Captain, who had not seen her since she was a baby.

"You'd better say Alec's great girl," said Uncle Mac, who professed to be madly jealous of his brother.

"Here I am, sir," and Rose appeared from behind the curtains, looking as if she had rather have stayed there.

"Saint George Germain, how the mite has grown!" cried Captain Jem as he tumbled the boys out of his lap and rose to greet the tall girl like a gentleman as he was. But somehow, when he shook her hand, it looked so small in his big one, and her face reminded him so strongly of his dead brother, that he was not satisfied with so cold a welcome, and with a sudden softening of the keen eyes he took her up in his arms, whispering, with a rough cheek against her smooth one, "God bless you, child! Forgive me if I forgot you for a minute, and be sure that not one of your kinsfolk is happier to see you here than Uncle Jem."

That made it all right; and when he set her down, Rose's face was so bright it was evident that some spell had been used to banish the feeling of neglect that had kept her moping behind the curtain so long.

Then everyone sat round and heard all about the voyage home— how the Captain had set his heart on getting there in time to keep Christmas; how everything had conspired to thwart his plan; and how, at the very last minute, he had managed to do it and had sent a telegram to Archie, bidding him keep the secret and be ready for his father at any moment, for the ship got into another port and he might be late.

Then Archie told how that telegram had burned in his pocket all dinnertime; how he had to take Phebe into his confidence, and how clever she was to keep the Captain back till the speech was over and he could come in with effect.

The elders would have sat and talked all the evening, but the young folks were bent on having their usual Christmas frolic; so after an hour of pleasant chat, they began to get restless, and having consulted together in dumb show, they devised a way to very effectually break up the family council.

Steve vanished, and sooner than the boys imagined Dandy could get himself up, the skirl of the bagpipe was heard in the hall, and the bonny piper came to lead Clan Campbell to the revel.

"Draw it mild, Stevie, my man; ye play unco weel, but ye mak a most infernal din," cried Uncle Jem, with his hands over his ears, for this accomplishment was new to him and "took him all aback," as he expressed it.

So Steve droned out a Highland reel as softly as he could, and the boys danced it to a circle of admiring relations. Captain Jem was a true sailor, however, and could not stand idle while anything lively was going on; so, when the piper's breath gave out, he cut a splendid pigeon-wing into the middle of the hall, saying, "Who can dance a fore-and-after?" and, waiting for no reply, began to whistle the air so invitingly that Mrs. Jessie "set" to him laughing like a girl; Rose and Charlie took their places behind, and away went the four with a spirit and skill that inspired all the rest to "cut in" as fast as they could.

That was a grand beginning, and they had many another dance before anyone would own they were tired. Even Fun See distinguished himself with Aunt Plenty, whom he greatly admired as the stoutest lady in the company; plumpness being considered a beauty in his country. The merry old soul professed herself immensely flattered by his admiration, and the boys declared she "set her cap at him," else he would never have dared to catch her under the mistletoe and, rising on the tips of his own toes, gallantly salute her fat cheek.

How they all laughed at her astonishment, and how Fun's little black eyes twinkled over this exploit! Charlie put him up to it, and Charlie was so bent on catching Rose that he laid all sorts of pitfalls for her and bribed the other lads to help him. But Rose was wide awake and escaped all his snares, professing great contempt for such foolish customs. Poor Phebe did not fare so well, and Archie was the one who took a base advantage of her as she stood innocently offering tea to Aunt Myra, whom she happened to meet just under the fatal bough. If his father's arrival had not rather upset him, I doubt if the dignified Chief would have done it, for he apologized at once in the handsomest manner and caught the tray that nearly dropped from Phebe's hands.

Jamie boldly invited *all* the ladies to come and salute him; and as for Uncle Jem, he behaved as if the entire room was a grove of mistletoe. Uncle Alec slyly laid a bit of it on Aunt Peace's cap and then softly kissed her; which little joke seemed to please her very much, for she liked to have part in all the home pastimes, and Alec was her favorite nephew.

Charlie alone failed to catch his shy bird, and the oftener she escaped the more determined he was to ensnare her. When every other wile had been tried in vain, he got Archie to propose a game with forfeits.

"I understand that dodge," thought Rose, and was on her guard so carefully that not one among the pile soon collected belonged to her.

"Now let us redeem them and play something else," said Will, quite unconscious of the deeply laid plots all about him.

"One more round and then we will," answered the Prince, who had now baited his trap anew.

Just as the question came to Rose, Jamie's voice was heard in the hall, crying distressfully, "Oh, come quick, quick!" Rose started up, missed the question, and was greeted with a general cry of "Forfeit! Forfeit!" in which the little traitor came to join.

"Now I've got her," thought the young rascal, exulting in his fun-loving soul.

"Now I'm lost," thought Rose, as she gave up her pincushion with a sternly defiant look that would have daunted anyone but the reckless Prince. In fact, it made even him think twice and resolve to "let Rose off easy," she had been so clever.

"Here's a very pretty pawn, and what shall be done to redeem it?" asked Steve, holding the pincushion over Charlie's head, for he had insisted on being judge, and kept that for the last.

"Fine or superfine?"

"Super."

"Hum, well, she shall take old Mac under the mistletoe and kiss him prettily. Won't he be mad, though?"—and this bad boy chuckled over the discomfort he had caused two harmless beings.

There was an impressive pause among the young folks in their corner, for they all knew that Mac *would* "be mad," since he hated nonsense of this sort and had gone to talk with the elders when the game began. At this moment he was standing before the fire, listening to a discussion between his uncles and his father, looking as wise as a young owl and blissfully unconscious of the plot against him.

Charlie expected that Rose would say, "I won't!" therefore he was rather astonished, not to say gratified, when, after a look at the victim, she laughed suddenly and, going up to the group of gentlemen, drew her *uncle* Mac under the mistletoe and surprised him with a hearty kiss.

"Thank you, my dear," said the innocent gentleman, looking much pleased at the unexpected honor.

"Oh, come; that's not fair," began Charlie. But Rose cut him short by saying, as she made him a fine curtsy, "You said 'Old Mac,' and though it was very disrespectful, I did it. That was your last chance, sir, and you've lost it."

He certainly had, for as she spoke, Rose pulled down the mistletoe and threw it into the fire, while the boys jeered at the crestfallen Prince and exalted quick-witted Rose to the skies.

"What's the joke?" asked young Mac, waked out of a brown study by the laughter, in which the elders joined.

But there was a regular shout when, the matter having been explained to him, Mac took a meditative stare at Rose through his goggles and said in a philosophical tone, "Well, I don't think I should have minded much if she *had* done it."

That tickled the lads immensely, and nothing but the appearance of a slight refection would have induced them to stop chaffing the poor Worm, who could not see anything funny in the beautiful resignation he had shown on this trying occasion.

Soon after this, the discovery of Jamie curled up in the sofa corner, as sound asleep as a dormouse, suggested the propriety of going home, and a general move was made.

They were all standing about the hall lingering over the goodnights, when the sound of a voice softly singing "Sweet Home" made them pause and listen. It was Phebe, poor little Phebe, who never had a home, never knew the love of father or mother, brother or sister, who stood all alone in the wide world, yet was not sad nor afraid, but took her bits of happiness gratefully and sung over her work without a thought of discontent.

I fancy the happy family standing there together remembered this and felt the beauty of it, for when the solitary voice came to the burden of its song, other voices took it up and finished it so sweetly that the old house seemed to echo the word "home" in the ears of both the orphan girls, who had just spent their first Christmas under its hospitable roof.

CHAPTER 21

A SCARE

"BROTHER ALEC, you surely don't mean to allow that child to go out such a bitter cold day as this," said Mrs. Myra, looking into the study, where the doctor sat reading his paper one February morning.

"Why not? If a delicate invalid like yourself can bear it, surely my hearty girl can, especially as *she* is dressed for cold weather," answered Dr. Alec with provoking confidence.

"But you have no idea how sharp the wind is. I am chilled to the very marrow of my bones," answered Aunt Myra, chafing the end of her purple nose with her somber glove.

"I don't doubt it, ma'am, if you *will* wear crepe and silk instead of fur and flannel. Rosy goes out in all weathers and will be none the worse for an hour's brisk skating."

"Well, I warn you that you are trifling with the child's health and depending too much on the seeming improvement she has made this year. She is a delicate creature for all that, and will drop away suddenly at the first serious attack, as her poor mother did," croaked Aunt Myra with a despondent wag of the big bonnet.

"I'll risk it," answered Dr. Alec, knitting his brows, as he always did when any allusion was made to that other Rose.

"Mark my words, you will repent it." And with that awful prophecy, Aunt Myra departed like a black shadow.

Now it must be confessed that among the doctor's failings—and he had his share—was a very masculine dislike of advice which was thrust upon him unasked. He always listened with respect to the great-aunts, and often consulted Mrs. Jessie; but the other three ladies tried his patience sorely by constant warnings, complaints, and counsels. Aunt Myra was an especial trial, and he always turned contrary the moment she began to talk. He could not help it, and often laughed about it with comic frankness. Here now was a sample of it, for he had just been thinking that Rose had better defer her run till the wind went down and the sun was warmer. But Aunt Myra spoke, and he could not resist the temptation to make light of her advice and let Rose brave the cold. He had no fear of its harming her, for she went out every day, and it was a great satisfaction to him to see her run down the avenue a minute afterward with her skates on her arm, looking like a rosy-faced Eskimo in her sealskin suit, as she smiled at Aunt Myra stalking along as solemnly as a crow.

"I hope the child won't stay out long, for this wind *is* enough to chill the marrow in younger bones than Myra's," thought Dr. Alec half an hour later, as he drove toward the city to see the few patients he had consented to take for old acquaintance' sake.

The thought returned several times that morning, for it *was* truly a bitter day, and in spite of his bearskin coat, the doctor shivered. But he had great faith in Rose's good sense, and it never occurred to him that she was making a little Casabianca of herself, with the difference of freezing instead of burning at her post.

You see, Mac had made an appointment to meet her at a certain spot and have a grand skating bout as soon as the few lessons he was allowed were over. She had promised to wait for him, and did so with a faithfulness that cost her dear, because Mac forgot his appointment when the lessons were done and became absorbed in a chemical experiment, till a general combustion of gases drove him out of his laboratory. Then he suddenly remembered Rose and would gladly have hurried away to her, but his mother forbade his going out, for the sharp wind would hurt his eyes.

"She will wait and wait, Mother, for she always keeps her word, and I told her to hold on till I came," explained Mac, with visions of a shivering little figure watching on the windy hilltop.

"Of course, your uncle won't let her go out such a day as this. If he does, she will have the sense to come here for you, or to go home again when you don't appcar," said Aunt Jane, returning to her *Watts on the Mind.*

"I wish Steve would just cut up and see if she's there, since I can't go," began Mac anxiously.

"Steve won't stir a peg, thank you. He's got his own toes to thaw out, and wants his dinner," answered Dandy, just in from school and wrestling impatiently with his boots.

So Mac resigned himself, and Rose waited dutifully till dinnertime assured her that her waiting was in vain. She had done her best to keep warm, had skated till she was tired and hot, then stood watching others till she was chilled; tried to get up a glow again by trotting up and down the road, but failed to do so, and finally cuddled disconsolately under a pine tree to wait and watch. When she at length started for home, she was benumbed with the cold and could hardly make her way against the wind that buffeted the frostbitten rose most unmercifully.

Dr. Alec was basking in the warmth of the study fire after his drive, when the sound of a stifled sob made him hurry to the door and look anxiously into the hall. Rose lay in a shivering bunch near the register, with her things half off, wringing her hands, and trying not to cry with the pain returning warmth brought to her half-frozen fingers.

"My darling, what is it?" And Uncle Alec had her in his arms in a minute.

"Mac didn't come—I can't gct warm—the fire makes me ache!" And with a long shiver Rose burst out crying, while her teeth chattered, and her poor little nose was so blue, it made one's heart ache to see it.

In less time than it takes to tell it, Dr. Alec had her on the sofa rolled up in the bearskin coat, with Phebe rubbing her cold feet while he rubbed the aching hands, and Aunt Plenty made a comfortable hot drink, and Aunt Peace sent down her own footwarmer and embroidered blanket "for the dear."

Full of remorseful tenderness, Uncle Alec worked over his new patient till she declared she was all right again. He would not let her get up to dinner, but fed her himself, and then forgot his own while he sat watching her fall into a drowse, for Aunt Plenty's cordial made her sleepy.

She lay so several hours, for the drowse deepened into a heavy sleep, and Uncle Alec, still at his post, saw with growing anxiety that a feverish color began to burn in her cheeks, that her breathing was quick and uneven, and now and then she gave a little moan, as if in pain. Suddenly she woke up with a start, and seeing Aunt Plenty bending over her, put out her arms like a sick child, saying wearily, "Please, could I go to bed?"

"The best place for you, deary. Take her right up, Alec; I've got the hot water ready, and after a nice bath, she shall have a cup of my sage tea and be rolled up in blankets to sleep off her cold," answered the old lady cheerily as she bustled away to give orders.

"Are you in pain, darling?" asked Uncle Alec as he carried her up.

"My side aches when I breathe, and I feel stiff and queer; but it isn't bad, so don't be troubled, Uncle," whispered Rose, with a little hot hand against his cheek.

But the poor doctor did look troubled, and had cause to do so, for just then Rose tried to laugh at Debby charging into the room with a warming pan, but could not, for the sharp pain that took her breath away and made her cry out.

"Pleurisy," sighed Aunt Plenty, from the depths of the bathtub.

"Pewmonia!" groaned Debby, burrowing among the bedclothes with the long-handled pan, as if bent on fishing up that treacherous disease.

"Oh, is it bad?" asked Phebe, nearly dropping a pail of hot water in her dismay, for she knew nothing of sickness, and Debby's sugges-tion had a peculiarly dreadful sound to her.

"Hush!" ordered the doctor in a tone that silenced all further predictions and made everyone work with a will.

"Make her as comfortable as you can, and when she is in her little bed I'll come and say good night," he added when the bath was ready and the blankets browning nicely before the fire.

Then he went away to talk quite cheerfully to Aunt Peace about its being "only a chill"; after which he tramped up and down the hall, pulling his beard and knitting his brows, sure signs of great inward perturbation.

"I thought it would be too good luck to get through the year without a downfall. Confound my perversity! Why couldn't I take Myra's advice and keep Rose at home. It's not fair that the poor child should suffer for my sinful overconfidence. She shall *not* suffer for it! Pneumonia, indeed! I defy it!" And he shook his fist in the ugly face of an Indian idol that happened to be before him, as if that particularly hideous god had some spite against his own little god-dess.

In spite of his defiance his heart sunk when he saw Rose again, for the pain was worse, and the bath and blankets, the warming pan and piping-hot sage tea, were all in vain. For several hours there was no rest for the poor child, and all manner of gloomy forebodings haunted the minds of those who hovered about her with faces full of the tenderest anxiety.

In the midst of the worst paroxysm Charlie came to leave a mes-sage from his mother and was met by Phebe coming despondently downstairs with a mustard plaster that had brought no relief.

"What the dickens is the matter? You look as dismal as a tomb-stone," he said as she held up her hand to stop his lively whistling.

"Miss Rose is dreadfully sick."

"The deuce she is!"

"Don't swear, Mr. Charlie; she really is, and it's Mr. Mac's fault." And Phebe told the sad tale in a few sharp words, for she felt at war with the entire race of boys at that moment.

"I'll give it to him, make your mind easy about that," said Charlie with an ominous doubling up of his fist. "But Rose isn't dangerously ill, is she?" he added anxiously as Aunt Plenty was seen to trot across the upper hall, shaking a bottle violently as she went.

"Oh, but she is, though. The doctor don't say much, but he don't call it a 'chill' anymore. It's 'pleurisy' now, and I'm *so* afraid it will be *pewmonia* tomorrow," answered Phebe with a despairing glance at the plaster.

Charlie exploded into a stifled laugh at the new pronunciation of *pneumonia,* to Phebe's great indignation.

"How can you have the heart to do it, and she in such horrid pain? Hark to that, and then laugh if you darst," she said with a tragic gesture and her black eyes full of fire.

Charlie listened and heard little moans that went to his heart and made his face as sober as Phebe's. "Oh, Uncle, please stop the pain and let me rest a minute! Don't tell the boys I wasn't brave. I try to bear it, but it's so sharp I can't help crying."

Neither could Charlie when he heard the broken voice say that; but, boylike, he wouldn't own it, and said pettishly, as he rubbed his sleeve across his eyes, "Don't hold that confounded thing right under my nose; the mustard makes my eyes smart."

"Don't see how it can, when it hasn't any more strength in it than meal. The doctor said so, and I'm going to get some better," began Phebe, not a bit ashamed of the great tears that were bedewing the condemned plaster.

"I'll go!" And Charlie was off like a shot, glad of an excuse to get out of sight for a few minutes.

When he came back all inconvenient emotion had been disposed of, and having delivered a box of the hottest mustard procurable for money, he departed to "blow up" Mac, that being his next duty in his opinion. He did it so energetically and thoroughly that the poor Worm was cast into the depths of remorseful despair and went to bed that evening feeling that he was an outcast from among men and bore the mark of Cain upon his brow.

Thanks to the skill of the doctor, and the devotion of his helpers,

Rose grew easier about midnight, and all hoped that the worst was over. Phebe was making tea by the study fire, for the doctor had forgotten to eat and drink since Rose was ill, and Aunt Plenty insisted on his having a "good, cordial dish of tea" after his exertions. A tap on the window startled Phebe, and looking up, she saw a face peering in. She was not afraid, for a second look showed her that it was neither ghost nor burglar, but Mac, looking pale and wild in the wintry moonlight.

"Come and let a fellow in," he said in a low tone, and when he stood in the hall he clutched Phebe's arm, whispering gruffly, "How is Rose?"

"Thanks be to goodness, she's better," answered Phebe with a smile that was like broad sunshine to the poor lad's anxious heart.

"And she will be all right again tomorrow?"

"Oh, dear, no. Debby says she's sure to have rheumatic fever, if she don't have noo-monia!" answered Phebe, careful to pronounce the word rightly this time.

Down went Mac's face, and remorse began to gnaw at him again as he gave a great sigh and said doubtfully, "I suppose I couldn't see her?"

"Of course not at this time of night, when we want her to go to sleep!"

Mac opened his mouth to say something more, when a sneeze came upon him unawares, and a loud "Ah rash hoo!" awoke the echoes of the quiet house.

"Why didn't you stop it?" said Phebe reproachfully. "I daresay you've waked her up."

"Didn't know it was coming. Just my luck!" groaned Mac, turning to go before his unfortunate presence did more harm.

But a voice from the stairhead called softly, "Mac, come up; Rose wants to see you."

Up he went, and found his uncle waiting for him.

"What brings you here at this hour, my boy?" asked the doctor in a whisper.

"Charlie said it was all my fault, and if she died I'd killed her. I couldn't sleep, so I came to see how she was, and no one knows it but Steve," he said with such a troubled face and voice that the doctor had not the heart to blame him.

Before he could say anything more a feeble voice called "Mac!" and with a hasty "Stay a minute just to please her, and then slip away, for I want her to sleep," the doctor led him into the room.

The face on the pillow looked very pale and childish, and the smile that welcomed Mac was very faint, for Rose was spent with pain, yet could not rest till she had said a word of comfort to her cousin.

"I knew your funny sneeze, and I guessed that you came to see how I did, though it is very late. Don't be worried. I'm better now, and it is my fault I was ill, not yours; for I needn't have been so silly as to wait in the cold just because I said I would."

Mac hastened to explain, to load himself with reproaches, and to beg her not to die on any account, for Charlie's lecture had made a deep impression on the poor boy's mind.

"I didn't know there was any danger of my dying." And Rose looked up at him with a solemn expression in her great eyes.

"Oh, I hope not; but people do sometimes go suddenly, you know, and I couldn't rest till I'd asked you to forgive me," faltered Mac, thinking that Rose looked very like an angel already, with the golden hair loose on the pillow and the meekness of suffering on her little white face.

"I don't think I shall die; Uncle won't let me; but if I do, remember I forgave you."

She looked at him with a tender light in her eyes, and seeing how pathetic his dumb grief was, she added softly, drawing his head down: "I wouldn't kiss you under the mistletoe, but I will now, for I want you to be sure I do forgive and love you just the same."

That quite upset poor Mac; he could only murmur his thanks and get out of the room as fast as possible, to grope his way to the couch at the far end of the hall and lie there till he fell asleep, worn out with trying not to "make a baby" of himself.

CHAPTER 22

SOMETHING TO DO

WHATEVER DANGER THERE MIGHT HAVE BEEN from the effects of that sudden chill, it was soon over, though of course Aunt Myra refused to believe it, and Dr. Alec cherished his girl with redoubled vigilance and tenderness for months afterward. Rose quite enjoyed being sick, because as soon as the pain ended the fun began, and for a week or two she led the life of a little princess secluded in the Bower, while everyone served, amused, and watched over her in the most delightful manner. But the doctor was called away to see an old friend who was dangerously ill, and then Rose felt like a young bird deprived of its mother's sheltering wing; especially on one afternoon when the aunts were taking their naps, and the house was very still within while snow fell softly without.

"I'll go and hunt up Phebe; she is always nice and busy and likes to have me help her. If Debby is out of the way we can make caramels and surprise the boys when they come," Rose said to herself as she threw down her book and felt ready for society of some sort.

She took the precaution to peep through the slide before she entered the kitchen, for Debby allowed no messing when she was round. But the coast was clear, and no one but Phebe appeared, sitting at the table with her head on her arms apparently asleep. Rose was just about to wake her with a "Boo!" when she lifted her head, dried her wet eyes with her blue apron, and fell to work with a resolute face on something she was evidently much interested in. Rose could not make out what it was, and her curiosity was greatly excited, for Phebe was writing with a sputtering pen on some bits of brown paper, apparently copying something from a little book.

"I *must* know what the dear thing is about, and why she cried and then set her lips tight and went to work with all her might," thought Rose, forgetting all about the caramels, and going round to the door, she entered the kitchen, saying pleasantly, "Phebe, I want something to do. Can't you let me help you about anything? Or shall I be in the way?"

"Oh, dear, no, miss; I always love to have you round when things are tidy. What would you like to do?" answered Phebe, opening a drawer as if about to sweep her own affairs out of sight; but Rose stopped her, exclaiming, like a curious child, "Let me see! What is it? I won't tell if you'd rather not have Debby know."

"I'm only trying to study a bit; but I'm so stupid I don't get on much," answered the girl reluctantly, permitting her little mistress to examine the poor contrivances she was trying to work with.

A broken slate that had blown off the roof, an inch or two of pencil, an old almanac for a reader, several bits of brown or yellow paper ironed smoothly and sewed together for a copybook, and the copies sundry receipts written in Aunt Plenty's neat hand. These, with a small bottle of ink and a rusty pen, made up Phebe's outfit, and it was little wonder that she did not "get on" in spite of the patient persistence that dried the desponding tears and drove along the sputtering pen with a will.

"You may laugh if you want to, Miss Rose. I know my things are queer, and that's why I hide 'em; but I don't mind since you've found me out, and I ain't a bit ashamed except of being so backward at my age," said Phebe humbly, though her cheeks grew redder as she washed out some crooked capitals with a tear or two not yet dried upon the slate.

"Laugh at you! I feel more like crying to think what a selfish girl I am, to have loads of books and things and never remember to give you some. Why didn't you come and ask me, and not go struggling along alone in this way? It was very wrong of you, Phebe, and I'll never forgive you if you do so again," answered Rose, with one hand on Phebe's shoulder while the other gently turned the leaves of the poor little copybook.

"I didn't like to ask for anything more when you are so good to me all the time, miss, dear," began Phebe, looking up with grateful eyes.

"Oh, you proud thing! Just as if it wasn't fun to give away, and I had the best of it. Now, see here, I've got a plan and you mustn't say no, or I shall scold. I want something to do, and I'm going to teach you all I know; it won't take long." And Rose laughed as she put her arm around Phebe's neck and patted the smooth dark head with the kind little hand that so loved to give.

"It would be just heavenly!" And Phebe's face shone at the mere idea; but fell again as she added wistfully, "Only I'm afraid I ought not to let you do it, Miss Rose. It will take time, and maybe the doctor wouldn't like it."

"He didn't want me to study much, but he never said a word about teaching, and I don't believe he will mind a bit. Anyway, we can try it till he comes, so pack up your things and go right to my room and we'll begin this very day; I'd truly like to do it, and we'll have nice times, see if we don't!" cried Rose eagerly.

It was a pretty sight to see Phebe bundle her humble outfit into her apron and spring up as if the desire of her heart had suddenly been made a happy fact to her; it was a still prettier sight to see Rose run gayly on before, smiling like a good fairy as she beckoned to the other, singing as she went,

"The way into my parlor is up a winding stair,
And many are the curious things I'll show you when
you're there.
Will you, will you walk in, Phebe dear?"

"Oh, won't I!" answered Phebe fervently, adding, as they entered the Bower, "You are the dearest spider that ever was, and I'm the happiest fly."

"I'm going to be very strict, so sit down in that chair and don't say a word till school is ready to open," ordered Rose, delighted with the prospect of such a useful and pleasant "something to do."

So Phebe sat demurely in her place while her new teacher laid forth books and slates, a pretty inkstand and a little globe; hastily tore a bit off her big sponge, sharpened pencils with more energy than skill, and when all was ready gave a prance of satisfaction that set the pupil laughing.

"Now the school is open, and I shall hear you read, so that I may know in which class to put you, Miss Moore," began Rose with great dignity, as she laid a book before her scholar and sat down in the easy chair with a long rule in her hand.

Phebe did pretty well, only tripping now and then over a hard word, and pronouncing *identical* "identickle" in a sober way that tickled Rose, though never a smile betrayed her. The spelling lesson which followed was rather discouraging; Phebe's ideas of geography were very vague, and grammar was nowhere, though the pupil protested that she tried so hard to "talk nice like educated folks" that Debby called her "a stuck-up piece who didn't know her place."

"Debby's an old goose, so don't you mind her, for she will say 'nater,' 'vittles,' and 'doos' as long as she lives, and insist that they are right. You do talk very nicely, Phebe; I've observed it, and grammar will help you and show why some things are right and others ain't—are not, I mean," added Rose, correcting herself, and feeling that she must mind her own parts of speech if she was to serve as an example for Phebe.

When the arithmetic came the little teacher was surprised to find her scholar quicker in some things than herself, for Phebe had worked away at the columns in the butcher's and baker's books till she could add so quickly and correctly that Rose was amazed and felt that in this branch the pupil would soon excel the teacher if she kept on at the same pace. Her praise cheered Phebe immensely, and they went bravely on, both getting so interested that time flew unheeded till Aunt Plenty appeared, exclaiming, as she stared at the two heads bent over one slate, "Bless my heart, what is going on now?"

"School, Auntie. I'm teaching Phebe, and it's great fun!" cried Rose, looking up with a bright face.

But Phebe's was brighter, though she added, with a wistful look, "Maybe I ought to have asked leave first; only when Miss Rose proposed this, I was so happy I forgot to. Shall I stop, ma'am?"

"Of course not, child; I'm glad to see you fond of your book and to find Rose helping you along. My blessed mother used to sit at work with her maids about her, teaching them many a useful thing in the good old fashion that's gone by now. Only don't neglect your work, dear, or let the books interfere with the duties."

As Aunt Plenty spoke, with her kind old face beaming approvingly upon the girls, Phebe glanced at the clock, saw that it pointed to five, knew that Debby would soon be down, expecting to find preparations for supper under way, and hastily dropping her pencil, she jumped up, saying, "Please, can I go? I'll clear up after I've done my chores."

"School is dismissed," answered Rose, and with a grateful "Thank you, heaps and heaps!" Phebe ran away singing the multiplication table as she set the tea ditto.

That was the way it began, and for a week the class of one went on with great pleasure and profit to all concerned; for the pupil proved a bright one and came to her lessons as to a feast, while the young teacher did her best to be worthy the high opinion held of her, for Phebe firmly believed that Miss Rose knew *everything* in the way of learning.

Of course the lads found out what was going on, and chaffed the girls about the "seminary," as they called the new enterprise; but they thought it a good thing on the whole, kindly offered to give lessons in Greek and Latin gratis, and decided among themselves that "Rose was a little trump to give the Phebe bird such a capital boost."

Rose herself had some doubts as to how it would strike her uncle and concocted a wheedlesome speech which should at once convince him that it was the most useful, wholesome, and delightful plan ever devised. But she got no chance to deliver her address, for Dr. Alec came upon her so unexpectedly that it went out of her head entirely. She was sitting on the floor in the library, poring over a big book laid open in her lap, and knew nothing of the long-desired arrival till two large, warm hands met under her chin and gently turned her head back so that someone could kiss her heartily on either cheek, while a fatherly voice said, half reproachfully, "Why is my girl brooding over a dusty encyclopedia when she ought to be running to meet the old gentleman who couldn't get on another minute without her?"

"Oh, Uncle! I'm so glad! And so sorry! Why didn't you let us know what time you'd be here, or call out the minute you came? Haven't I been homesick for you? And now I'm so happy to have you back I could hug your dear old curly head off," cried Rose as the encyclopedia went down with a bang, and she up with a spring that carried her into Dr. Alec's arms, to be kept there in the sort of embrace a man gives to the dearest creature the world holds for him.

Presently he was in his easy chair with Rose upon his knee smiling up in his face and talking as fast as her tongue could go, while he watched her with an expression of supreme content as he stroked the smooth round cheek or held the little hand in his, rejoicing to see how rosy was the one, how plump and strong the other.

"*Have* you had a good time? *Did* you save the poor lady? *Aren't* you glad to be home again with your girl to torment you?"

"Yes, to all those questions. Now tell me what you've been at, little sinner? Aunty Plen says you want to consult me about some new and remarkable project which you have dared to start in my absence."

"She didn't tell you, I hope?"

"Not a word more except that you were rather doubtful how I'd take it, and so wanted to 'fess' yourself and get round me as you always try to do, though you don't often succeed. Now, then, own up and take the consequences."

So Rose told about her school in her pretty, earnest way, dwelling on Phebe's hunger for knowledge and the delight it was to help her, adding, with a wise nod, "And it helps me too Uncle, for she is so quick and eager I have to do my best or she will get ahead of me in some things. Today, now, she had the word 'cotton' in a lesson and asked all about it, and I was ashamed to find I really knew so little that I could only say that it was a plant that grew down South in a kind of a pod and was made into cloth. That's what I was reading up when you came, and tomorrow I shall tell her all about it, and indigo too. So you see it teaches me also, and is as good as a general review of what I've learned, in a pleasanter way than going over it alone."

"You artful little baggage! That's the way you expect to get round me, is it? That's not studying, I suppose?"

"No, sir, it's teaching; and please, I like it much better than having a good time all by myself. Besides, you know, I adopted Phebe and promised to be a sister to her, so I am bound to keep my word, am I not?" answered Rose, looking both anxious and resolute as she waited for her sentence.

Dr. Alec was evidently already won, for Rose had described the old slate and brown paper copybook with pathetic effect, and the excellent man had not only decided to send Phebe to school long before the story was done, but reproached himself for forgetting his duty to one little girl in his love for another. So when Rose tried to look meek and failed utterly, he laughed and pinched her cheek and answered in that genial way which adds such warmth and grace to any favor, "I haven't the slightest objection in the world. In fact, I was beginning to think I might let you go at your books again, moderately, since you are so well; and this is an excellent way to try your powers. Phebe is a brave, bright lass, and shall have a fair chance in the world, if we can give it to her, so that if she ever finds her friends they need not be ashamed of her."

"I think she has found some already," began Rose eagerly.

"Hey? What? Has anyone turned up since I've been gone?" asked Dr. Alec quickly, for it was a firm belief in the family that Phebe would prove to be "somebody" sooner or later.

"No, her best friend turned up when *you* came home, Uncle," answered Rose with an approving pat, adding gratefully, "I can't half thank you for being so good to my girl, but she will, because I know she is going to make a woman to be proud of, she's so strong and true, and loving."

"Bless your dear heart, I haven't begun to do anything yet, more shame to me! But I'm going at it now, and as soon as she gets on a bit, she shall go to school as long as she likes. How will that do for a beginning?"

"It will be 'just heavenly,' as Phebe says, for it is the wish of her life to 'get lots of schooling,' and she will be *too* happy when I tell her. May I, please?—it will be so lovely to see the dear thing open her big eyes and clap her hands at the splendid news."

"No one shall have a finger in this nice little pie; you shall do it all yourself, only don't go too fast, or make too many castles in the air, my dear; for time and patience must go into this pie of ours if it is to turn out well."

"Yes, Uncle, only when it *is* opened, won't 'the birds begin to sing'?" laughed Rose, taking a turn about the room as a vent for the joyful emotions that made her eyes shine. All of a sudden she stopped and asked soberly, "If Phebe goes to school, who will do her work? I'm willing, if I can."

"Come here and I'll tell you a secret. Debby's 'bones' are getting so troublesome, and her dear old temper so bad, that the aunts have decided to pension her off and let her go and live with her daughter, who has married very well. I saw her this week, and she'd like to have her mother come, so in the spring we shall have a grand change, and get a new cook and chamber-girl if any can be found to suit our honored relatives."

"Oh, me! How can I ever get on without Phebe? Couldn't she stay, just so I could see her? I'd pay her board rather than have her go, I'm *so* fond of her."

How Dr. Alec laughed at that proposal, and how satisfied Rose was when he explained that Phebe was still to be her maid, with no duties except such as she could easily perform between school hours.

"She is a proud creature, for all her humble ways, and even from us would not take a favor if she did not earn it somehow. So this arrangement makes it all square and comfortable, you see, and she will pay for the schooling by curling these goldilocks a dozen times a day if you let her."

"Your plans are always *so* wise and kind! That's why they work so well, I suppose, and why people let you do what you like with them. I really don't see how other girls get along without an Uncle Alec!" answered Rose with a sigh of pity for those who had missed so great a blessing.

When Phebe was told the splendid news, she did not "stand on her head with rapture," as Charlie prophesied she would, but took it quietly, because it was such a happy thing she had no words "big and beautiful enough to thank them in," she said; but every hour of her day was brightened by this granted wish, and dedicated to the service of those who gave it.

Her heart was so full of content that it overflowed in music, and the sweet voice singing all about the house gave thanks so blithely that no other words were needed. Her willing feet were never tired of taking steps for those who had smoothed her way; her skillful hands were always busy in some labor of love for them, and on the face fast growing in comeliness there was an almost womanly expression of devotion, which proved how well Phebe had already learned one of life's great lessons—gratitude.

CHAPTER 23

PEACEMAKING

"Steve, I want you to tell me something," said Rose to Dandy, who was making faces at himself in the glass while he waited for an answer to the note he brought from his mother to Aunt Plenty.

"P'raps I will, and p'raps I won't. What is it?"

"Haven't Arch and Charlie quarreled?"

"Daresay; we fellows are always having little rows, you know. I do believe a sty is coming on my starboard eye." And Steve affected to be absorbed in a survey of his yellow lashes.

"No, that won't do; I want to know all about it; for I'm sure something more serious than a 'little row' is the matter. Come, please tell me, Stevie, there's a dear."

"Botheration! You don't want me to turn telltale, do you?" growled Steve, pulling his topknot, as he always did when perplexed.

"Yes, I do" was Rose's decided answer—for she saw from his manner that she was right, and determined to have the secret out of him if coaxing would do it. "I don't wish you to tell things to everyone, of course, but to me you may, and you must, because I have a right to know. You boys need somebody to look after you, and I'm going to do it, for girls are nice peacemakers and know how to manage people. Uncle said so, and he is never wrong."

Steve was about to indulge in a derisive hoot at the idea of her looking after them, but a sudden thought restrained him and suggested a way in which he could satisfy Rose and better himself at the same time.

"What will you give me if I'll tell you every bit about it?" he asked, with a sudden red in his cheeks and an uneasy look in his eyes, for he was half ashamed of the proposition.

"What do you want?" And Rose looked up rather surprised at his question.

"I'd like to borrow some money. I shouldn't think of asking you, only Mac never has a cent since he's set up his old chemical shop, where he'll blow himself to bits someday, and you and Uncle will have the fun of putting him together again." And Steve tried to look as if the idea amused him.

"I'll lend it to you with pleasure, so tell away," said Rose, bound to get at the secret.

Evidently much relieved by the promise, Steve set his topknot cheerfully erect again and briefly stated the case.

"As you say, it's all right to tell *you,* but don't let the boys know I blabbed, or Prince will take my head off. You see, Archie don't like some of the fellows Charlie goes with, and cuts 'em. That makes Prince mad, and he holds on just to plague Arch, so they don't speak to one another, if they can help it, and that's the row."

"Are those boys bad?" asked Rose anxiously.

"Guess not, only rather wild. They are older than our fellows, but they like Prince, he's such a jolly boy; sings so well, dances jigs and breakdowns, you know, and plays any game that's going. He beat Morse at billiards, and that's something to brag of, for Morse thinks he knows everything. I saw the match, and it was great fun!"

Steve got quite excited over the prowess of Charlie, whom he admired immensely and tried to imitate. Rose did not know half the danger of such gifts and tastes as Charlie's, but felt instinctively that something must be wrong if Archie disapproved.

"If Prince likes any billiard-playing boy better than Archie, I don't think much of his sense," she said severely.

"Of course he doesn't; but, you see, Charlie and Arch are both as proud as they can be and won't give in. I suppose Arch *is* right, but I don't blame Charlie a bit for liking to be with the others sometimes, they are such a jolly set." And Steve shook his head morally, even while his eye twinkled over the memory of some of the exploits of the "jolly set."

"Oh, dear me!" sighed Rose. "I don't see what I can do about it, but I wish the boys would make up, for Prince can't come to any harm with Archie, he's so good and sensible."

"That's the trouble; Arch preaches, and Prince won't stand it. He told Arch he was a prig and a parson, and Arch told him he wasn't a gentleman. My boots! Weren't they both mad though! I thought for a minute they'd pitch into one another and have it out. Wish they had, and not gone stalking round stiff and glum ever since. Mac and I settle our rows with a bat or so over the head, and then we are all right."

Rose couldn't help laughing as Steve sparred away at a fat sofa pillow to illustrate his meaning; and having given it several scientific whacks, he pulled down his cuffs and smiled upon her with benign pity for her feminine ignorance of this summary way of settling a quarrel.

"What droll things boys are!" she said with a mixture of admiration and perplexity in her face, which Steve accepted as a compliment to his sex.

"We are a pretty clever invention, miss, and you can't get on without us," he answered with his nose in the air. Then, taking a sudden plunge into business, he added, "How about that bit of money you were going to lend me? I've told, now you pay up."

"Of course I will! How much do you want?" And Rose pulled out her purse.

"*Could* you spare five dollars? I want to pay a little debt of honor that is rather pressing." And Steve put on a mannish air that was comical to see.

"Aren't all debts honorable?" asked innocent Rose.

"Yes, of course; but this is a bet I made, and it ought to be settled up at once," began Steve, finding it awkward to explain.

"Oh, don't bet; it's not right, and I know your father wouldn't like it. Promise you won't do so again, please promise!" And Rose held fast the hand into which she had just put the money.

"Well, I won't. It's worried me a good deal, but I was joked into it. Much obliged, cousin, I'm all right now." And Steve departed hastily.

Having decided to be a peacemaker, Rose waited for an opportunity, and very soon it came.

She was spending the day with Aunt Clara, who had been entertaining some young guests and invited Rose to meet them, for she thought it high time her niece conquered her bashfulness and saw a little of society. Dinner was over, and everyone had gone. Aunt Clara was resting before going out to an evening party, and Rose was waiting for Charlie to come and take her home.

She sat alone in the elegant drawing room, feeling particularly nice and pretty, for she had her best frock on, a pair of gold bands her aunt had just given her, and a tea-rose bud in her sash, like the beautiful Miss Van Tassel, whom everyone admired. She had spread out her little skirts to the best advantage and, leaning back in a luxurious chair, sat admiring her own feet in new slippers with rosettes almost as big as dahlias. Presently Charlie came lounging in, looking rather sleepy and queer, Rose thought. On seeing her, however, he roused up and said with a smile that ended in a gape, "I thought you were with Mother, so I took forty winks after I got those girls off. Now, I'm at your service, Rosamunda, whenever you like."

"You look as if your head ached. If it does, don't mind me. I'm not afraid to run home alone, it's so early," answered Rose, observing the flushed cheeks and heavy eyes of her cousin.

"I think I see myself letting you do it. Champagne always makes my head ache, but the air will set me up."

"Why do you drink it, then?" asked Rose anxiously.

"Can't help it, when I'm host. Now, don't *you* begin to lecture; I've had enough of Archie's old-fashioned notions, and I don't want any more."

Charlie's tone was decidedly cross, and his whole manner so unlike his usual merry good-nature that Rose felt crushed and answered meekly, "I wasn't going to lecture, only when people like other people, they can't bear to see them suffer pain."

That brought Charlie round at once, for Rose's lips trembled a little, though she tried to hide it by smelling the flower she pulled from her sash.

"I'm a regular bear, and I beg your pardon for being so cross, Rosy," he said in the old frank way that was so winning.

"I wish you'd beg Archie's too, and be good friends again. You never were cross when *he* was your chum," Rose said, looking up at him as he bent toward her from the low chimney piece, where he had been leaning his elbows.

In an instant he stood as stiff and straight as a ramrod, and the heavy eyes kindled with an angry spark as he said in his high and mighty manner, "You'd better not meddle with what you don't understand, cousin."

"But I do understand; it troubles me very much to see you so cold and stiff to one another. You always used to be together, and now you hardly speak. You are so ready to beg my pardon I don't see why you can't beg Archie's, if you are in the wrong."

"I'm not!" This was so short and sharp that Rose started, and Charlie added in a calmer but still very haughty tone: "A gentleman always begs pardon when he has been rude to a lady, but one man doesn't apologize to another man who has insulted him."

"Oh, my heart, what a pepperpot!" thought Rose, and hoping to make him laugh, she added slyly: "I was not talking about men, but boys, and one of them a Prince, who ought to set a good example to his subjects."

But Charlie would not relent, and tried to turn the subject by saying gravely, as he unfastened the little gold ring from his watch-guard, "I've broken my word, so I want to give this back and free you from the bargain. I'm sorry, but I think it a foolish promise and don't intend to keep it. Choose a pair of earrings to suit yourself, as my forfeit. You have a right to wear them now."

"No, I can only wear one, and that is no use, for Archie will keep *his* word I'm sure!" Rose was so mortified and grieved at this downfall of her hopes that she spoke sharply and would not take the ring the deserter offered her.

He shrugged his shoulders and threw it into her lap, trying to look cool and careless but failing entirely, for he was ashamed of himself and out of sorts generally. Rose wanted to cry, but pride would not let her, and being very angry, she relieved herself by talk instead of tears. Looking pale and excited, she rose out of her chair, cast away the ring, and said in a voice that she vainly tried to keep steady, "You are not at all the boy I thought you were, and I don't respect you one bit. I've tried to help you be good, but you won't let me, and I shall not try anymore. You talk a great deal about being a gentleman, but you are not, for you've broken your word and I can never trust you again. I don't wish you to go home with me. I'd rather have Mary. Good night."

And with that last dreadful blow, Rose walked out of the room, leaving Charlie as much astonished as if one of his pet pigeons had flown in his face and pecked at him. She was so seldom angry that when her temper did get the better of her it made a deep impression on the lads, for it was generally a righteous sort of indignation at some injustice or wrongdoing, not childish passion.

Her little thunderstorm cleared off in a sob or two as she put on her things in the entry closet, and when she emerged she looked the brighter for the shower. A hasty good night to Aunt Clara—now under the hands of the hairdresser—and then she crept down to find Mary the maid. But Mary was out, so was the man, and Rose slipped away by the back door, flattering herself that she had escaped the awkwardness of having Charlie for escort.

There she was mistaken, however, for the gate had hardly closed behind her when a well-known tramp was heard, and the Prince was beside her, saying in a tone of penitent politeness that banished

Rose's wrath like magic, "You needn't speak to me if you don't choose, but I must see you safely home, cousin."

She turned at once, put out her hand, and answered heartily, "*I* was the cross one. Please forgive me, and let's be friends again."

Now that was better than a dozen sermons on the beauty of forgiveness, and did Charlie more good, for it showed him how sweet humility was and proved that Rose practiced as she preached.

He shook the hand warmly, then drew it through his arm and said, as if anxious to recover the good opinion with the loss of which he had been threatened, "Look here, Rosy, I've put the ring back, and I'm going to try again. But you don't know how hard it is to stand being laughed at."

"Yes, I do! Ariadne plagues me every time I see her, because I don't wear earrings after all the trouble I had getting ready for them."

"Ah, but her twaddle isn't half as bad as the chaffing *I* get. It takes a deal of pluck to hold out when you are told you are tied to an apron string, and all that sort of thing," sighed Charlie.

"I thought you had a 'deal of pluck,' as you call it. The boys all say you are the bravest of the seven," said Rose.

"So I am about some things, but I *cannot* bear to be laughed at."

"It is hard, but if one is right, won't that make it easier?"

"Not to me; it might to a pious parson like Arch."

"Please don't call him names! I guess *he* has what is called moral courage, and *you* physical courage. Uncle explained the difference to me, and moral is the best, though often it doesn't look so," said Rose thoughtfully.

Charlie didn't like that and answered quickly, "I don't believe he'd stand it any better than I do, if he had those fellows at him."

"Perhaps that's why he keeps out of their way, and wants you to."

Rose had him there, and Charlie felt it, but would not give in just yet, though he was going fast, for somehow, in the dark he seemed to see things clearer than in the light and found it very easy to be confidential when it was "only Rose."

"If he was my brother, now, he'd have some right to interfere," began Charlie in an injured tone.

"I wish he was!" cried Rose.

"So do I," answered Charlie, and then they both laughed at his inconsistency.

The laugh did them good, and when Prince spoke again, it was in a different tone—pensive, not proud nor perverse.

"You see, it's hard upon me that I have no brothers and sisters. The others are better off and needn't go abroad for chums if they don't like. *I* am all alone, and I'd be thankful even for a little sister."

Rose thought that very pathetic, and overlooking the uncomplimentary word "even" in that last sentence, she said, with a timid sort of earnestness that conquered her cousin at once, "Play I was a little sister. I know I'm silly, but perhaps I'm better than nothing, and I'd dearly love to do it."

"So should I! And we will, for you are not silly, my dear, but a very sensible girl, we all think, and I'm proud to have you for a sister. There, now!" And Charlie looked down at the curly head bobbing along beside him, with real affection in his face.

Rose gave a skip of pleasure and laid one sealskin mitten over the other on his arm as she said happily, "That's so nice of you! Now, you needn't be lonely anymore, and I'll try to fill Archie's place till he comes back, for I know he will, as soon as you let him."

"Well, I don't mind telling *you* that while he was my mate I never missed brothers and sisters, or wanted anyone else; but since he cast me off, I'll be hanged if I don't feel as forlorn as old Crusoe before Friday turned up."

This burst of confidence confirmed Rose in her purpose of winning Charlie's mentor back to him, but she said no more, contented to have done so well. They parted excellent friends, and Prince went home, wondering why "a fellow didn't mind saying things to a girl or woman which they would die before they'd own to another fellow."

Rose also had some sage reflections upon the subject, and fell asleep thinking that there were a great many curious things in this world, and feeling that she was beginning to find out some of them.

Next day she trudged up the hill to see Archie and, having told him as much as she thought best about her talk with Charlie, begged him to forget and forgive.

"I've been thinking that perhaps I ought to, though I *am* in the right. I'm no end fond of Charlie, and he's the best-hearted lad alive; but he can't say no, and that will play the mischief with him if he does not take care," said Archie in his grave, kind way. "While Father was home, I was very busy with him, so Prince got into a set I don't like. They try to be fast, and think it's manly, and they flatter him and lead him on to do all sorts of things—play for money, and bet, and loaf about. I hate to have him do so, and tried to stop it, but went to work the wrong way, so we got into a mess."

"He is all ready to make up if you don't say much, for he owned to me he *was* wrong; but I don't think he will own it to you, in words," began Rose.

"I don't care for that; if he'll just drop those rowdies and come back, I'll hold my tongue and not preach. I wonder if he owes those fellows money, and so doesn't like to break off till he can pay it. I hope not, but don't dare to ask; though, perhaps, Steve knows, he's always after Prince, more's the pity." And Archie looked anxious.

"I think Steve does know, for he talked about debts of honor the day I gave him—" There Rose stopped short and turned scarlet.

But Archie ordered her to "fess" and had the whole story in five minutes, for none dared disobey the Chief. He completed her affliction by putting a five-dollar bill into her pocket by main force, looking both indignant and resolute as he said, "Never do so, again; but send Steve to me if he is afraid to go to his father. Charlie had nothing to do with that; *he* wouldn't borrow a penny of a girl, don't think it. But that's the harm he does Steve, who adores him, and tries to be like him in all things. Don't say a word; I'll make it all right, and no one shall blame you."

"Oh, me! I always make trouble by trying to help, and then letting out the wrong thing," sighed Rose, much depressed by her slip of the tongue.

Archie comforted her with the novel remark that it was always best to tell the truth, and made her quite cheerful by promising to heal the breach with Charlie as soon as possible.

He kept his word so well that the very next afternoon, as Rose looked out of the window, she beheld the joyful spectacle of Archie and Prince coming up the avenue, arm in arm, as of old, talking away as if to make up for the unhappy silence of the past weeks.

Rose dropped her work, hurried to the door, and opening it wide, stood there smiling down upon them so happily that the faces of the lads brightened as they ran up the steps eager to show that all was well with them.

"Here's our little peacemaker!" said Archie, shaking hands with vigor.

But Charlie added, with a look that made Rose very proud and happy, "And *my* little sister."

CHAPTER 24

WHICH?

"UNCLE, I have discovered what girls are made for," said Rose the day after the reconciliation of Archie and the Prince.

"Well, my dear, what is it?" asked Dr. Alec, who was "planking the deck," as he called his daily promenade up and down the hall.

"To take care of boys," answered Rose, quite beaming with satisfaction as she spoke. "Phebe laughed when I told her, and said she thought girls had better learn to take care of themselves first. But that's because *she* hasn't got seven boy cousins as I have."

"She is right, nevertheless, Rosy, and so are you, for the two things go together, and in helping seven lads you are unconsciously doing much to improve one lass," said Dr. Alec, stopping to nod and smile at the bright-faced figure resting on the old bamboo chair after a lively game of battledore and shuttlecock, in place of a run which a storm prevented.

"Am I? I'm glad of that, but really, Uncle, I do feel as if I *must* take care of the boys, for they come to me in all sorts of troubles and ask advice, and I like it *so* much. Only I don't always know what to do, and I'm going to consult you privately and then surprise them with my wisdom."

"All right, my dear; what's the first worry? I see you have something on your little mind, so come and tell Uncle."

Rose put her arm in his and, pacing to and fro, told him all about Charlie, asking what she could do to keep him straight, and be a real sister to him.

"Could you make up your mind to go and stay with Aunt Clara a month?" asked the doctor when she ended.

"Yes, sir; but I shouldn't like it. Do you really want me to go?"

"The best cure for Charlie is a daily dose of Rose water, or Rose and water; will you go and see that he takes it?" laughed Dr. Alec.

"You mean that if I'm there and try to make it pleasant, he will stay at home and keep out of mischief?"

"Exactly."

"But *could* I make it pleasant? He would want the boys."

"No danger but he'd have the boys, for they swarm after you like bees after their queen. Haven't you found that out?"

"Aunt Plen often says they never used to be here half so much before I came, but I never thought *I* made the difference, it seemed so natural to have them round."

"Little Modesty doesn't know what a magnet she is; but she will find it out someday." And the doctor softly stroked the cheek that had grown rosy with pleasure at the thought of being so much loved. "Now, you see, if I move the magnet to Aunt Clara's, the lads will go there as sure as iron to steel, and Charlie will be so happy at home he won't care for these mischievous mates of his; I hope," added the doctor, well knowing how hard it was to wean a seventeen-year-old boy from his first taste of what is called "seeing life," which, alas! often ends in seeing death.

"I'll go, Uncle, right away! Aunt Clara is always asking me, and will be glad to get me. I shall have to dress and dine late, and see lots of company, and be very fashionable, but I'll try not to let it hurt me; and if I get in a puzzle or worried about anything, I can run to you," answered Rose, goodwill conquering timidity.

So it was decided, and without saying much about the real reason for this visit, Rose was transplanted to Aunt Clara's, feeling that she had a work to do, and very eager to do it well.

Dr. Alec was right about the bees, for the boys did follow their queen, and astonished Mrs. Clara by their sudden assiduity in making calls, dropping in to dinner, and getting up evening frolics. Charlie was a devoted host and tried to show his gratitude by being very kind to his "little sister," for he guessed why she came, and his heart was touched by her artless endeavors to "help him be good."

Rose often longed to be back in the old house, with the simpler pleasures and more useful duties of the life there; but having made up her mind, in spite of Phebe, that "girls were made to take care of boys," her motherly little soul found much to enjoy in the new task she had undertaken.

It was a pretty sight to see the one earnest, sweet-faced girl among the flock of tall lads, trying to understand, to help and please them with a patient affection that worked many a small miracle unperceived. Slang, rough manners, and careless habits were banished or bettered by the presence of a little gentlewoman; and all the manly virtues cropping up were encouraged by the hearty admiration bestowed upon them by one whose good opinion all valued more than they confessed; while Rose tried to imitate the good qualities she praised in them, to put away her girlish vanities and fears, to be strong and just and frank and brave as well as modest, kind, and beautiful.

This trial worked so well that when the month was over, Mac and Steve demanded a visit in their turn, and Rose went, feeling that she would like to hear grim Aunt Jane say, as Aunt Clara did at parting, "I wish I could keep you all my life, dear."

After Mac and Steve had had their turn, Archie and Company bore her away for some weeks; and with them she was so happy, she felt as if she would like to stay forever, if she could have Uncle Alec also.

Of course, Aunt Myra could not be neglected, and with secret despair, Rose went to the "Mausoleum," as the boys called her gloomy abode. Fortunately, she was very near home, and Dr. Alec dropped in so often that her visit was far less dismal than she expected. Between them, they actually made Aunt Myra laugh heartily more than once; and Rose did her so much good by letting in the sunshine, singing about the silent house, cooking wholesome messes, and amusing the old lady with funny little lectures on physiology, that she forgot to take her pills and gave up Mum's Elixir; because she slept so well, after the long walks and drives she was beguiled into taking, that she needed no narcotic.

So the winter flew rapidly away, and it was May before Rose was fairly settled again at home. They called her the "Monthly Rose," because she had spent a month with each of the aunts, and left such pleasant memories of bloom and fragrance behind her that all wanted the family flower back again.

Dr. Alec rejoiced greatly over his recovered treasure; but as the time drew near when his year of experiment ended, he had many a secret fear that Rose might like to make her home for the next twelvemonth with Aunt Jessie, or even Aunt Clara, for Charlie's sake. He said nothing, but waited with much anxiety for the day when the matter should be decided; and while he waited he did his best to finish as far as possible the task he had begun so well.

Rose was very happy now, being out nearly all day enjoying the beautiful awakening of the world, for spring came bright and early as if anxious to do its part. The old horse chestnuts budded around her windows, green things sprang up like magic in the garden under her hands, hardy flowers bloomed as fast as they could, the birds sang blithely overhead, and every day a chorus of pleasant voices cried, "Good morning, cousin; isn't it jolly weather?"

No one remembered the date of the eventful conversation which resulted in the doctor's experiment (no one but himself at least); so when the aunts were invited to tea one Saturday they came quite unsuspiciously, and were all sitting together having a social chat when brother Alec entered with two photographs in his hand.

"Do you remember that?" he said, showing one to Aunt Clara, who happened to be nearest.

"Yes, indeed; it is very like her when she came. Quite her sad, unchildlike expression, and thin little face with the big dark eyes."

The picture was passed round, and all agreed that "it was very like Rose a year ago." This point being settled, the doctor showed the second picture, which was received with great approbation and pronounced a "charming likeness."

It certainly was, and a striking contrast to the first one, for it was a blooming, smiling face, full of girlish spirit and health, with no sign of melancholy, though the soft eyes were thoughtful and the lines about the lips betrayed a sensitive nature.

Dr. Alec set both photographs on the chimney piece and, falling back a step or two, surveyed them with infinite satisfaction for several minutes, then wheeled round, saying briefly, as he pointed to the two faces, "Time is up; how do you think my experiment has succeeded, ladies?"

"Bless me, so it is!" cried Aunt Plenty, dropping a stitch in her surprise.

"Beautifully, dear," answered Aunt Peace, smiling entire approval.

"She certainly *has* improved, but appearances are deceitful, and she had no constitution to build upon," croaked Aunt Myra.

"I am willing to allow that, as far as mere health goes, the experiment *is* a success," graciously observed Aunt Jane, unable to forget Rose's kindness to her Mac.

"So am I; and I'll go farther, for I really do believe Alec has done wonders for the child; she will be a beauty in two or three years," added Aunt Clara, feeling that she could say nothing better than that.

"I always knew that he would succeed, and I'm so glad you all allow it, for he deserves more credit than you know, and more praise than he will ever get," cried Aunt Jessie, clapping her hands with an enthusiasm that caused Jamie's little red stocking to wave like a triumphal banner in the air.

Dr. Alec made them a splendid bow, looking much gratified, and then said soberly, "Thank you; now the question is, shall I go on?— for this is only the beginning. None of you know the hindrances I've had, the mistakes I've made, the study I've given the case, and the anxiety I've often felt. Sister Myra is right in one thing—Rose *is* a delicate creature, quick to flourish in the sunshine, and as quick to droop without it. She has no special weakness, but inherits her mother's sensitive nature and needs the wisest, tenderest care to keep a very ardent little soul from wearing out a finely organized little body. I think I've found the right treatment, and with you to help me, I believe we may build up a lovely and noble woman who will be a pride and comfort to us all."

There Dr. Alec stopped to get his breath, for he had spoken very earnestly and his voice got a little husky over the last words. A gentle murmur from the aunts seemed to encourage him, and he went on with an engaging smile, for the good man was slyly trying to win all the ladies to vote for him when the time came.

"Now, I don't wish to be selfish or arbitrary, because I am her guardian, and I shall leave Rose free to choose for herself. We all want her, and if she likes to make her home with any of you rather than with me, she shall do so. In fact, I encouraged her visits last winter, that she might see what we can all offer her and judge where she will be happiest. Is not that the fairest way? Will you agree to abide by her choice, as I do?"

"Yes, we will," said all the aunts, in quite a flutter of excitement at the prospect of having Rose for a whole year.

"Good! She will be here directly, and then we will settle the question for another year. A most important year, mind you, for she has got a good start and will blossom rapidly now if all goes well with her. So I beg of you, don't undo my work, but deal very wisely and gently with my little girl, for if any harm come to her, I think it would break my heart."

As he spoke, Dr. Alec turned his back abruptly and affected to be examining the pictures again; but the aunts understood how dear the child was to the solitary man who had loved her mother years ago, and who now found his happiness in cherishing the little Rose who was so like her. The good ladies nodded and sighed, and telegraphed to one another that none of them would complain if not chosen, or even try to rob Brother Alec of his "Heart's Delight," as the boys called Rose.

Just then the pleasant sound of happy voices came up from the garden, and smiles broke out on all serious faces. Dr. Alec turned at once, saying, as he threw back his head, "There she is; now for it!"

The cousins had been a-Maying, and soon came flocking in laden with the spoils.

"Here is our bonny Scotch rose with all her thorns about her," said Dr. Alec, surveying her with unusual pride and tenderness as she went to show Aunt Peace her basket full of early flowers, fresh leaves, and curious lichens.

"Leave your clutter in the hall, boys, and sit quietly down if you choose to stop here, for we are busy," said Aunt Plenty, shaking her finger at the turbulent clan who were bubbling over with the jollity born of spring sunshine and healthy exercise.

"Of course, we choose to stay! Wouldn't miss our Saturday high tea for anything," said the Chief, as he restored order among his men with a nod, a word, and an occasional shake.

"What is up? A court-martial?" asked Charlie, looking at the assembled ladies with affected awe and real curiosity, for their faces betrayed that some interesting business was afloat.

Dr. Alec explained in a few words, which he made as brief and calm as he could; but the effect was exciting, nevertheless, for each of the lads began at once to bribe, entice, and wheedle "our cousin" to choose his home.

"You really ought to come to us for mother's sake, as a relish, you know, for she must be perfectly satiated with boys," began Archie, using the strongest argument he could think of at the moment.

"Oh, do! We'll never slam, or bounce at you or call you 'fraid cat,' if you only will," besought Geordie and Will, distorting their countenances in the attempt to smile with overpowering sweetness.

"And I'll always wash my hands 'fore I touch you, and you shall be my dolly, 'cause Pokey's gone away, and I'll love you *hard*," cried Jamie, clinging to her with his chubby face full of affection.

"Brothers and sisters ought to live together; especially when the

brother needs someone to make home pleasant for him," added
Charlie, with the wheedlesome tone and look that Rose always
found so difficult to resist.

"You had her longest, and it's our turn now; Mac needs her more
than you do, Prince, for she's 'the light of his eyes,' he says. Come,
Rose, choose us, and I'll never use the musky pomade you hate again
as long as I live," said Steve, with his most killing air as he offered
this noble sacrifice.

Mac peered wistfully over his goggles, saying in an unusually wide-
awake and earnest way, "Do, cousin, then we can study chemistry
together. My experiments don't blow up very often now, and the
gasses aren't at all bad when you get used to them."

Rose meantime had stood quite still, with the flowers dropping
from her hands as her eyes went from one eager face to another,
while smiles rippled over her own at the various enticements offered
her. During the laugh that followed Mac's handsome proposition,
she looked at her uncle, whose eyes were fixed on her with an expression of love and longing that went to her heart.

"Ah, yes," she thought, "*he* wants me most! I've often longed to
give him something that he wished for very much, and now I can."

So when, at a sudden gesture from Aunt Peace, silence fell, Rose
said slowly, with a pretty color in her cheeks, and a beseeching look
about the room, as if asking pardon of the boys, "It's very hard to
choose when everybody is so fond of me; therefore I think I'd better
go to the one who seems to need me most."

"No, dear, the one you love the best and will be happiest with,"
said Dr. Alec quickly, as a doleful sniff from Aunt Myra and a murmur of "My sainted Caroline" made Rose pause and look that way.

"Take time, cousin; don't be in a hurry to make up your mind, and
remember, 'Codlin's your friend,' " added Charlie, hopeful still.

"I don't want any time! I *know* who I love best, who I'm happiest
with, and I choose Uncle. Will he have me?" cried Rose in a tone
that produced a sympathetic thrill among the hearers, it was so full
of tender confidence and love.

If she really had any doubt, the look in Dr. Alec's face banished it without a word, as he opened wide his arms, and she ran into them, feeling that home was there.

No one spoke for a minute, but there were signs of emotion among the aunts, which warned the boys to bestir themselves before the waterworks began to play. So they took hands and began to prance about uncle and niece, singing, with sudden inspiration, the nursery rhyme

Ring around a Rosy!

Of course that put an end to all sentiment, and Rose emerged laughing from Dr. Alec's bosom, with the mark of a waistcoat button nicely imprinted on her left cheek. He saw it, and said with a merry kiss that half effaced it, "This is my ewe lamb, and I have set my mark on her, so no one can steal her away."

That tickled the boys, and they set up a shout of

Uncle had a little lamb!

But Rose hushed the noise by slipping into the circle, and making them dance prettily—like lads and lasses round a Maypole; while Phebe, coming in with fresh water for the flowers, began to twitter, chirp, and coo, as if all the birds of the air had come to join in the spring revel of the eight cousins.